Cover Design: Hang Le
Cover Photography: Wander Aguiar
Cover Model: Adrea & Alex
Editing: Hot Tree Editing
Proofreading: Deaton Author Services
Paperback Formatting: Jersey Girl Designs

The following story contains sexual situations and strong language. It is intended for adult readers.

Forever AFTER ALL

NEW YORK TIMES BESTSELLING AUTHOR

KAYLEE RYAN

OTHER TITLES BY KAYLEE RYAN

With You Series
Anywhere with You | More with You | Everything with You

Soul Serenade Series
Emphatic | Assured | Definite | Insistent

Southern Heart Series
Southern Pleasure | Southern Desire | Southern Attraction | Southern Devotion

Unexpected Arrivals Series
Unexpected Reality | Unexpected Fight | Unexpected Fall | Unexpected Bond
Unexpected Odds

Riggins Brothers Series
Play by Play | Layer by Layer
Piece by Piece | Kiss by Kiss | Touch by Touch

Standalone Titles
Tempting Tatum | Unwrapping Tatum | Levitate
Just Say When | I Just Want You
Reminding Avery | Hey, Whiskey | Pull You Through | Beyond the Bases
Remedy | The Difference
Trust the Push

Entangled Hearts Duet
Agony | Bliss

Cocky Hero Club
Lucky Bastard

Box Sets
Series Starter - Kaylee Ryan

CO-WRITTEN WITH LACEY BLACK

Fair Lakes Series
It's Not Over | Just Getting Started
Can't Fight It

Standalone Titles

Boy Trouble | Home to You

Prologue

MCKENNA

SEVEN YEARS OLD

I GRIP THE ROPE LADDER AS I CLIMB TO THE TREEHOUSE. THE ROPE IS ROUGH AND ITCHY under my hands, but I don't care. I'm mad at Corbin. We were playing hide and seek, and he was supposed to count to one hundred, but he skipped. I heard him. I wasn't done hiding, and he tagged me out. He's not playing fair, so I'm not playing at all.

Making it into the treehouse, I see my and Laramie's Barbie dolls we were playing with before her brother, Rip, and his stupid friend, Corbin, convinced us to play tag with them. Who wants to play hide and seek when you can play with Barbies?

We were getting ready to have a wedding. Laramie has Ken in a nice suit, and my Barbie is in her wedding dress. Standing the two side by side, I start the wedding. I don't need Laramie for this. I can have fun on my own.

Walking the two next to each other across the floor of the treehouse, I stop just beside the other Barbie set up to be the preacher. Every wedding needs a preacher. That's how they have it on TV.

"Dearly beloved," I say in a man's voice. 'Cause the one I see on TV on that movie Momma watched last night was a man. "We're getting married today," I say in the same voice.

"McKenna! You up there?"

I freeze when I hear Rip's voice. I don't want to play with them. I want to play up here. "Go away."

I start again. "Dearly beloved," I say just as Rip's head appears through the hole in the floor.

"What are you doing, Kenna?" he asks. His head tilts to the side, and it's the same thing my mommy does when she's asking me what I'm doing. Rip's the only one who ever calls me Kenna. Everyone else calls me Mac.

"Playing."

"I can see that. Why aren't you playing with us?" he asks as he climbs the rest of the way into the treehouse.

Rip is older than me by two years. His sister is my best friend, and she's seven like me. "Because stupid Corbin cheated. He didn't count all the way, and I was still hiding."

"Come on. I'll make him give you an extra turn at being it." He tries to coax me.

"No. Ken and Barbie are getting married." I ignore him and start again, "Dearly beloved—" only for him to stop me.

"I'll play with you," he says, reaching for Ken.

"No. Boys can't play Barbies." I reach for Ken but Rip moves so fast that I can't.

"Can too," he counters.

"No. This is girls only."

"You're in my treehouse."

"It's Laramie's too, and she's my best friend."

"I'm your friend," he says, his voice low. "How about we get married instead? That way, I'm not playing with Barbies."

Dropping Barbie, I cross my arms over my chest and glare at him. "Are you going to make fun of me?" Rip and Corbin call us babies all the time for playing Barbies. "I'm not a baby," I say as an afterthought.

"No. How about we have the wedding, and then I'll make sure that Corbin gives you an extra turn?"

I think about it, and I really do want to play with them. My feelings were hurt, but I like it when Rip and Corbin play with us.

"Fine. You have to sit next to me." Rip moves to sit next to me. "And we're supposed to lock arms like this." I link my arm with his.

"Who's going to marry us?"

"I will. You don't know how to do it." I clear my throat and start yet again. "Dearly beloved," I start. "These two people are getting married. Do you, Rip, take McKenna to be your awful wife?" I say in my man's voice.

"Yep."

"No. You're supposed to say 'I do.'" I shake my head at him.

"Sorry. I do."

"Do you McKenna take Rip to be your awful husband?"

"I do," I say in my own voice.

"You can kiss your bride."

"Wait, we have to kiss?" Rip curls his lip.

I sigh in frustration. "That's how it goes, Rip," I say, defeated.

"Fine. Let's get this over with. Close your eyes." I do as he says, closing my eyes and puckering my lips. When his lips touch mine, I feel... funny, and I don't know what it means.

"Eww! Dude, you got girl cooties!" Corbin yells.

Rip and I pull apart, opening our eyes to find Corbin with his head stuck through the floor. "Shut it," Rip fires back.

"I can't believe you kissed her. Are we playing or what?" Corbin asks.

"Yeah, and McKenna gets an extra turn. You cheated."

Corbin rolls his eyes. "Fine," he grumbles. "Let's go." His head disappears, and I can hear him yelling down to Laramie, telling her that we were kissing.

"We were not!" I yell back. Only we were.

"Did I do it right?" Rip asks.

"Yes." I nod. "And we live happily forever after all. We can go play hide and seek now." I stand, something Rip can't do. He's too tall.

"Finally. I'll go first in case you need help getting down."

"I can do it on my own."

"But I'm older. It's my job to do it." With no further arguing, he climbs down the ladder and calls for me to come down.

I'm angry that he thinks I need his help, and I miss the final step of the rope and begin to fall. Rip reaches out and catches me. "I've got you, Kenna," he says quietly. He helps me stand, his eyes watching me. Once he's satisfied, he tags my arms and screams, "McKenna's it!"

We spend the rest of the day playing tag. It's not until I'm at home later when I realize I kissed a boy.

Chapter One

RIP

THE FLAMES OF THE FIRE DANCE, LIGHTING UP THE DARK SKY. IT'S THE PERFECT NIGHT FOR a bonfire. Over the blaze, I watch as McKenna brings the bottle of Boone's Farm to her lips. I can't help but feel nostalgic. We've spent many summer nights out in this field. When McKenna left for college, it just didn't feel the same. Not to me, and not to my little sister, Laramie, her best friend. We just sort of stopped having bonfires. However, tonight is a special occasion. McKenna graduated from law school two weeks ago.

She's wicked smart, having graduated high school with an associate's degree. She left for Harvard to finish her undergrad and attend law school. Her trips home were few and far between, and we all missed her.

I missed her.

"You know," Laramie says, "you'd think now that we're legal drinking age, we'd move onto something better than Boone's Farm," she says, holding the half-empty bottle in the air.

"Speak for yourself. I'm an in-debt college graduate," McKenna tells her. "Besides, there's nothing wrong in indulging in a little Boone's." As if she needs to prove her point, her bottle is back to her lips as she takes a healthy drink. Laramie cheers her on, making us all laugh.

"Right." My sister laughs. "Miss Attorney at Law." She smiles at McKenna.

"Not yet. I still have to pass the bar exam."

"Please," Laramie chides. "You've got this."

"It's damn good to have you home," my best friend, Corbin, says, wrapping his arm around her shoulders. McKenna gives him a blinding smile as she returns his embrace.

My eyes never leave the two of them as they dance around, acting a fool. "What's up with you?" Colby, Corbin's younger brother, asks, plopping down on the back of the tailgate beside me.

"Nothing."

"You look like you could murder my brother."

I have to force myself to turn and look at him. "Maybe you should slow down on those." I nod to the bottle of beer in his hand.

"Yeah, okay," he says, laughing off my comment.

"What are you two fuddy-duddies doing over there?" my sister calls out.

"Your girl is lit," I tell Colby.

"I know." I can hear the smile in his voice. My sister and Colby have been dating and still going strong since Laramie's senior year of high school.

"Is she going home with you?" I ask him. I know the answer. Even though Laramie technically still lives at home, she's never there. She's always staying over at Colby's.

"Nah, we're staying at your place tonight."

"Really?" I laugh.

"Yep. Her idea." He points to my sister.

"When are you going to make an honest woman out of her?"

"Soon." He's evasive, but that's Colby. The only thing he's ever transparent about is how he feels about my baby sister. What he doesn't know is that I know he's already talked to Mom and Dad. I know he plans to ask her to marry him, and if I know Colby, his "soon" is just that. Soon.

"Come on." Laramie appears in front of us. She grabs onto Colby's hand

and tugs. He lets her, like the pussy he is for her, and follows her to the other side of the fire.

I watch as he pulls her into his arms, and they begin to slow dance. The smile on my sister's face as she stares up at him is the same smile she had when she was eighteen. My eyes stray to McKenna and Corbin, but it's just Corbin in the light of the flames. I scan the surroundings, and that's when I see her headed my way.

"Rip, will you go with me?" she asks.

I don't need her to clarify. I know what she needs. She and Laramie both used to come to me for this very same reason, that is until Colby appeared in the picture. I don't hesitate to jump off the tailgate and link my fingers with hers. Fuck, I've missed her. Stopping at the back of my truck, I grab the roll of toilet paper and the small paper bag for trash that we can toss into the fire.

"My hero," she says, her voice sugary sweet.

"You know, it's just us. You don't really need me," I remind her. Not that I mind. It's been too damn long since I've spent this kind of time with her. She barely came home while she was in college. She was always studying, taking a full course load, or working at her part-time job at a local law firm. Besides, I don't know how many times I've preached to her and my sister never to wander off alone at a field party, or any party for that matter.

"Rip, you can't break tradition," she says, leaning into me.

I can't hold in my chuckle. When we reach the big oak tree, I hand her the toilet paper and the bag and turn my back. "You doing okay?" I ask when I hear her cursing under her breath.

"Yep. Good. Ah," she says, and I find myself again not able to hold onto my laughter. "Are you laughing at me, Rip Callahan?"

"You're cute as hell, McKenna."

"Men. You don't know how lucky you are. All you have to do is just whip it out, and you're good to go. I have to balance myself and not pee on my clothes."

It's on the tip of my tongue to ask her if she wants me to help her strip out of her clothes, but I refrain. McKenna has always been beautiful. I never would have thought she could be any more attractive, that is until I saw her walk into my parents' house yesterday afternoon. Her hair is longer, and her body, she's filled out, and she's now all woman. Something that eighteen-year-old McKenna was lacking when she left for college.

Don't get me wrong, she was beautiful, and I wanted her with a fierceness that I can't explain. I've noticed subtle changes in her over the years when our paths crossed, but tonight is the first time I've really got to spend any amount of time with her. Her visits were always quick, as she had to get back to work in Massachusetts.

"You need help?" I ask when I hear more cursing and rustling around.

"Nope." She appears beside me and slips her arm in the crook of mine.

Arm in arm, we walk back to the fire. I stop us at the truck to toss the toilet paper back into the cab. After leading us to the fire, McKenna tosses the small paper bag into the flames, and as soon as we're in sight, Colby looks over at me and grins. "It's about time," he says, smirking.

"Hey, you try squatting and not getting any on your clothes," McKenna fires back, making everyone laugh.

"This one's for you, ladies," Corbin says as he turns up the music. Laramie pulls McKenna from my side, and they begin to dance around the fire. When the song turns slow, Colby stands and wraps my sister in his arms. McKenna backs away with tears in her eyes as the couple dances to Train's "Marry Me" like no one is watching.

"Do you know something that I don't?" I whisper to McKenna when she comes to stand next to me.

"Just watch," she says, leaning her head on my shoulder. There are tears shimmering in her eyes, and I know that this is it. He's going to do it, and my guess is that he's been waiting for McKenna to come home. So that my sister's best friend could be here to witness the moment. As the song ends, Colby gathers Laramie's hands in his and drops to one knee.

My sister stills, placing her hand over her mouth. As we draw closer, I can see she also has tears in her eyes. "Laramie, I've loved you for longer than I can remember." Colby's voice is strong. Clear. "These past six years have been more than I ever could have asked for. Now, I'm just hoping you're willing to give me the rest of yours. I want to spend a lifetime with you. Will you marry me?"

My sister drops to her knees in front of him and pulls him into a kiss. "Yes!" She tilts her head back and shouts at the night sky, "Yes! Yes! Yes!" She pulls him into a kiss that I'm not sure I should be witnessing from my little sister.

They stand, and Colby pulls her close. The smiles on their faces are matching, and I couldn't be happier for the two of them.

Damn, my little sis is getting married.

"Hell yeah! Welcome to the family." Corbin rushes to them and hugs them both. When he steps back, I step in and do the same, followed by McKenna.

"Congratulations, man." I shake Colby's hand. "Lara," I say, my throat growing thick. I pull her into a hug. "The first of our group to get married," I muse, releasing her back to her fiancé.

"Oh, no, they're not the first," Corbin says, holding his hands up in the air, one of them holding a bottle of beer. "That title goes to the two of you." He points to McKenna and me.

"You might want to slow down on those, bud." I aim to the bottle of beer in his hands. I'm pretending like I don't know what he's talking about, yet the memory is my most vivid from my childhood.

"Do you two remember the day I walked in on you two—" He gestures to McKenna and then me. "—in the treehouse, and you were getting married?" He laughs.

"Stop." McKenna laughs with him. "I was seven."

Corbin gives me a mischievous grin. "It's been what? Sixteen years? You think you two still have it in you?" He wags his eyebrows. "I'm thinking we need a reenactment."

"I think Lara and Colby should do the reenactment," I speak up, turning the heat from McKenna and me.

"Nope. That's bad luck," Corbin fires back.

"No, it's not," McKenna argues.

"Yep. It's bad luck to pretend to marry the person you're actually going to marry," Laramie explains. I can tell by the look in my sister's eyes that she knows she's talking shit and no such theory exists. I mean, that's what wedding rehearsals are for, right?

"Colbs, I think we need to cut her off." McKenna makes a slashing motion across her neck. "She's had enough."

"Hush." Laramie's grin grows wider. "Besides, it's not a true reenactment unless it's the original actors."

"We're not actors," I counter. My sister waves her hand in the air. "And we're already married," I say, joking.

"Nope. Single as a Pringle." McKenna holds up her hand, showing she's not wearing a ring. That pleases me more than it should.

"What's the matter, Callahan?" Corbin goads. "You afraid to catch McKenna's cooties?"

"Are you twelve?" I ask him. My heart races at the thought of my lips touching hers. One time in my life, I kissed her. I was nine years old, and the memory is one I will never forget. I'm twenty-five. What does that say about me?

He brings his beer to his lips and makes a show of draining the bottle. "Nope. Are you a pussy?" he asks.

From beside me, McKenna bursts into laughter.

"Really?" I ask her. I'm trying very hard to remain stone-faced, but I can't do that when she laughs like that. So carefree. So beautiful.

"If I remember correctly, you volunteered to play with me that day," she muses, tapping her index finger against her chin.

"You really wanna do this?" My eyes stay trained on hers. There's a part of me that wants her to say yes, and a part of me that is worried that I won't be able to stop once my lips mold with hers.

She nods. "I mean, unless you're scared?" The corner of her mouth tilts up in a smile.

"It's just a show for our fans," I say, making them all laugh. "I'm only getting married once in real life. It's definitely not going to be some snap decision at a bonfire," I tell them.

"Oh, hush." My sister laughs. "Just humor me."

Fuck it. Reaching over, I take the new beer that Corbin just opened out of his hands and down the entire thing. "Let's do this," I tell them.

Corbin claps his hands together, as does my sister, as I'm placed on one side of the fire, while McKenna is led to the opposite so she can "walk down the aisle" to me, or at least that's what Laramie is mumbling about. My hands are sweaty, but I know if I wipe them on my jeans, Corbin will call me out. That fucker never misses anything. Hence the reason we're performing this little charade. I made the mistake of telling him how good she looked yesterday, and well, now here we are.

My reluctance has nothing to do with being a pussy, or being scared. It's not because I think McKenna has cooties. I mentally roll my eyes with that one. No, it's because I've had a thing for my sister's best friend for years. She was the first girl I ever kissed, and tonight, she's too fucking tempting. Her long brown hair cascades down her back. Those short cutoff jean shorts that make her legs look incredible and that tank top that does nothing to hide the impressive tits that live just below the surface of the fabric. I'm hesitant because I'm not sure once my lips touch hers that I'll be able to stop. I've been fighting this for a long damn time.

At first, I wanted to wait until she graduated. I'm two years older than her, and I thought that was the right thing to do. Then she announced she was accepted to Harvard for prelaw with the dreams of following in her grandpa's footsteps. Telling her then would have only caused pain for both of us. No way was I going to interfere with her living her dream. This time she's home for good. She's back, and I'm not sure I have the willpower to resist her.

"You nervous?" Corbin smirks.

"Terrified," I say, deadpan. That's not the truth, but not a complete lie either. I'm cautious. That's a better way to describe it.

"Yo, Lara, you ready?" Corbin calls out.

"Colby, you have to walk her down the aisle," Laramie calls back.

"I thought this was a reenactment. That didn't happen." I know, because even though I was nine years old, that's one of my most vivid memories of my childhood. That day I kissed McKenna Dawson on the lips is the day I realized she wasn't just my little sister's best friend.

"Ready," Laramie calls out.

I'm staring off into the darkness of the night, trying to keep my shit together, when I feel an elbow in my side. "Dude, you're supposed to only have eyes for your wife," Corbin tells me. His eyes are glassy, but he's not too far gone to not know what he's doing. With a roll of my eyes for him, I turn toward the fire and watch as Colby walks McKenna around the flames, stopping just before she gets to me. My hands tremble to touch her.

McKenna is all smiles as she links her arm with mine and glances up at me. "You ready, handsome?" she asks in a Southern drawl that's not her own.

"Shh," Corbin scolds before I can reply. He clears his throat and begins. "Dearly beloved, we are gathered here today to join Rip Callahan and McKenna Dawson in holy matrimony." He yammers on with random words that I'm not entirely sure are involved in a wedding. I've been to a few, but usually, I check out after the first line until the "you may kiss the bride" portion of the event. That's usually my cue that it's time for drinks. Even if I wanted to pay attention, I wouldn't be able to, though. Not with her on my arm like she is.

"Rip, do you take McKenna to be your lawfully wedded wife?"

I'm looking down at her, and she's looking up at me. The glow of the fire dances in her brown eyes. She takes my breath away, and I'm finding it hard to breathe.

"Rip, buddy. You're supposed to say, 'I do,'" Corbin whispers, but we can all hear him.

I swallow hard. My eyes never leaving hers. "I do."

"McKenna, do you take Rip to be your lawfully wedded husband?" Corbin repeats the question. My hair that's now hanging just below my ears blows into my eyes. McKenna raises her hand and tucks it behind my ear. Once she's finished, her palm rests against my cheek. "I do," she whispers.

This feels real.

Intimate.

"By the power vested in me, by the bonfire gods and the state of Texas—" Corbin laughs at himself "—I now pronounce you husband and wife. You may kiss your bride."

I don't hesitate to bend my head and press my lips to hers briefly. Way too briefly before I'm pulling away. I need to maintain control. I can't devour her as I want. I watch as her eyes flutter open and lock on mine.

"Boo!" Corbin says loudly. "You call that a kiss. You're fired. Both of you."

"Encore," my sister begins to chant, and it only takes a couple of seconds for Corbin and Colby to start cheering right along with her.

"What do you think, Kenna?" I ask, placing my hands on her hips and pulling her close.

"I think we better give them what they want." That's what she says, but the way her eyes are hooded and her body leans into mine, I think it's what she wants too.

I want it. I want her. I have for such a long fucking time that my tightly spun control snaps. With one hand around her waist, I slide the other under her hair to grip the back of her neck. Then, I kiss her. Not for the fake wedding, not for the show our friends are demanding.

No. I kiss the hell out of her for me, and I finally got the answer to a question that's always plagued me. Her lips are indeed as soft as they look.

My tongue glides past her lips, and we begin a battle, both giving as much as we're taking. I don't hear our friends. I don't hear the crackling of the fire. The only sound I can make out is the moan that rises from somewhere deep in her chest, leading me to release one of my own.

She's fucking incredible.

Chapter Two

MCKENNA

MY KNEES WOBBLE, BUT THAT'S OKAY BECAUSE RIP HAS HIS BIG, STRONG ARMS WRAPPED around me, holding me tight. His mouth is pressed against mine, and I meet his tongue stroke for stroke.

I'm kissing Rip!

This man, he's nothing like the boy who stole my first kiss all those years ago, but then again, he is. He's still my best friend's older brother. He's still in control, and I'm still falling for his charms. His hair is longer, falling just shy of his shoulders, and his body is more defined, and I know he's put on some muscle. I can feel the difference beneath the palm of my hands that rest on his chest. The day I left for college, he gave me a big hug telling me to be safe and to chase my dreams. Rip five years ago was buff. Rip today is a work of sculpted perfection.

I can't stop the moan that pulls from deep in my chest from escaping, and in turn, Rip produces one of his own. His arms tug me closer, and I go willingly. Rip Callahan has always been my kryptonite. I just never told him. Sure, I confessed to my best friend that I kinda sorta had a thing for her older brother in high school. Laramie begged me to let her set me up with him. She claimed she could see it in his eyes that he had a thing for me as well. However, I knew that I was going off to college and that there was a very strong possibility that if I let myself fall into Rip, I would never leave.

He slows the kiss and presses his forehead against mine. Neither one of us speak while we both try to catch our breath.

"Damn, bro." Corbin steps next to us and places his hand on Rip's shoulder. "That's what I'm talking about." He cheers before dropping his hand and disappearing.

"You good?" Rip asks quietly.

My hands move to hold him around his waist. Sliding my hand under his T-shirt, I feel the smooth, warm skin of his back. I melt into him, needing to be closer. "Never been better. You?" I ask, pulling back so I can look into his eyes. Rip and I have never shied away from touching one another. I've always felt comfortable around him. However, tonight this is more than comfortable. It feels right.

His eyes soften. "Never been better," he tosses my words back at me. As if he needs to mimic my every move, his fingers slip under the hem of my shirt, just above the waistline of my shorts. I shiver at the contact of his skin against mine.

I don't know how long we stand here, staring into each other's eyes, testing the waters, feeling one another, but the spell is somehow broken when Laramie tackles us both in a hug.

"Academy Award, right there." She chuckles. "That was awesome."

My eyes are still locked on him, and the corner of his mouth tilts in a smile. "Go love on your fiancé," he tells his sister with zero malice or heat.

"Oh, I'm going to love on him all right." Laramie laughs when Rip shakes his head.

"Come here you." Colby slides his arm around her waist and leads them to a chair, where he proceeds to pull her into his lap.

I stand frozen, my arms motionless around Rip, his arms still around me. Neither one of us willing nor ready to break this connection between us.

"I gotta piss," Corbin states as he clumsily walks toward the front of his truck.

"You all right, man?" Rip asks him. He's always been the one taking care of our little group.

Corbin waves him off.

"Don't worry, I have his keys," Colby tells us.

"McKenna, come sit. I miss you," my best friend calls over to us.

Rip smiles at me and moves to stand beside me. His entire hand slides up the back of my shirt as he guides me to the lawn chair that's next to his sister and Colby. He doesn't move his hand until he takes the chair, and to my surprise, he tugs me down onto his lap. He wraps his strong arms around me, and just like nothing happened, Laramie starts firing off questions, just like she did when I arrived at her parents' place yesterday afternoon to surprise her.

"Tell me about this bar exam," she says, snuggling into Colby's embrace.

"Lara, you just got engaged. I'm sure you don't want to talk about my boring summer internship."

"We could talk about that kiss and this." She points her finger at me, snuggled in her brother's lap.

I lean forward to stand, but Rip's hold is firm. "Stay," he whispers, his lips next to my ear. A shiver races through me from the feel of his hot breath against my skin. Reaching down beside the chair, he grabs my bottle of Boone's Farm and hands it to me.

"I take the test in two weeks. I can't actually practice law until I pass, but I'll still be helping Gramps out at the firm until then. I can do everything but represent a client," I explain. "I should really be studying right now," I confess.

"That's what I thought." Laramie grins.

"So, how long does it take to get your test results?" Colby asks.

"It just depends. I've heard anywhere from six to twelve weeks. I think it depends on how many are taking it at any given time. Right now, there are a lot of graduates, so my guess is closer to twelve weeks."

"You know you're going to nail it, right?" Laramie asks.

My shoulders slump. "I hope so."

Rip's arms tighten around me, and I turn to look at him. I lose my breath when he leans in and kisses my bare shoulder. "You've got this, Kenna," he says softly. His words are just for me, and they make my insides flutter.

Glancing at the bottle of Boone's Farm in my hands, I place it on the ground. I think I've had enough. My mind and my body are starting to play tricks on me. I'm starting to think that Rip might actually be interested. At least for tonight. I could never have just one night with him, so it's time for me to slow my roll where the alcohol consumption is concerned. Although, that kiss was toe curling, and now he's holding me. We might have hugged, and not shied away from touching one another growing up, but this is altogether different. He's never given me any indication that he wants more, but tonight, well, tonight feels like more. I'm terrified to think of this anything other than just being caught up in the moment, and a little bit of alcohol. I'm afraid to let myself want more where he's concerned.

"I've missed you," Laramie tells me. "I'm so glad you were here for tonight, and you're going to be here for the wedding."

"When is the wedding?" I ask, trying to ignore the way Rip's hand slides up the back of my tank top. The feel of the rough pad of his thumb on my skin is driving me insane. "Well, I'm here for whatever you need," I tell her before she can respond. Corbin staggers back to the fire, plopping down on the cooler, drawing my attention away for a moment.

"Well, we're going to have to set a date. Soon." She turns to smile at her fiancé. "Right, Colbs?"

"Anything you want," he says, kissing her temple. I know he means exactly that. He will make damn sure that their wedding is everything Laramie ever dreamed of. He waited for me to be home to propose. Colby and Laramie are solid, and he would do anything for her, and she him. I have no doubt that the two of them are going to have a very long, happy marriage. My heart warms. I'm so happy for the two of them.

"So, wedding planning?"

Like I knew she would, Laramie dives into the conversation about her upcoming nuptials. I listen, fighting the urge to drink my bottle of wine, all while sitting on Rip's lap with one of his arms locked tight around me, while the other drives me crazy as he caresses my skin. I really could use a drink, but I know better. I need to sober up a little.

"I'm done," Corbin says, staggering to his feet.

"I should get home too," I say, trying to stand, and yet again, Rip keeps me from doing so. "I've got you," he says, his voice low and husky. "Colbs, you got Lara?" he asks.

"Yeah, we're headed to your place."

I feel Rip nod. "Corbin, get in the truck. I'll drive."

Corbin waves him off and staggers to Rip's truck. I watch as he stops and struggles to pull open the back door. He finally, after several tries, is able to pull it open and climb inside.

"You coming with us?" Laramie asks me.

"Nah, I'll just walk home from here."

"She's coming with us," Rip says.

Part of me wants to argue with him. Part of me wants to tell him I can make my own decisions. The other part, well, it's not ready to leave him or his warm embrace just yet. Sure, I've been drinking, but I'd like to think I'm sober enough to make an informed decision. I know what I'm doing. Well, I know the choice that I'm making. I know that I busted my ass in college on the other side of the country from my family and friends, and I've missed them. I know that tonight is my last free night before I hibernate studying for the bar exam, and I want to soak up every moment. I also know that here tonight, I'm living out a childhood dream. I've always crushed on Rip, and to have his hands and lips on me, well, if he's not ready to let that go, then neither am I.

We can deal with the consequences later.

"Ready?" Rip asks. His hand taps my thigh, and this time he lets me stand. My legs are weak, and it has nothing to do with the alcohol and everything to do with the man who has his hand pressed firmly on the small of my back, leading me to his truck. He opens the driver's door, and before I know what's happening, his hands are on my hips, and he's lifting me into his truck. "I'm going to make sure the fire is out. I'll be right back." I'm surprised when he leans in and presses a kiss to the corner of my mouth.

"He's whipped." Corbin laughs from his seat in the back as I slide over to the passenger side of the truck.

I ignore his drunk statement. "You doing okay back there, bud?" I ask instead.

"Fine as frog hair, my friend." His speech is slow and a little slurred.

Rip is back in no time, sliding behind the wheel. "What are you doing over there?" he asks me.

"Riding home?"

He pats the seat next to him. "This is your spot. It's our wedding night, after all." He gives me a lopsided grin, and even though I know I should stay put, I find myself lifting the console yet again and sliding to the middle of the bench seat to sit next to him.

"Better," he mumbles, placing his arm around me, and putting the truck in Drive. He expertly maneuvers us through the bumpy field with one hand. Not that I would think anything else. Rip has been driving these fields since his legs were long enough to reach the pedals.

"Are you sure?" I ask again. "I can go home. You're going to have a full house."

"I have the room," he says, and leaves it at that.

I know he has the room. Laramie has sent me pictures of the house he remodeled on the family farm. It's huge and gorgeous. I don't know why a single man needs that much space, but then again, his house is full of family history. If I remember correctly, his great-great-grandparents built it. It was old and rundown, but you'd never know it now. Rip has restored it to be a beautiful, modern farmhouse. At least from the pictures I've seen. Instead of arguing with him and asking him to take me home, I ride quietly, enjoying the feel of his arm around me.

When Rip pulls up to his house, I wish it was daylight so that I could see the building. The view from the cab of his truck, with just the headlights, isn't enough. I guess I'll have to wait until in the morning.

"You need help inside?" Rip turns to look at Corbin in the back seat.

"You going to hold me close like that girl of yours?" Corbin sniggers. I stiffen at the mention of a girl. Laramie didn't mention he had a girlfriend.

"Nope," Rip replies. "My wife is the only one I'll be holding tonight," he teases, giving my shoulder a gentle squeeze.

"Told ya, McKenna, pussy-whipped," Corbin says before opening the back door and falling out of the truck.

Rip smiles at me. "You would think he would learn."

"Does this happen a lot?" I inquire.

"More than it should. Corbin's all about the good time."

"And you're not?"

"Sure. I like to have a good time, but drinking to where I can't stand or even climb out of a truck without falling on my ass doesn't sound like a good time."

"I've seen you wasted," I tell him.

"Yeah. When I was younger. Adulting takes brain cells, and I can't run this farm without them. Come on. Let me get his drunk ass inside." He pushes open the door and climbs out. I scoot across the seat, ready to jump from his tall-ass truck, when his hands find my hips once again. "I've got you," he says huskily.

When my feet hit the ground, I take a step back. Being this close to Rip is making my head spin. He referred to me as his wife, and although I know he was joking, I didn't hate it. Not in the least little bit.

"Come on, James, let's get your ass inside."

"Wait, tonight is your wedding night. You're finally going to go all the way with your dream girl," he slurs.

Rip chuckles softly. I wait for him to reject the idea or call Corbin out on his claims, but neither happens. Instead, he slides his arm around Corbin's waist and slowly walks him up the wraparound porch.

"Babe, can you grab my keys and phone?" Rip calls out.

I stand frozen. *Babe.* My heart flutters in my chest. Turning back to the truck, I step up on the running boards, grab his keys from the ignition, and search around for his phone. Pulling my phone out of my pocket, I use the flashlight to search on and under the seat. I don't see it anywhere. I go to step down and lose my footing. I'm prepared to fall when two strong arms wrap around me.

"Easy, beautiful," Rip says softly.

"S-Sorry. I couldn't find your phone," I tell him once my feet are planted firmly on the ground.

He pats his shorts pockets and grins. "Oops." He smiles, pulling his phone out of his pocket.

"Here are your keys." I hold out my shaking hand.

Rip takes the keys and then laces his fingers through mine. "You ready for bed, or do you need to wind down a little?" he asks, guiding me into the house with his hands still linked with mine.

"Uh, wh-what is everyone else doing?"

"Lara and Colby are in the spare bedroom. Corbin is passed out on the couch." I open my mouth to say something. I'm not sure what when he beats me to it. "I was hoping we could maybe watch some TV or something?"

"Sure, yeah, we can do that." I'm relieved at the offer. I'm here for him, so I'm not ready for tonight to end. Not yet.

With our hands linked, he leads me down the hall and pushes open a door. It's a bedroom. A huge bedroom decorated in black and gray. It's very masculine, and it smells like him. Glancing around the room, I spot a huge TV that takes up almost the entire wall. "Were you going for the movie theatre vibe?" I point at the TV.

Rip's laughter wraps around me like a warm embrace. "This room is huge, and I didn't want to have to squint to see the TV."

"Got ya. Maybe you should have your eyes checked," I tease.

"I've got twenty-twenty vision." His eyes roam over my body. My skin flushes from his attention. Clearing his throat, he lets go of my hand and opens a dresser drawer. "You can sleep in this," he says, handing me a T-shirt. "Bathroom is through that door." He points to a door on the left side of the room.

"Thanks." I offer him a smile and make my way to the bathroom. Once inside, I shut the door and turn the lock. I need a minute. I've hung out with

Rip hundreds of times, and we've watched countless hours of TV together, with and without his sister. However, this time feels different. We're no longer kids, and my body's reaction to his says that it's all too aware of that fact.

Now, here I am in his bathroom, changing into one of his shirts—the lawyer in me is overanalyzing. Rip is just being Rip. He's always been nice to me, and that's no different now. However, what I thought was a childhood crush is back in full force, and I need to learn how to keep my libido in check around him. He's Rip, my best friend's older brother.

I can do this.

I change into the shirt he gave me. He's so tall that it hangs to my knees, so I take off my shorts and fold them neatly with my tank top, setting them on the chair that sits in the corner. This bathroom is huge, so big in fact that all five of us could fit in the shower and not touch one another. It's beautiful with the dark tile, contrasted with the white molding. Rip really did an amazing job on this place.

Taking a deep breath for courage, I twist the lock and turn the handle. Rip is lying on the bed, sans shirt, now in a pair of basketball shorts. His muscular arm is resting behind his head while the other pats the mattress next to him.

"Come lie down."

I try to hide the tremble in my knees as I walk to the bed and climb on, settling beside him. He surprises me when he moves my way, places his arm around me, and points the remote at the TV.

I'm reeling from what's transpired tonight. There is hope in my heart, that this is leading to something more. I don't have a crystal ball to tell me what the future holds. What I do know is that I can't resist him. Not like this.

Chapter Three

RIP

NO WAY IN HELL CAN I HAVE HER IN MY BED AND NOT HOLD HER. IT'S PHYSICALLY impossible. She leans into my side, and I can feel her body relax. Fuck me, but this is more than I ever expected tonight, but I'll be damned if I'm not going to enjoy every second of my time with her.

"What do you want to watch?" My fingers tap the button on the remote, scrolling mindlessly through the channels.

"Meh, I don't really watch much television. My nose is usually buried in a book, or I'm working."

"Yeah? At the law firm close to school, right?" I pretend like I don't already know the exact details of the last five years, not only has she worked at the big city law firm, she's worked at a coffee shop just off of campus. When Laramie talks about McKenna, I soak up every morsel of information like a sponge. I told myself it was because she was a childhood friend, my sister's best, but lying here with her in my arms, I know that was just an excuse. One I told myself to feel better about needing to know about her life away from me.

"A coffee shop just off campus. I was part-time at the law firm, so I did both. I didn't get many hours at the coffee shop, but it was extra cash." I feel her shoulders shrug. "I usually picked up a few shifts on the weekends."

"All work and no play?" I hit the power button to turn off the TV and toss the remote onto the nightstand. There's nothing more interesting than the woman in my arms.

"Pretty much." She laughs. "I worked hard to keep my grades up to be accepted to law school. I took a full course load of classes each semester. Add in work and time for studying, and there's not much time for play. Then when law school actually started, it was even more studying."

"Surely the men in Massachusetts were beating down your door," I tease her. There's a knot in my gut thinking about some hoity-toity lawyer type swooping her off her feet. Not that I can be pissed. I've never told her that I think she's the most beautiful woman I've ever laid eyes on.

"Yeah, not really. I'm a country girl through and through. It's all Ivy league sweater vest types, and that's just not my thing." Her nose scrunches up, and I wrangle with the idea of pressing my lips there.

The tension in my gut releases. "You can take the girl out of the country," I say, making her smile.

She shifts so that she's lying on her side, and I do the same. "I don't really fit in there, not like I do here. Everyone is so uptight, and it's just not me. However, their law program is outstanding, and my education was important. I wanted to be the best lawyer that I can be."

"You're happy to be home?" I know the answer. I heard her talking to Laramie about it earlier, but I want her to tell me too. I need to hear her say it. Something primal in me needs to hear her say she's home to stay.

"Yes," she agrees. "I've missed this place so much. The people," she whispers, looking up at me. "Anyway, Gramps is ready to retire. Although, I hope I can work side by side with him for a little while at least."

"You're going to be a kickass attorney," I say, tucking some loose strands of hair behind her ear.

"You think so?" A lazy smile tilts her lips.

"I know so."

"What makes you so sure?" There's a vulnerability in her voice that I didn't expect.

"Come on now. You know my wife wouldn't be anything but kickass in everything she does."

"Stop." She giggles, swatting at my arm playfully.

I grab her hand and lace her fingers with mine. "Real talk, McKenna, you're amazing." From the way her eyes widen, we both know I'm no longer talking about her career choice.

She opens her mouth to speak, but no words fill the air between us. Our eyes are locked in this intense stare that has me feeling all kinds of things that I wasn't prepared to feel. I've always had a thing for her, but this is on another level.

Want. Need. Desire. Longing.

Her hand breaks away from mine, and she reaches up to run her fingers through my hair. "It's long." She smiles.

"Yeah."

"What made you grow it out?"

"It just kind of happened, really. I needed a haircut, but I was working on the house, and between that and running the farm during the day, I just didn't have time. It started to grow, and I decided to just let it stay long."

"Let me guess, chicks dig it?"

"Not sure. There's only one I'm worried about."

"Oh." Her demeanor changes. "I didn't realize you were seeing someone."

"I'm not." Reaching out, I place my hand on the small of her back and pull her closer. "There is someone," I say, my voice sounding husky even to my own ears. I know I should stop now. I shouldn't be touching her like this, but I can't. Not when she's here in my house. In my bed. In my arms. I know that she's been drinking, and I'm not trying to take advantage of her, but damn, she feels good lying next to me.

"Rip." My name rolling off her tongue is the sweetest sound I've ever heard. Her voice is filled with desire, and I have no choice but to assume that her desire is for me.

"How drunk are you, McKenna?" I ask.

"Buzzed."

"Do you know where you are?"

"Yes."

"Tell me."

"I'm at your house."

"Whose bed are you in?"

"Yours."

Resting my palm against her cheek, I gently trace her bottom lip with my thumb. "Can I kiss you, McKenna?"

"You want to kiss me?"

I lean in a little closer. Our mouths are now barely a breath apart. "More than anything."

"Am I dreaming?" she asks as her eyes flutter closed. Her tongue sneaks out and wets her lips.

"Open your eyes, beautiful." I wait as her eyes slowly open. "This isn't a dream, but you're a damn dream come true." Tired of wasting time, I close the breath's distance and press my lips to hers.

Her lips are subtle and soft, just as they were earlier. I didn't have the time to appreciate them then, but now I do, and I plan to do just that. I want to appreciate the hell out of her. I could kiss her for hours and be perfectly content. Her hand grips my arm as if she's worried I'll pull away. Not a chance. I need more.

Cautiously, I trace her lips with my tongue, asking for entrance. She gives me what I want when she opens for me, her taste exploding on my tongue.

I need her closer.

My hand returns to the small of her back. Applying light pressure, I mold our bodies together. There isn't a part of her that's not touching a part of me. I don't know how many times I've imagined us in this very situation, in my bed. I'm fucking twenty-five years old, and this woman has me feeling like I'm a randy teenager all over again.

I deepen the kiss and realize McKenna is the only woman in the world that could have me feeling this way.

Out of control.

Fueled by lust.

It's all McKenna, and I want to soak up every second of this experience with her. My hand slides under her shirt. *My shirt.* I allow my fingers to trace the silky-smooth skin of her back, and my tongue lazily explores her mouth. Neither of us is in a hurry. I'm not sure what she's thinking, but for me, I want time to slow down. I want to stop it, right here at this moment, with the beautiful, intoxicating woman in my arms.

In my bed.

Her phone ringing from my nightstand has me ending the kiss and pulling back. "You need to get that?" I ask her.

She pulls in a deep breath as if she needs to work harder to breathe. I know the feeling. "Yeah, I should see who it is."

Reluctantly, I pull away from her, reaching over to the nightstand and handing her the phone. I see my sister's face smiling at me, and I bite back a groan. If Laramie pulls her away from me right now, I'm going to be pissed.

"Hey," McKenna answers, clearing her throat. "Yeah, I'm here. I'm... uh...

in Rip's room. We're watching a movie." She's quiet as her face turns red. "I'll see you in the morning, Lara." She shakes her head, ending the call.

"Everything okay?"

"Yeah. She was just checking to see if I was here. I guess they went to the kitchen for food and didn't see me on the couch."

"I would never have you sleep on the couch. You'll sleep here in my bed. I'll take the couch in my office."

"I can sleep on the couch, Rip. It's fine." Her eyes roam over my body and if I wasn't already hard as stone, I would be now.

"My bed's more comfortable." I smirk.

"You want to share?" Her eyes widen. "I mean, I could have gone home."

"With you? Absolutely. And you are exactly where you're supposed to be." My words cause a light blush to coat her cheeks. "Here, I'll plug that in for you." Holding my hand out for her phone, she gives it to me. Rolling over, I fumble with the cord to plug it in and turn off the lamp, bathing the room in darkness. Rolling back over, I reach for her, and she comes willingly into my arms.

"You good?"

"Yeah." She settles into my chest, and I can't help but think about how right this feels. This is where she belongs.

"How many women have had the opportunity to try out this more comfortable mattress?" she asks into the silence of the room. There's a hesitancy in her voice as if she's afraid of the answer. She shouldn't be.

"Just you."

I feel her lift her head from my chest. I wish I could see her big brown eyes. "Come on now. I'm a big girl. I can handle it."

"Just you, McKenna. This is my home. I don't bring women here."

"Oh." I feel her start to move away, but I hold tight, keeping my arms around her. "I should go...." Her voice trails off.

"You should lie back down." I hold my breath, waiting to see what she'll do. When she finally lies back down, I can feel the stiffness in her body, and that just won't do. "They're not you, McKenna."

"I don't understand."

"This is my home. I've spent countless hours renovating this place. It's special to me."

"It's beautiful."

You're beautiful. "I don't share this part of my life with just anyone."

"So you're telling me that I made the cut?"

"No. What I'm telling you is that you're the one and only. At least when it comes to this room and this bed. You're it." I can't stop the word vomit from spewing from my mouth. I'm sure I've said too much. I'm sure she's going to have questions, and I don't know how to answer them. She's been home less than forty-eight hours, and here I am staking my claim. I've stayed silent all these years, not wanting to scare her away, and now here I am laying all of my cards on the table. I wanted her to follow her dreams and then come home. That's why I've kept my desire for her all to myself. I could never live with myself if I held her back in any way.

She's quiet, and I know she's trying to work out the meaning of my words in her head. I probably shouldn't have said anything, but I couldn't seem to stop myself. However, my feelings are not new to me, but to her, I'm sure they're a shock. I've done a good job—at least I think I have—of hiding what she does to me. My control slipped when she climbed into my bed.

"Rip?"

"Yeah, baby?" The term of endearment seems to have her finally relaxing again in my arms.

"Will you kiss me?"

"My fucking pleasure," I mutter, before searching for her lips in the dark of the room. Our lips mold together as if they were two pieces to a puzzle. She shifts, and I pull her on top of me.

I get lost in her kiss. My hands roam her body, sliding again under the oversized T-shirt she's wearing. Her skin is so damn soft, and I moan from the feel under my fingertips.

My cock is hard as steel. Even through the shorts I'm wearing, I can feel the heat of her. I want nothing more than to strip her bare and bury myself inside her. I want to make her mine. However, I know it's not the right time. Not yet. I've blindsided her, and she's been drinking. I want us both sober the first time I feel her from the inside.

I know that McKenna Dawson is my forever. My hope is that I have a chance to prove that to her. That's not tonight, though. I swore years ago I would always do right by her. Blue balls be damned. I won't push her for more.

One day soon, if I have my way, I'll be able to make her my wife for real, and we'll get our forever after all.

I smile against her lips as I remember her words at our first wedding all those years ago. We were just kids, but I knew then that McKenna would change my life. I just didn't know how.

I lose track of time as we make out like teenagers. It's sometime in the middle of the night that I wrap my body around hers, and we fall into a deep sleep. In fact, it's safe to say it's the best night of sleep I've had in my entire life, and it was a mere few hours at best.

Chapter Four

MCKENNA

WHEN RIP'S LIPS PRESS AGAINST MY SHOULDER, I CAN'T STOP THE SMILE THAT TAKES over my face. Not that he can see it in this position. We're still in his bed, and from the looks of the light coming in through the blinds, the sun is high in the sky. His arms are wrapped tightly around me, and his hard cock is pressing into my ass.

It's not a bad way to wake up.

Speaking of waking up, I should slide out of his arms and head home. He was saying things last night that have my mind all jumbled. I was buzzed, but I knew what I was doing when I asked him to kiss me. It was that or ask him to explain what he meant when he said I was it. He said I was the one and only woman in his bed.

My heart leaps in my throat as the teenager in me who crushed on him appears with full sixteen-year-old giddiness. I would never have expected to be staying the night in his bed, let alone in his arms. Top both of those things with his words, and I'm a swoony, girly mess of twisted emotions.

"Morning," his deep raspy voice greets me.

There's a flutter in my chest at the sound of his gruff, sleep-laced voice. Turning in his arms, I don't try to hide my smile when I see his long hair mussed and his eyes still heavy from sleep. He's a sight to behold. "Morning." My hands have a mind of their own as I reach out and push his hair out of his eyes.

"What's the plan for today?" he asks.

"Uh... I'm not sure. I'm sure Laramie is going to want to talk wedding plans."

His grin grows wider. "I'm sure you're right. Is there anything you want to do?"

"I need to study for the bar exam."

"Today?" he asks, and is that disappointment that I hear?

"I should."

"Kenna." He leans in and presses his lips to my forehead. "Give me today. I promise I'll do whatever I can the next two weeks to help you study, but I just... you're here, and I'm not ready to give you back to books just yet."

"You gave me up to books, did you?" I tease.

Something crosses his face, but he quickly masks it. "I missed you. Please." He juts out his lip in a pout, which is needless. He had me at "I'm not ready to give you back to books."

"Fine. One more day, but if I fail, it's on you." I point at him, trying to sound stern when we both know I'm anything but.

"Thank you." He leans in and presses a kiss to my lips. I didn't know what to expect in the light of day. It certainly wasn't more kisses, and him holding me as if I'm precious to him. "And taking a break will help clear your head. What would you like to do? Anything you've been wanting to do?" His hand on my back pulls me a little closer, which is fine with me. I don't think I'll ever be close enough to him to meet my satisfaction.

"Not specifically other than just relax. That's not something I've done much of the last five years," I confess.

His brow furrows. "Tell me what you want to do, baby. Whatever it is, as long as it's not studying, I'll make it happen."

I'm able to pretend to not be affected. I pretend that lying here in his arms, his kisses, and his whispered terms of endearment aren't affecting me. This isn't us. We've always been close. There's not much to do in small-town Texas, and since his sister is my best friend, we naturally became close as well. Not this close. Not the kissing kind of close. A hug here or there and a hand offered to help me out of the truck or off a stump sitting around a bonfire, not sharing kisses that leave me breathless, and not sleeping in each other's arms.

This is new for us.

I don't hate it.

I just don't know what it means.

"You hungry?" he asks.

"Yes. And I need a shower and a toothbrush."

"You can use my shower, and there are spare toothbrushes I get from the dentist in the bottom drawer."

"I uh... just assumed I would go home for those things. I need clean clothes." Something crosses over his face but leaves just as quickly as it appeared.

"You could do that," he says cautiously. "Or I could give you some of the clothes that Laramie leaves here for nights like this. You shower while I make you breakfast."

"Rip, you don't have to do that. You already took care of me and let me stay here last night."

"Neither of those things were a hardship, Kenna." His eyes are soft as he waits for my answer.

Kenna. He's the only person who calls me that. Everyone else uses my full name or calls me Mac. Rip is the only one, and I'll admit being here with him, hearing the name only he calls me rolling off his lips, is affecting me more than it should. I've really missed him.

"You sure?"

"Spending more time with you? Yes, beautiful, I'm sure." His chocolate eyes are watching me intently, waiting for my reply.

"Depends. What are you making for breakfast?" I ignore the fact he called me beautiful. That's new as well. This softer side of Rip is not something I'm used to. He's always been nice to me, but this... this is an all-new level.

"Anything you want," he counters.

I pretend to be thinking about what I want when I already know what sounds good. "Pancakes and bacon. Extra crispy."

"Deal." He pulls me close and kisses my forehead. "Go shower. I'll send Laramie in with some clothes."

"What's she going to think? I mean, I slept in your bed. Now I'm showering in your bathroom, and you're making me breakfast." I know Laramie isn't going to say a word, except maybe encourage me to go for it. She knows I used to think the sun rose and set with her brother. She's always had this theory that Rip and I would live happily ever after, and we could be sisters. At least she used to.

Rip throws the covers off and climbs out of bed. I watch as he stretches, his muscles rippling, giving all new meaning to his name. It's fitting. I wonder if that even crossed his parents' minds when they were naming him.

I watch as he moves around the bed and tugs the covers off me as well. He offers me his hand to help me stand. Once I'm steady on my feet, he pulls me into his arms in a hug that rivals all hugs. I can feel his morning wood pressing into my belly, and I swallow hard. He's not hiding it, and I can't help but wonder is it more than just the "morning," or is that rocket in his pocket for me?

"What do you think, Kenna? You're the only one I'm worried about," he says, pulling out of the hug, keeping his hands resting on my hips.

"What is this, Rip? What's going on here?"

He smiles, his eyes crinkling at the corners. "This is us, Kenna." His lips find their way to mine, and morning breath be damned, he kisses me like I'm his. "Now. Go get in the shower. I'll send Laramie. Be thinking about what you want to do today." He taps my hip and releases me.

I stay rooted to my spot as I watch him walk out of his room. Part of me wants to call Laramie and give her a heads-up. I know she and Colby are in one of the guest rooms. The other part of me just needs time to process this. I don't know what's going on. Rip has never acted this way with me before. Not that I'm complaining. I'll take his attention, his hugs, and his kisses any day of the week. Then again, I remember when Laramie called me last night, and I told her I was in Rip's room watching a movie. I believe her exact words were "Finally" before she hung up the phone.

"Knock knock." I hear Laramie say before she pushes the bedroom door open. I'm still standing in the same spot, trying to process the last twenty-four hours. My best friend's grin is huge as she wags her eyebrows. "The man of the house requested some clothes for his lady friend," she says in an exaggerated Southern drawl.

"Stop," I say, spluttering with laughter.

"What's with this"—she waves her hand in the air around me—"statue look?"

"Nothing. Just needed some clothes to take a shower."

"These?" She holds up a stack of clothes.

"Thank you." I reach for them, but she pulls them away.

"First, let's set some ground rules."

"What kind of ground rules?" I wasn't expecting rules from her. "Never mind, I should just go home to shower and change."

"Oh, no, you don't, sister. You're staying." She grins wickedly, and I brace myself for what she says next. "We have one rule and one rule only."

My hands settle on my hips, and I mock glare at her. "Let's hear it."

"All future conversations regarding you and my brother, we shall refer to him as Hans. When it's not directly related to what happened in this room last night, he can be Rip."

"What?" I ask, holding in my laughter.

"I should have prefaced this with I love that you spent the night in his room, and I need all the details. But... he's my brother, and eww, I don't want to hear about his moves, so when you talk about your sexy times, he shall be referred to as Hans."

"You're crazy." I shake my head.

"You love me," she sings, dropping to the bed with a bounce. "Wait, maybe I shouldn't be sitting here." She scrunches up her nose.

"Stop. Nothing happened."

"You mean to tell me you had my brother all to yourself in his bed, in his clothes"—she points to the shirt I'm wearing—"and nothing happened?"

"That's what I'm telling you."

"Mac," she exhales. "I was kidding about the Hans thing. You know that, right? You can talk to me."

"Nothing happened. Well, I mean, I woke up with his arms around me, and his, you know, pressed against my ass, but that's it. We might have kissed a few times," I confess. "Oh, and he hugged me before he went downstairs to make me breakfast."

"He didn't try anything?"

"Nope." I'm not the least bit shocked. Rip has never been a player. He's always respected the women he's dated. Maybe he changed while I was away at school, but something tells me he didn't. That's just not who he is.

"Huh."

"Huh? What do you mean, huh?"

"I just… thought that he would, that's all. He's always asking about you and just thought there might be something there. I expected more than a few kisses and a hug."

"He asks about me?"

She nods. "Yeah, pretty frequently. I thought maybe he was finally pulling his head out of his ass and claiming you as his."

I don't know why I'm fighting this attraction. I guess I'm waiting for the other shoe to drop. It always does. "We both know that's not going to happen." I'm not sure what's going on between us, but it feels too good to be true. I don't want to get my hopes up.

"I guess we'll see."

I can tell she's not convinced that's not what's happening. However, I was here in the moment, and a hug and some tonsil hockey and words spoken in the moment isn't exactly what futures are made of. Even him dropping the word beautiful isn't enough to justify what she thinks might be happening.

"These should work." She points to the clothes on the bed. "What are you doing today that you needed to shower here?"

"I— Nothing that I know of. He did mention hanging out. He just told me he could get me some of your clothes that you keep here and that he was going down to start breakfast."

She wags her eyebrows. "He's into you."

"Stop it. You're going to get my hopes up. Besides, we both know Rip could have any woman he wants." I hold up my hand when she starts to argue. "You know I'm right," I tell her.

"Whatever you say, Mac. I'm going to shower with my fiancé. I'll see you downstairs." With a wag of her eyebrows, she jumps off the bed and leaves the room.

Grabbing the clothes she brought for me from the bed, I lock myself in his bathroom. His scent surrounds me.

I can't believe, after crushing on him as hard as I did, that I'm finally here, in his room. That I slept in his bed, in his arms last night. The teenager McKenna would be thrilled at this turn of events.

Who am I kidding? The adult McKenna is too.

AFTER MY SHOWER, I TOOK MY TIME GETTING DRESSED. LUCKILY LARAMIE AND I ARE THE same size, just like we've always been, and we have the same taste in clothes. She gave me a pair of cutoff jean shorts and a tank top. Some might think it's weird to wear your best friend's bra and panties, but they're clean, and this is Laramie, my very best friend. There are worse things I could be wearing. The outfit is perfect for the Texas summer heat. Knowing I've stalled long enough, I pull open his bedroom door and make my way downstairs.

"There she is. I thought you fell back asleep," Rip says as soon as I enter the kitchen.

"Sorry, the shower was too nice not to indulge." I take a look around the room. The long kitchen island has six barstools. Colby and Laramie are occupying two on one end, while Rip and Corbin take up two on the opposite, leaving two in the middle. I spy a plate full of crispy bacon and pancakes and have to bite down on my cheek to keep from smiling.

"Kenna," Rip says, my name pulling my attention away from breakfast. He's standing with a plate that I assume is for me as he places it on the island next to where he was sitting. "Come and eat."

"Why didn't you make my plate?" Corbin asks.

"Because you don't have legs like McKenna," Colby fires back.

"Is that how it is?" Corbin chuckles.

My eyes are locked on Rip. He smiles and shrugs before pulling out the barstool next to him, motioning for me to sit.

My eyes flash to my best friend, who's grinning from ear to ear. She mouths, "Told you," before turning back around and focusing on her plate.

My feet carry me to the seat Rip insisted that I take, and I sit.

"What do you want to drink?" Rip asks.

"Oh, I can get it." I start to stand, but his hand on my shoulder stops me.

He bends close, his hot breath brushing across my face. Goose bumps break out on my skin when he says, "Tell me what you want, Kenna."

You. The deep timbre of his voice and the way that his hand traces down my bare arm tells me he's not just asking what I want to drink. At least I don't think he is. I've not dated much. I wasn't kidding when I told Rip the guys at school were not my type. Give me a man in boots and well-worn jeans any day over sweater vests and loafers. "Juice is fine."

"You want some coffee too?"

"Um… sure. I can get it," I offer again.

"Let me take care of you," he says, his voice low and only for me. He stands and walks around the counter, pulling a mug out of the cabinet and pouring me a cup of coffee. "Black?"

"Yeah. Thanks." I take the offered cup when he hands it to me. I sip the nectar of the gods while I watch him also pour me a small glass of juice and slide it across the island. When he takes his seat next to me, I set my coffee down and settle down to eat. Just before I take my first bite, his large hand lands on my thigh. I pause and glance over at him out of the corner of my eye, but he's just taken a huge bite of bacon, his head turned toward Corbin, listening to whatever it is he's saying.

Turning to my left, I look over at Laramie, who's ignoring me for her fiancé. I get it. They just got engaged last night, but I need backup. I don't know what's happening here. It's as if I came home to the twilight zone. Every dream I've ever had about Rip wanting me is suddenly the only thing I can think about. Five years ago, before I left for college, I would have given anything for him to notice me. Here I am five years later, and I'm preening from his attention. I don't know what any of this means.

"You not hungry?" Rip asks, pulling me from my thoughts.

"No. It's good. Thank you."

"You okay?" He gives my thigh a gentle squeeze.

No. I am not okay. Why are you touching me? Please don't ever stop. Instead, I say, "Yeah, just still tired, I guess. Thank you for this."

He leans in close. "You're welcome." He pulls away and digs into his breakfast as though nothing has changed. Like he's not spinning my mind or my heart in circles. I want to ask him what all of this means. I want to know if his kisses, and his tender touch, mean something to him, like it does to me, but part of me thinks this attraction between us is all in my head. He's just being flirty and friendly.

That's all it is.

Right?

Chapter Five

RIP

I CAN'T STOP TOUCHING HER. IF SHE'S CLOSE TO ME, I HAVE TO HAVE MY HANDS ON HER. I can't seem to stop myself. I've wanted her for so long, and when she walked into my parents' place two days ago, something inside me shifted. That something craves her with an intensity I've never experienced before. I've always wanted her; she's gorgeous. What's surprising to me is the need that I have for her and the depth of my feelings that I never realized were there. The reality that she's home for good, and that I could finally have everything I've ever wanted, is a lot to take in.

I want her to be mine.

"So, what are we doing today?" Corbin asks from his seat next to me. He's resting his arm on the island, his chin propped up on his hand. It's easy to see he's hungover from last night.

All of our plates are empty, even McKenna's, which makes me smile. I don't know why, but something about the fact that I cooked for her, that I'm taking care of her, has my heart swelling in my chest. It's a new feeling, one I've never felt before, but it's one I could quickly get used to. I knew I cared about her. Hell, she's been in my life since we were kids. But this intensity, this need to be with her all the time, the yearning to feel her in my arms, it's new and unexpected.

I shrug and turn to look at McKenna. "You said you wanted to relax.

Anything specific you have in mind?" Whatever she wants to do, I hope it involves me. I want all of her time.

"Oh, you don't have to entertain me." She's quick to reply.

I lean in close, getting a whiff of my body wash, and my cock stirs, knowing she smells like me. "We talked about this," I remind her. "I want to spend time with you." *You need to relax, and I need you.* "Tell me what you want to do today."

"I'm up for anything."

I look past McKenna to my sister. "Lara?"

She places her hand on McKenna's shoulder. "Don't you have to study?"

"Yeah, but uh... Rip talked me into taking the day off."

My sister winks at McKenna, then looks past her to me. "The lake. Today is the perfect day to soak up some sun."

"Kenna?"

"Sure, I'm good with that."

"You sure?" I only want to do what will make her happy. She deserves the break.

"I'm sure," she says, leaning toward me just a little. "I need to check in with Grams and Gramps, just out of courtesy."

"I'll drive you over. You text me when you're ready to head to the lake."

"Oh, you don't have to do that. I can walk. And you don't have to wait for me. I can meet you there."

"I'll drive you," I counter. I don't even address that she can meet us there. The others can do what they want. I'm going to wait for her.

"Rip," she sighs, and my cock twitches. I love the sound of my name falling from her lips.

"Kenna, I'll drive you over. It's not a big deal. I'll head into town and grab some ice for the cooler and some stuff for the lake. It's on the way." I know she lives just across the field, but it's at least a fifteen-minute walk, if not more, and it's hot as hell out today. It's supposed to be pushing the high nineties. Besides, that's all the more time I have to spend with her.

"You know he's stubborn," Laramie chimes in.

"Fine. Thank you."

"I'm ready when you are." I stand and grab her plate and mine and place them in the dishwasher.

"What about my plate?" Corbin asks, smirking.

"Are your legs broken?"

"Nope," he says, popping the *p*. Then he turns his gaze to McKenna with her long legs in those short-ass shorts. "Mac's aren't either," he says. I can't see his face because he's looking at her, but I know he's kidding. At least I think he is. As one of my best friends, he knows I've had a thing for McKenna since before she left for college. He would never try to swoop in and claim her as his. I know that, but it doesn't stop the growl in my voice.

"James," I say, calling him by his last name. It's a warning, and everyone here knows it.

"Watch out, bro," Colby tells him. "You're about to wake the beast."

Corbin throws his head back and laughs. "Stop, my head can't take it," he says, pressing his fingertips against his temple.

It serves him right. "That's what you get," I tell him. Walking back around the island, I place my hand on McKenna's back as she stands. I want to slide my hand under her tank top to feel her soft skin. "Ready?" I leave my hand above her clothing.

"Yeah, I just need to run upstairs and get my clothes," she says, her face flushed.

"I'll throw them in the wash with mine and give them back to you."

"Really, that's not necessary."

"I'll wash them," I say, guiding her to the front door. "I'm heading into town. Any requests?" I toss over my shoulder on my way to the front door.

"Get stuff for sandwiches, and I'll make them up when you get back," Laramie answers.

I throw my hand in the air in a wave, not bothering to look back. Once we reach the front door, I grab my keys from the bowl that sits on a small table in the entryway. "After you," I say, pulling the door open.

"Thanks," McKenna says softly.

Once the door is shut, my hand goes back to the small of her back, and I guide her to the passenger side of my truck. When I reach for the door handle, she stops me with her hand on my arm.

"You don't have to open doors for me, Rip."

I smile down at her. "If a man isn't opening doors for you, Kenna, he's not worth your time."

"Are you saying that you're worth my time?" She seems shocked at her own question.

Letting go of the handle, I lean in until her back is pressed against the door of my truck. I brace my arms above her head, my palms flat resting on the window. "I don't know," I say, staring down into her big brown eyes. "I want to be."

Her intake of breath tells me that she's surprised.

I want to kiss her. It wouldn't take much for me to lean in just a little further and press my lips to hers. I already know what her lips feel like, pressed firmly against mine. That doesn't mean I don't need to feel them again. Closing the distance, I do exactly that and kiss her. I take my time, tracing her lip with my tongue, before pulling back. "Let's get you home to visit with your grandparents." I try like hell not to lean in and devour her. Dropping my hands, I wait for her to move so I can open the door for her.

Not another word is spoken as she climbs in, and I shut the door. I don't need her words. I saw the heat in her eyes, and the rapid rise and fall of her chest. She's just as affected by that kiss as I am.

Taking my time walking around the back of the truck, I adjust my cock in my jeans. I meant what I told her. I don't know if I'm good enough. To be honest, I'm not sure there is a man out there who is, but I want to be. I know she and I need to talk. I need to tell her what I'm thinking, what I'm feeling, but that opens the opportunity for her to push me away. Right now, she's letting me kiss her and hold her. I need to take this slow. At least I need to try to until we talk.

"Thanks for the ride," she says once I'm settled behind the wheel.

"You're welcome. Any special requests for the lake?"

"No, not really. Whatever is fine."

"You sure?"

"Yeah, just the thought of being there and relaxing is enough."

"I'm proud of you," I tell her. "We've missed you." *I've missed you.* "But I'm so fucking proud of you for chasing your dreams."

"Thanks." Her reply is softly spoken. "I can't wait to be done with the bar exam. I feel as though I've lived with my nose stuck in a book my entire life. This was always the goal, to finish law school and come home to work with Gramps. I'm so close I can taste it."

"You're going to nail it, Kenna," I say, pulling into her grandparents' driveway. "You're badass like that." I put the truck in Park. "They're proud of you, and I know they're glad to have you home," I say, pointing at the house.

"Yeah, Gramps keeps telling me he's ready to retire. He's keeping the practice open for me. I really hope that I get a little time for us to work together."

"I know he's been looking forward to this as well. I'm sure he's going to slowly make his transition." In fact, I know he is. I keep an eye on Harold and Agnes and have dinner at their place at least once a week. McKenna is the light of their life.

"I know. They saved me." She looks over at me. "Gramps fought the courts for me, and that's why I want to be a lawyer. I want to fight for those who can't fight for themselves."

"You're amazing." I lean in and press my lips to hers. "Now, go say hi to Harold and Agnes for me. Call me or text me when you're ready for me to pick you up."

"I can—" I hold my index finger to her lips to stop her.

"Call me, Kenna. I'm not going to the lake without you." I wouldn't be much fun watching the clock, wondering when she was going to get there anyway.

Her shoulders relax. "Okay. Thank you again. For everything."

"My pleasure, beautiful."

Her cheeks instantly turn a light shade of pink as she reaches for the handle and climbs out of the truck. I should have opened the door for her and walked her to the door, but I know me. I know I would never leave. Not unless she made me. I crave her. Sleeping with her in my arms, waking up the same way, I want that every day and every night. I should never have let it get that far because now, she's all I can think about.

Pulling out of her grandparents' driveway, I point my truck toward town. Mentally I'm making a list of the things I know she loves. At least, I hope she still loves them. My girl wants a relaxing day, and that's what she's going to get. Making sure to buy her favorite things will show her that I pay attention. She's not just my sister's best friend, and it's time I let her see that.

We're going to have to have that talk, and soon.

I know she's stressed about passing the bar. I'll hold off until she takes the exam, but after that, all bets are off. I'm ready to make her mine.

Chapter Six

MCKENNA

MY FEET FEEL AS THOUGH THEY'RE FILLED WITH LEAD AS I WALK AWAY FROM HIS TRUCK. I made a mistake. I should never have agreed to stay at his place last night, and I should never have stayed in his bed. It took one night for all of those hopes and dreams for what we might one day be to come rushing back. Only this time, I'm not a teenager, and neither is he. We're both adults, and my crush is heading into the "more" category. That's an issue seeing as our lives are too entwined. I'm home for good, and this isn't just a fling I can walk away from.

Walking into the house, I smell Gram's baking something. "It smells good in here," I call out.

"McKenna." She smiles wide when I walk into the kitchen. "How was the bonfire?"

"Good. We all stayed at Rip's instead of going back to Laramie's."

"Oh, well, that was nice of him to let everyone stay at his place. He's such a nice boy."

"Um, Gram, I wouldn't describe Rip as a boy. He's definitely all man." Thoughts of waking up in his arms with his hard length pressed against me flash in my mind. All man indeed.

"Is he now?" she asks with a knowing smile.

Gram and Gramps raised me. They're my only family, and we're close, so of course, they both know about my past schoolgirl crush on Rip. "Yep." I know that my face is flushed. I can feel the heat as it creeps up from my neck to my cheeks. I'm a grown woman. Talking about him shouldn't make me blush.

"I didn't expect you home. It's been ages since you've seen your friends."

"It's been ages since I've seen you and Gramps. Speaking of, where is he?"

"He's out back meddling in the garden. And you're young, McKenna, and you work so hard. You deserve some downtime with your friends."

"We're going to the lake later today," I say as the back door opens and Gramps comes in, carrying a couple of tomatoes.

"Look, Agnes." He grins. "They're coming on early this year." He stops next to me, leaning in and kissing my cheek. "Mac," he says affectionately, in a way only he can. "You feeling all right? You look flushed."

"Oh, she's fine. We were just discussing Rip," Gram says, teasing me.

"Stop!" I laugh. "There is nothing going on with Rip and me. He's Laramie's brother. We were all close growing up. You know that." I sound defensive even to my own ears. I don't really know what's going on with Rip. What I do know is last night and yesterday, that's not normal for us. I've never slept in his bed, and he's never called me beautiful.

"Nice young man," Gramps adds.

"Enough about Rip. How's the garden?" I ask Gramps.

"Good, good." He nods. "These beauties will taste mighty fine on a juicy cheeseburger for dinner." He sets the tomatoes on a paper towel on the counter.

"The homegrown ones do taste better than the ones you buy at the grocery store," I agree.

"What's this about the lake?" Gramps asks, taking a seat next to me.

"A group of us are going to the lake later."

"It's a good day for it. Why are you going later instead of while the sun is high in the sky?"

"I wanted to come home and see you and Grams. I feel like I've barely seen you since I've been home."

"Go on, enjoy your day," Gramps encourages me. "We miss you, Mac, but you deserve some fun. Remember, I went through law school, and it's a lot harder now than it was back then. Call your friends, and go have some fun."

"I want to spend time with the two of you too," I tell him. "I'll be honest, Gramps. I'm not really feeling the love right now."

"Trust me, darlin', there's more love for you in this old heart than you could ever understand." He taps his hand on his chest.

"He's right, you know. You need to be hanging out with your friends and relaxing. I know you're worried about the bar, but, honey, you have to take some time to breathe and soak up the sun. It will do wonders to clear your mind. We love you, but you're home now, McKenna." She smiles softly. "Go, have fun." Grams waves her hand at me. "Have you eaten? I can make you something before you go," she offers.

"Yes. Rip made pancakes and bacon."

"Extra crispy?" she asks.

"Yep," I say, popping the *p*.

"Train him right, sweetheart." Gramps chuckles. "Agnes, what do you say we call Mary and Tom and see if they want to go grab some ice cream?"

"Sounds like a plan to me. McKenna, take these with you." She hands me a plastic container.

"What is it?"

"Chocolate chip cookies. I made them this morning."

"Are you sure?"

"Of course I am. You know I love to bake. I just had an itch to do so this morning. It's nice to spend time in the kitchen just because I want to. This is my happy place. We'll never be able to eat all of them on our own. Now, call your friends. Go have fun."

I stand and pull Grams into a hug. "Thank you, and thank you for the cookies. Love you."

"I love you too," she says as we pull out of our embrace.

"Gramps." I walk to him with my arms wide open, and he doesn't hesitate to wrap me in a hug. "Love you."

"Love you too. Have fun and be safe. If you need us…." His voice trails off.

"I know. Call you. I'll probably stay with Laramie tonight like we were supposed to last night. Oh, I forgot to tell you. Laramie and Colby got engaged last night!"

"He finally did it." Grams smiles. "Tell them we said congratulations."

"I will. I guess I need to go change. Enjoy your ice cream." With a wave over my shoulder, I head upstairs to my room. The same one that hasn't changed at all since the day I left for college.

Digging into my dresser, I pull out my black bikini. It's from two summers ago. I don't have much time for leisure. I need to go shopping to pick up a new one. This one will have to do. Besides, it's barely used. Quickly, I strip out of the clothes that Lara let me borrow and grab the bikini.

"Damn, I better call Rip." Grabbing my phone from the dresser, I send him a text.

Me: Hey. Change of plans. I'll be ready for the lake when you are.

Not ten seconds later, my phone is ringing, and Rip's name flashes on the screen. "Hey," I greet him.

"Why the change of plans? I told you I didn't mind waiting on you."

"I know. I appreciate that. Gram and Gramps insisted I go and hang out with friends. So, I'm getting changed now."

"Changed?"

"Into my suit?"

"Right now?"

"Yes. I'm, uh, actually naked talking to you. I was just sending a quick text. I didn't expect you to call me."

"You're naked?" His voice is low and gruff.

"I am." My voice is sultry, and I wasn't even trying. That's just what he does to me.

"I'm almost home. I'll stop and get you before I go back to my place to grab the cooler."

"Are you sure? I can meet you there," I offer.

"Kenna, I'll be right there. Just— Fuck, I'm on my way." With that, the call ends.

Tossing my phone on the bed, I rush to get dressed, wondering what I might have said to upset him. He sounded upset, but there is nothing I can think of. Unless he's mad I offered to meet him at his place. Surely not. Shit, I'm doing it again. I have to stop comparing every man to my father. I know that Rip is his own man, but other than Gramps, my experience is that if something is wrong... it's my fault. I can hear my therapist, Maggie, in my head telling me that all men are not my father. I know that, rationally, but the little girl in me sometimes forgets.

Slipping a pair of my own cutoff jean shorts and a tank top over my bikini, I slip my feet back into my flip-flops. After sliding my phone into my back pocket, I grab a small tote from my closet. Across the hall, I grab a towel, some sunscreen, and a few hair ties out of the bathroom and shove them into my tote. The only thing I need is my wallet. After searching my room, and downstairs, I remember that I left it at Rip's before we went to the field for the fire. It looks like I'd have been going back to his place today regardless.

I'm in the living room saying goodbye when I hear his truck pull up. "That's Rip. I'll see you later. I'll be sure to let you know if I'm not coming home." With a hug and a kiss on the cheek to each of them, I'm headed toward the door.

"Oh," I say when I pull open the door to find Rip standing on the front porch.

He takes his time, letting his eyes roam over me. When he's had his fill, his eyes find mine. "You got everything you need?"

"Yes." I hold up a small tote.

"Why don't you grab some clothes for tomorrow. Just in case," he suggests.

"Good point. I need to wash Laramie's from today to give them back to her."

"Just toss them in your bag. I can wash them. She leaves them at my place anyway."

"You don't have—" The look he gives me shuts me up.

"Are we really going to argue over laundry twice in one day?" he asks, wearing an amused smile.

"Fine. I'll be right back. Gram and Gramps are in the living room. You want to come in and say hi?"

"I can't."

"What do you mean you can't? They love you."

"Kenna—" He looks down at his crotch and back up to me. "I can't."

My eyes travel to where he was looking, and I gasp. He's hard. Clearly, *obviously* hard. "Oh!" I say a little too loud. "Your... um, yeah, okay. I'll be... I'll be right back." On shaking knees, I turn to head back into the house to get

Laramie's clothes and some extras for me.

"Kenna?"

I freeze and turn to look at him. His eyes are smoldering. I swallow hard. "Yeah?"

"This is your fault."

"M-My fault?"

He nods and takes a step closer so we're nose to nose, barely a breath apart. "You were naked when I talked to you. This is what happens when I think about you naked." With that, he pulls back. "I'll be in the truck. Tell them I said hi." He points inside the house.

I turn back around and rush upstairs. "Forgot something!" I call out. My knees feel weak, and my heart is beating like a heavy drum in my chest.

I did that?

Me?

The thought of me naked did that?

I can't think about that right now. Grabbing a backpack from the closet, I toss in the clothes I borrowed from Laramie, as well as a change of clothes for me, a bra, panties, shorts, and a tank. Across the hall, I grab my own toothbrush and call it good.

I'm on the bottom step when I remember the cookies. Making a detour to the kitchen, I place the container in my tote bag for the beach.

"Bye again," I call over my shoulder as I rush out the door. Once I'm on the front porch, my steps slow, and I focus on pulling in even breaths. Rip reaches over and pushes open my door before settling back behind the wheel of his truck.

"All set?"

"Y-Yes."

"Everyone is still at my place. Laramie is going to make sandwiches while

I get the cooler packed."

"I can help."

"You're supposed to be relaxing."

"Trust me, making some sandwiches and packing a cooler is relaxing."

"I don't want you working today. This is supposed to be a break for you."

"It's not working. It's making food and drinks, both of which you need in order to live. So, it's not work. I'm just trying to live." He glances over at me, and I give him a knowing grin.

"You're going to kick ass at this lawyer thing, aren't you?" he asks with humor lacing his voice.

"You know it," I reply as he pulls into his driveway. Together, we carry in the bags from the store.

"Hey. I'm going to…." Laramie's voice trails off when she sees me in the kitchen with Rip. "I was just going to call you to see when you wanted to head out." She looks from me to her brother.

"Gram and Gramps insisted I go, so here I am."

"Here you are," she echoes. "And you called Rip?"

I nod. "Yeah. He insisted I call him when I was ready to go."

"Interesting." She grins.

"Are we making sandwiches or not?" I try to steer the conversation from whatever it is she finds interesting about her brother having me call him.

Before she can answer, Rip places his hand on my hip. He leans down, and I think he's going to kiss me. Instead, he says, in a voice clearly just for me, "I'm going to go load the cooler." With a quick tap, he releases me and walks out the door.

"Looks like you and my brother might be getting your forever after all." Laramie grins.

"Stop. He's just being nice."

"Uh-huh. That"—she points at my hip—"wasn't just nice. That's something my fiancé would do to me. He's got it bad. You both do."

"Sandwiches." I toss the lunchmeat at her across the counter.

She starts singing "U Got It Bad" by Usher, and we both dissolve in a fit of laughter.

I don't know if she's right about Rip, but she's hit the nail on the head when it comes to me. What I thought was a schoolgirl crush is now so much more. I don't know what the future holds for us, but I'm not going to stress over it. I'm just going to enjoy hanging out, and whatever happens, happens.

Chapter Seven

RIP

I'M NOT EVEN TRYING TO KEEP MY HANDS TO MYSELF. I'VE TRIED, AND I JUST DON'T HAVE the willpower. Not when it comes to McKenna. Not anymore. That's why my hand is currently resting on her thigh as I point my truck toward the lake. Laramie and Colby insisted they drive separately. Well, Laramie insisted, and like the lovesick fool Colby is for my little sister, he agreed. Corbin and a few of our other friends are already there. He's called and texted me what feels like a million times asking when we're showing up. Speaking of, my phone vibrates from the cupholder.

"You going to get that?" McKenna asks.

"Nope."

"Why not?"

"I'm driving. I'm sure it's just Corbin. You can check it. Tell him we're on our way."

"You want me to get into your phone?" she asks, surprised.

"You can, or if you don't feel like dealing with him, just let it ride. He'll see us soon enough."

"It's not that. It's just, aren't guys' cell phones off-limits? Especially single guys?"

"Not mine. Not to you." *I'm not single, at least not in my mind.*

"So, you're just going to let me go through your phone?"

"Yep." Glancing over, I see her face masked in surprise. "What? You think I'm hiding naked pictures or numbers or something?"

"I don't know. I just— There's this guy who was in a lot of my classes. One day before class started, he and his buddies were moaning and groaning about his girlfriend getting into his phone. From the sound of it, he'd been getting nudes from half the state, and they were all saved on his phone."

"You think I'm that guy?" I draw lazy circles on her thigh with my thumb.

"N-No," she answers. Is it my touch that has her stumbling over her words? Or the conversation?

"Good, because I'm not. There's nothing in my phone that you can't see or have access to. Go on, take a look." I nod to my phone in the cupholder.

"No, that's okay. I don't need to look. Besides, it's none of my business what's in your phone."

"Well, I say it's your business. I'm an open book for you, McKenna." My phone rings again, and I laugh. "Just answer it." I can't let go of the wheel, and I'm not going to stop touching her. She's Corbin's only shot at finding out where we are.

"Fine." She reaches for the phone and taps the screen placing it on speaker. "Hello."

"Mac?" Corbin asks, confused.

"Hey, Corbin."

"Where's Rip?"

"He's driving."

"Are you two on your way?"

"Yeah, we're about ten minutes out."

"So, you and my boy, huh?" he asks. I make a mental note to kick his ass.

"Rip volunteered for me to ride with him."

"I bet he did." Corbin chuckles. "Y'all got food? I'm starving."

"Yes, we have food." She shakes her head. "I think you'll survive until we get there."

"What took you so long?"

"I was visiting with my grandparents, and Rip had to go to the store, and then we made sandwiches." She lists off everything we've done today.

"Yo, James, you're up!" someone yells from the background.

"That's Russ. We're playing corn hole. I gotta go." With that, the line goes dead.

"He's still the same whirlwind he's always been." McKenna laughs as she places my phone back into the cupholder.

"Did you expect anything less?" I ask with a quick glance in her direction.

"Nope." I can hear the smile in her voice.

"So, you ever plan on upgrading this old truck?" she asks.

"Shh, you're going to hurt her feelings."

Laughter, the most incredible sound, fills the cab of the truck. "Oh, I wouldn't want to do that."

"They don't make them like they used to," I tell her as I turn onto the road that leads us to the lake.

"Right, because a radio that doesn't play cassette tapes and has power windows are an abomination," she teases.

Parking the truck, I lift the console. My phone goes flying into the back seat, but I ignore it and pull her toward me. She squeals with laughter. "No, but most of the new trucks no longer have bench seats, which means I can't have my girl sitting next to me." We're close, so close it would only take minuscule effort from either of us for our lips to connect.

"You think she'd be mad that I'm in her spot?" Her question is breathless.

Before I can reply, there's a loud banging on the window that has us pulling apart. Looking over, I see Corbin standing there with a wide-ass grin on his face. I make a mental note to get him back. One day he's going to fall hard, and I have a long-ass mental list of ways to torture him like he so obviously enjoys torturing me.

"Right," McKenna says as she slides over to the passenger door and climbs out of the truck.

I take a minute to rake my hands over my face and focus on willing my cock to deflate. It's a wasted effort anytime I'm around her. Feeling a little more composed, I exit the truck, only to open the back door and search for my phone before we start unloading the food and snacks.

"Grab the cooler from the back," I tell Corbin.

"On it." He lowers the tailgate, grabs the cooler, and takes off walking toward our group of friends.

Laramie and Colby pull in, and together, the four of us work on getting everything unpacked. There are three huge picnic tables that are now covered with food and drinks, and our rowdy group settles around and digs in. Realizing I forgot something, I head back to the truck. In the back seat, I grab the old quilt I brought for McKenna to sit on. Tossing it on one of the lawn chairs, I take a seat at the picnic table, squeezing in next to McKenna and our friend Russ. He graduated with Corbin and me.

"This is for you," McKenna says, handing me a plate.

"Thanks." I lean over and kiss her cheek. Her eyes seem to glass over as she smiles up at me.

Russ, from his seat next to me, sighs. I turn to see what the fuss is about. "You calling it?" he asks, his voice low for only me to hear.

"Yep."

"I figured."

"She's always been mine."

"I just assumed it's been a while...." His voice trails off.

"When it comes to McKenna and assumptions, always assume that it's me. Always."

"What are you two whispering about over there?" Laramie asks from the table across from us.

"He's trying to steal my girl," I say, placing my arm around McKenna's shoulders.

"Stop." She snickers and pushes me away.

"Rope swing challenge," Corbin says before shoving the remainder of his sandwich into his mouth.

"You know Rip's going to win," Russ tells him. "He always does."

"Maybe not this time." Corbin smiles with glee, which tells me he's up to something.

"You been working on your technique?" I tease.

"Don't you worry about me, Callahan."

"What are the rules?" Josh, another friend of ours, asks.

"What are you talking about?" Stephanie, Josh's date, asks.

"We have rope swing challenges to see who can jump the farthest into the water."

"From where?" Stephanie asks.

"Up there." Colby points to the huge oak tree that stands tall on the far side of the lake.

"Do you two do it?" Stephanie looks at Laramie and then McKenna.

"Yeah." McKenna shrugs. "It's a good time."

"You can jump with me," Josh assures Stephanie.

"Together?"

"Yep." He wags his eyebrows.

"How do you get up there?" she asks, pointing toward the tree.

"We've created a well-worn path over the years," Laramie tells her.

"I'm not sure I can do it."

"It's easy. I'll go first." McKenna stands and pulls her tank top over her head. I swallow my tongue as I take her in. *Fuck me. She's a goddess.*

"Here." Corbin hands me a napkin, barely containing his laughter.

I wad it up and toss it on the table. "You think you've still got it?" I ask McKenna as she unzips her shorts and pulls them over her legs. My eyes trail the movement like a starving man sitting in front of a steak.

"Please," she scoffs. "I've got this."

"Prove it." I stand and pull my shirt over my head, tossing it on top of McKenna's neatly folded clothes on the bench seat of the picnic table.

"I'm taking bets." My sister laughs. "Mac's got this one in the bag."

I smile and shake my head. "You ready?" I ask McKenna.

"It's on, Callahan." She grins and takes off running toward the tree.

I sprint after her. Getting close, I wrap my arm around her waist and sling her up on my shoulder as I run the rest of the way to the tree. She's laughing and playfully swatting at my back. I grip the backs of her thighs, and my hands itch to explore her silky-smooth skin.

When we reach the tree, I slowly slide her down from my shoulder, letting every inch of her press against every hard inch of me. No, I'm not talking about my abs. Her eyes are wide as she stares up at me. Her hair has fallen into her eyes from her ride hanging upside down on my shoulder. I tuck the loose strands behind her ear. "Jump with me."

"W-What?"

She knows me too well, aware my words have a double meaning. I want her to jump into this with me. I want her to be mine. Fuck, I want to be hers. I want to see where this goes.

"The rope."

"Oh." Her face falls.

"Hey." I cradle her face in the palm of my hands. "That too," I whisper, leaning in close. I'm going to kiss her. After all this time, I'm going to make my intentions known to the girl who stole my heart when I was nine years old.

"What are you waiting on?" Corbin calls out.

"Fucking Corbin," I grumble, resting my forehead against hers. "Jump with me?" I ask again, trying to gain my composure.

"Okay."

Bending, I place my hands on her waist. "On the count of three," I say as I count off. When I get to three, I lift as she jumps and wraps her legs around my waist. My cock is hard and throbbing as she settles against me.

"Rip," she moans my name, and I debate stalking off into the field and having my way with her. If it weren't for the fact that I refuse for our first time to be in a damn wheat field, I would do just that.

I crave her.

Instead of ravishing her like I want, I ignore the fact that my cock is resting just between her thighs. I ignore the fact that there are two very thin pieces of clothing separating me from the promised land. "You ready?" I croak.

She nods.

"Hold onto me. Whatever you do, don't let go."

"Are you sure this thing will hold both of us?" she asks, staring up at the rope.

"You've seen couples do this countless times."

"That was a long time ago."

"I replaced the rope a few weeks ago. It's strong and secure. I promise." I press my nose against hers. "I won't let anything happen to you."

"Okay. Let's do it." Her voice is full of conviction. I want to beat on my chest that she's put her absolute trust in me.

"Getting old over here, Callahan!" Russ calls out.

Standing to my full height, I place my hands on the small of her back and pull her closer. "Lock your legs tight," I say as I grab the rope. "Ready?"

"Ready."

Tightening my grip, I rush toward the ledge, and we're flying over the lake. I release the rope and immediately wrap my arms around her. The water hits my back, and it feels like a knife, but the shrill sound of her laughter and the way she clings to me even after we hit the water is more than worth it. We surface, and I tread water to keep us afloat.

"Well?" I ask her.

"You kept me safe."

"Always, Kenna." I press my lips to her forehead just in time for her to release herself from my hold and swim toward the bank. I follow after her, only at a much slower pace, giving my cock time to settle. When I reach the bank, she's standing there with a towel over her shoulders, handing one out for me.

"Rip!" I turn over my shoulder to see Corbin, Colby, Josh, and Russ up on the hill by the swing. "Get your ass back up here."

I wave, then turn back to McKenna. "You good?"

"Yeah. I'm going to soak up some sunshine."

"Hold on a sec." I run over to the lawn chair, where I dropped the quilt, and grab it, bringing it back to where she's standing. Spreading the blanket out on the grass, I retrieve her bag, our clothes, and a bottle of water from the cooler. "Here." I hand her the water before placing our things on the blanket.

Her eyes flash to our clothes and back to me.

"You need help with your sunscreen?" I ask her.

"No. I think I'm good. You going to show them how it's done?" She nods toward the rope swing.

"Depends? You want me to sit with you?"

Her smile is bright and beautiful. "Go have fun. Just be safe?"

"Always." I want to lean in and kiss her. I almost do, but I think better of it. I know that my sister and Stephanie are close by. I settle for touching the tip of her nose with my index finger before turning and heading back up the hill.

That's how the rest of the afternoon goes.

The girls take a few turns on the rope to get cooled off, but they spend the majority of their time soaking up the sun, and I'm sure talking about my sister's engagement. As far as the guys and me, we do what we do best—goof off on a warm, sunny afternoon. My eyes wander to McKenna often. It's damn good to have her home. I can feel the change in me with her here, and I can't wait to see what happens next.

Chapter Eight

MCKENNA

I'VE SPENT THE LAST THREE DAYS WITH MY NOSE BURIED IN A BOOK. I'M SO CLOSE TO MY dream of becoming a lawyer, I can taste it.

Me.

I'm going to be a lawyer.

I've dreamed of being just like Gramps since I came to live with them. His knowledge of the legal system kept me with them. He saved me from my drug-addict mother. I would say parents, but dear old dad eventually bailed. Apparently, I ruined his life. Gram and Gramps have paid for countless therapy sessions for the messed-up insecurities and feelings I have toward my biological parents. My grandparents are my parents; they raised me and showed me love. I shudder every time I think about how my life would have turned out had my grandparents not fought for me.

"McKenna Dawson, Attorney at Law," I answer the phone.

"Mac," my best friend replies.

"Hey, Lara." I'd know her voice anywhere.

"Good to see you're practicing. Are you hiding from me?" she inquires.

"No. Why would you think that?"

"I haven't seen you since the lake on Saturday."

"That's because I've been buried in books. Studying my life away for the bar exam."

"I know. McKenna, you've got this. You're wicked smart, but there is such a thing as studying too much."

"Are you feeling neglected?" I tease.

"Yes. I am. You and me, we're going to the Silver Star tonight for dinner and drinks."

"What time?"

"Seven."

"Okay."

"Good. I'll pick you up."

"You don't have to do that."

"Mac," she sighs. "I'm picking you up. I'll see you at seven."

"Is this a date?" I joke. "You know I don't kiss on the first date."

Her laughter greets me through the line. "Stop it," she splutters. "I've missed you so much. I'll pick you up at seven."

"See ya then," I say, ending the call.

"Did I hear you right? You have a hot date tonight?" Grams asks.

"No. Not unless you count dinner and a drink with Laramie?"

She nods. "That's a date with an old friend. The best kind, in fact."

"I couldn't agree more. I think getting away from all of this"—I motion to the dining room table where my books are all spread out—"might do me some good."

"I think that's a great idea. You're going to burn yourself out. Your grandfather says you know the information. He said you did great when he was quizzing you last night."

"Yeah, well, Gramps is biased." I laugh.

"I think he's both." She grins. "Speaking of," she says as Gramps walks in the door, "what are you doing home so early?"

"Court was canceled, so I thought I'd come on home and see my girls."

"Good, you can tell this one she's going to overload that brain of hers," Grams teases.

"She's right, you know. Go on, get out of here. Get some fresh air."

"Are you getting sick of me, Gramps?"

"I'll never have enough of you, but I would like to spend more time with my wife." His eyes crinkle at the corners. "It's time for me to sit back and enjoy life and let my granddaughter take over the reins." He winks at me, and my chest swells with pride and love for them.

"Are you really going to trust me with your legacy?" I ask him. I know this is what we've always talked about, and a part of me still feels as though I'm not worthy. That little girl in me who was told she was a mistake is still inside me.

"McKenna—" He releases his hold on Grams and comes to stand next to me, bending to wrap his arms around me. "The office isn't my legacy, sweetheart. You are."

Hot tears prick my eyes. I nod as it's not possible to speak with the golf-ball-size lump of emotion clogging my throat.

"Now, now, enough of that. Don't be crying on me. Your grams will have me sleeping on the couch, and I didn't get married to sleep alone, Mac." He winks at me and smiles his familiar smile.

Gramps is one of those people who loves with his entire heart. He refuses to go to bed angry, and my grams is the moon and the stars in his eyes. He loves her fiercely and with a passion I've only witnessed between them. I dream of finding a man who loves me half as much as Gramps loves Gram.

She's the same with him.

Sure, I've seen them argue, but they're always respectful with one another, and no matter what the argument, the love between them is undeniable.

"Why don't you go out and get some fresh air? Call your friends and see if they want to do something? Get you out of this house and away from these books for a little while," Gramps suggests.

"You trying to get rid of me, old man?" I place my hands on my hips and try to glare at him, but it's impossible. We both know there's zero heat behind my words.

"I know what law school is like. I also know what the stress and worry over the bar exam are like. Trust me on this. Getting out of the house will do you some good. Clear your mind."

"Actually, Gram was saying the same thing. Laramie called, and we're going to dinner tonight."

"Wonderful. Here." He reaches into his wallet and hands me some cash. "Tonight is on me. Tell Laramie I said to show you a good time."

"This is Laramie we're talking about. That's a given." I laugh. "Thank you, Gramps. I love you." I kiss his cheek.

"Never a dull moment when that one's around," Gram says affectionately.

"Definitely not," I say, thinking about my best friend. I'll never forget the day we met, and we've been joined at the hip ever since. She's more than my best friend. She's my sister, and it has nothing to do with how I feel about her brother.

IT'S EARLY AFTERNOON, AND AFTER AN HOUR OF STUDYING, I NEED A BREAK. I STILL HAVE hours before I meet Laramie for dinner, so I decide to see what Grams is doing. Tossing my books to the side, I make my way downstairs, following the noise to the kitchen. Gram is frosting what looks like a cake. "You need some help?" I ask Gram.

"Oh, I think I'm good, but I would love the company." She smiles.

"Who's the cake for? It's adorable." I point to the bear cake she's working on.

"Oh, Sally Henson's little girl. She's turning three tomorrow."

"Are you staying busy with your cakes and pies and whatnot?" I ask, pulling up a stool at the island. I've been so lost in my world of studying that I feel like I've been neglecting them.

"I am. I've even had to turn people away, and you know I hate that."

"That's great. I'm so happy for you. I know you were nervous starting up your own business, but you're doing amazing."

"Don't go making me blush." She smiles warmly.

"Are you sure there isn't anything that I can help you with?"

"No. You work too much as it is."

"I'm taking a break, remember," I remind her.

"Yes, and do you know what taking a break means?" She raises her eyebrows, making me laugh.

"Fine, but I feel useless. It's been a really long time since I've been able to just sit with nothing to do."

"Well, I do need to drop this cake off and run to the store for supplies. Would you like to ride along?"

"I'm your girl, Gran."

"That you are." She smiles. We spend the next twenty minutes chatting while she finishes the cake. I miss being home.

"Thank you for your help. I'm going to box this up, and I'll be ready." She points to the bear cake.

"It's too cute." I smile at her before dashing up the stairs.

"THIS IS A HAUL," I TELL GRAMS AS WE PULL INTO THE DRIVEWAY. THE ENTIRE BACK OF HER van is full of baking supplies. After delivering the cake, we made her weekly run for supplies. I didn't expect the van to be loaded to max capacity. I was thinking a couple bags of flour and sugar, but no, we bought fifty-pound bags instead.

"I know." She grins.

"Is it like this every time you go shopping for supplies?"

"It is."

"I hate that you're lugging all this by yourself."

"Oh, I don't. Not usually. Rip usually stops by to help. Your grandfather swears he didn't put him up to it, but I'm not sure if I believe him."

"How does he know when you go?"

"Well, I'm somewhat a creature of habit. I always go shopping on Wednesday afternoons. I hate going at the beginning or at the end of the week and definitely not on weekends. The store is always packed."

Climbing out of her van, she opens the back, just as an old pickup truck comes barreling up the driveway. I stop and stare as Rip, in his faded blue jeans and sleeveless T-shirt, steps out of the truck and heads our way.

"Miss Agnes, you weren't planning on doing this without me, were you?" he asks, placing his hands on his hips.

"No." She waves him off. "Mac went with me today, so I was able to finish earlier than I usually do."

"I was watching for you," he tells her.

"Rip, I've told you I can handle this. I hate interrupting your workweek."

"It's fine. I do mostly paperwork on Wednesdays, and I can see you drive by from my office window." He winks at her, and she smiles.

"You're a good man, Rip Callahan," Gram says, patting him on the back.

Rip ducks under the back of the van, careful not to hit his head. "Kenna," he greets me. His voice is deep and husky and causes every single part of me to melt for him. Seriously, if I was ice cream, I'd be a puddle on the ground, and it has nothing to do with the Texas heat.

"Rip."

He winks at me, then begins to unload an armful of supplies and carry them into the house. With his help, it only takes three trips for each of us, with Rip carrying the majority of the load.

"Well, ladies, I need to get back to work."

"Thank you for your help. These are for you." Gram hands him a small container of something.

"Thank you. I have last week's container out in the truck."

Gram waves him off. "I'll get it some other time. You go on back to work. I appreciate your help."

"Have a good day," he tells her before turning his eyes to me. "Kenna, why don't you walk me out and I can give you that container?"

"Sure," I say, falling into step behind him.

"It's been a few days since I've seen you."

"Yeah, I've been studying nonstop. Gram and Gramps actually forced me to take a break this afternoon."

He nods. "I was hoping to get to spend more time with you now that you're home."

"I'm sure I'll see you around." It sounds like I'm brushing him off, but I'm not. I just need to process what all this new attention from him is. I mean I know what he says it is, but it's hard for me to grasp. It's confusing. On Saturday, when he drove me home from our day at the lake, he patted the seat next to him. I rode there in the center all the way home. His hand was on my thigh, driving me crazy. He walked me to the door, hugged the shit out of me, and kissed me on the forehead before stepping back and making sure I got inside safe.

That's the last I've seen of him. I don't know what any of this means, and the girl in me who had daydreamed about these exact moments doesn't have the guts to ask.

"Dinner tonight?" he asks.

"Sorry, I already made plans with Laramie."

"My sister is stealing my time with you too," he says softly.

"Another night?" I suggest. My voice quivers as my nerves take over. "Or not—" I stop talking when he steps in close.

"Anytime you want to see me, all you have to do is say the word. I'll be there."

My head tilts back as I stare up at him. "Tomorrow night?"

"My place. I'll make us dinner."

"Y-You don't have to do that. We can go out."

"Kenna." He pushes my hair back off my shoulder. "I'm making you dinner."

"Okay."

"What time will you be finished studying?"

"Never." I laugh nervously. "How about five?"

"Perfect. Come on over when you're done."

"Around five-thirty or six?" I suggest. I'll definitely need time to freshen up.

"I'll be ready for you. How about we eat at six? Will that give you time to change and do what you need to do?" He knows me so well.

I nod. "What can I bring?"

"Just you. Now give me a hug. I need to get back to work." He pulls me into his chest and wraps his strong arms around me. I don't hesitate to hug him back. I don't know how many hugs like this I'll get with him, so I'm taking what I can get. "Have fun tonight. Call me if you need a ride."

"We will."

With a wave, he's back in his truck and driving away from me. I watch him until I can no longer see him. It's not until I reach the door of the house that I realize I forgot the container. This should be fun to explain.

"Rip leave?" Gram asks.

"Yes."

"Where's the container?"

I look up to find her smirking. "He um... he thought he had it, but he didn't."

"I see." She grins. "Well, it's no worry. I can get it next time."

"Right. Next time. Let's get this put away." I keep my focus on the task at hand and pretend to ignore her knowing looks.

As I help Gram store all of her baking supplies, I can't help but think about Rip. About the change in him, at least when it comes to me, and the fact that he helps Gram every week. I wonder if Gramps did put him up to it. Regardless, the act has my heart swelling in my chest. I'm glad he helped to look out for them while I was gone.

It really is good to be home.

Chapter Nine

RIP

I'VE BEEN SITTING AT MY DESK FOR TWENTY MINUTES. I'VE STARED OUT THE WINDOW pretty much all that time. I wanted to beg McKenna to cancel on my sister, but I know they miss each other. I also wanted to ask her where they were going to dinner so that I could just happen to be there. I realize my thoughts are stalker-ish, so I refrained. Now, here I am, sitting and staring off into space, thinking of her.

My phone rings, pulling me out of my McKenna daze, and I laugh when I see it's my sister calling. "Lara," I answer.

"Big brother."

"What's up?"

"Oh, nothing. I just called to tell you that Colby might be reaching out to you. I'm having dinner with Mac tonight, so he might be lonely. He mentioned calling you and Corbin."

"Yeah? Where are the two of you headed?"

"Depends."

"On what?"

"You going to tell me what's going on between the two of you?"

"I don't know what you're talking about." It's not a complete lie. I don't know what's going on. I know that I want her. More today than I did at the lake on Saturday and more than the day she left for college. Time hasn't diminished my desire for her. It's fueled it.

"Come on now," she pries.

"I think I need to have this conversation with her first." Eleven words are all it takes for my sister to understand my feelings for her best friend.

"How long?"

"A while."

"How long is a while, Rip?"

"High school."

"Wow," she whispers. "I always thought maybe, I mean, I know she had a crush on you, but you never pursued her even when you had the chance." She's quiet, and so am I. What do I say to that? That I knew she was interested, but I was doing what I thought was best for her? "What are you going to do about it?"

"Still trying to figure that out." What I don't tell her is that I can't seem to keep my hands off her best friend or that McKenna is all that I can think about.

"I can help."

"No. I don't need your help."

"I'm her best friend. You need me," she says with confidence.

"I don't need your help," I say again, trying to steer her away from whatever point it is that she's trying to make.

"She's always had a thing for you."

I know. "She was always leaving for college."

"Rip Callahan, are you going to claim your girl?"

"If it's meant to be, it will be." That's what I tell her, and that's what I also keep telling myself. I want it to be—more than my next breath. I want to be able to call her mine.

"Well, I'm going to help you."

"Lara," I warn.

"Tonight, she and I are having dinner and drinks at the Silver Star. We're meeting there at seven."

"I'm not crashing her time with you. I know she misses you."

"Well, I miss her too, but I want this to happen. She could be my sister." She lets her proclamation hang between us.

"What, am I not a good enough sibling?"

"We can't share clothes."

"You and Kenna do that now."

"Figure it out," she says, calling an end to our back-and-forth banter. "I've never known you to back down from something that you want."

She's right. I don't, and when it comes to McKenna, I don't want to. "Who says I'm backing down?"

"Gah! Why are men so damn confusing?"

"Everything all right with you and Colby?"

"Yes! This is about you. You want her. Hell, it wouldn't surprise me if you were half in love with her, and I'm offering my help. I want you to get the girl, and you're being stubborn."

"I don't need your help, little sister."

"Well, you're getting it anyway. I'm team Rip and McKenna all the way."

Me too, little sister. Me too. "Have fun tonight. If you two need a ride, you call me." I leave no room for argument in my tone.

"Sure thing, big brother," she says, way too cheerily. "I'll talk to you soon."

"Was there a reason you called?"

"Nope. I'm good. Can't a girl just call her brother?"

"Laramie." I sigh.

"Gotta go. Bye, Rip!" The line goes dead.

I toss my phone on my desk. Resting my elbows on the dark mahogany wood, I bury my face in my hands. I've never wanted someone or anything, for that matter, as much as I want McKenna. My sister is right. I never back down from what I want, and this isn't me backing down. No, this is me planning for the long game. The end game. This is me wanting her for more than just a small moment in time, and I want her forever.

You can't rush forever.

I'M PACING THE LIVING ROOM, WEARING A PATH INTO THE HARDWOOD FLOORS, WHEN MY cell phone rings. It's Corbin. "Hello," I answer, continuing to pace.

"What are you getting into tonight?"

"Nothing much." Just driving myself crazy wanting to go into town, to the Silver Star specifically. Just to see her. Have I ever been this taken by a woman? No. No one has ever gotten to me like McKenna has.

"Colby and I are going to grab some food and a couple of beers. You in?"

"Where you going?"

"Silver Star. I guess Laramie and McKenna are going to be there. He wants to be close in case they need a ride home."

I stop pacing, and from my reflection, in the window, the scowl is gone, replaced with a smile. "I'm in."

Corbin's laughter is loud and boisterous as it flows through the line. "I figured as much. Meet us there?"

"When?"

"Thirty minutes?"

I don't need to look at the clock to know that it's seven. "I'll be there." I end the call. The girls will have had time to order and probably be started on dinner by the time we get there. I should probably feel guilty or like I'm spying on her, but I don't. I'm just going to be there in case she needs me. They can have their girl time. I'm just backup. If she doesn't need me, at least I'll get to see her. Lay my eyes on her. That's more than I can say for the past five years. I need to soak up as much time with her as I can. How else am I going to get her to fall in love with me?

Twenty minutes later, I'm pulling into the parking lot of the Silver Star Saloon. I don't see Corbin or Colby's trucks, but I spot my sister's car right away. I scan the lot looking for McKenna's and don't see it. They must have ridden together. I debate on going in alone, but that would be way too obvious. Instead, I turn off the truck and tap my fingers against the steering wheel as I wait for the guys to show up.

When Colby's truck pulls up, I grab my keys and my phone and meet him in front of our trucks. "Where's Corbin?"

"He's on his way. Let's grab a table."

I nod and follow him inside. As soon as the door closes behind me, my eyes are scanning, looking for her. I spot them at a high-top table. They both have plates of food and a beer in front of them. Something my sister says makes McKenna laugh. She throws her head back, and I swear the sound finds its way to my cock. That's nothing new when it comes to McKenna, but this time, the sound is stopped by my heart and squeezed it as well.

She takes my breath away.

Luckily for me, Colby is just as gone for my sister. I don't even have to suggest that we stop by their table and say hello. His feet carry him like a man on a mission. "Hey, you."

Laramie lifts her chin for a kiss. I'm envious as I turn to McKenna and her bright smile.

"Hi." She smiles up at me.

Unable to stop myself, I bend down and press my lips to her cheek.

"Hey," I whisper huskily.

"What are you guys doing here?"

"Just came to eat, and this one wanted to make sure Laramie didn't need a ride home." I point to Colby.

"Like you wouldn't have done that same thing if he hadn't. I know how protective you are of her," McKenna replies.

She's right. I am protective of my little sister. I also know that Colby's got her. Always. He loves her fiercely. I should feel guilty that I wasn't concerned about my sister, but I know that I don't have to be. Instead, all I could think about was McKenna. Seeing her, making sure she was okay. *I'm protective of you too.*

"He's got her," I say with confidence. "But who has you?" I ask. I reach out and push her hair over her shoulder. The silky strands feel so damn soft as they run through my fingers.

"I'm good, Rip."

"You are now," I assure her.

She opens her mouth to speak but quickly closes it. I've rendered her speechless. I don't know if that's a good thing or a bad thing, but I have this feeling I need to explain. Placing my hand on the back of her chair, I turn so that I'm blocking out everyone else. "I know you're strong and beautiful," I add. "I just want you to know you're not alone. I'm always going to be here." *Wanting you.*

"I love you both, but it's time for you to go," my sister says, breaking the spell we're under. I stand to my full height, keeping my hand on the back of McKenna's chair, letting my fingers lightly trace over her shoulder.

"Have fun, babe." Colby kisses her quickly.

I smile down at McKenna. "Have fun, babe." I wink at her and follow Colby to the small booth in the corner that gives us a clear view of their table.

Colby and I order drinks and wings, just as Corbin slides into the booth next to Colby. "Took you long enough," I tell him.

"Work sucked today," he explains.

"How's the build going?"

"Good." He nods. The waitress delivers our beers, and Corbin orders one for himself and an order of wings. "The homeowner keeps changing shit and gets pissed when we go over budget."

"I'd hate that part of your job," I tell him. Corbin and Colby both work for their father's construction company, James Construction.

"Tell me about it. Dad keeps hinting at retiring, wanting us to take over," Corbin says.

"What about you?" I ask Colby.

"It's part of the job, but I hate that shit."

"Why don't y'all hire someone to deal with the additions and the finances?"

"Not a bad idea," Colby agrees.

"It's always been a family thing," Corbin chimes in. "Wait." He turns to look at his brother. "What about Laramie?"

"What about her?"

"She said the other day she was ready for a change. She's been working at the hardware store since high school. She knows her way around the industry, and she's a lot less burly about these kinds of things than we are." He chuckles.

"She is going to be family." Corbin grins.

"Speaking of, you two set a date yet?" I ask, leaning back so the waitress can deliver our wings.

"Not yet. She's talking to McKenna about that tonight." He nods to where the girls are sitting. "I don't care when. Sooner rather than later if I have my choice."

My eyes travel to their table, and the girls have their phones out, I'm sure discussing dates. My heart gallops in my chest. I've married McKenna twice in my life, and I wouldn't hate it if we could do it again. Only this time for real. Baby steps. We'll get there.

"How's the farm?" Corbin asks.

"Same old. Just doing my thing," I tell him. We spend the next hour or so just shooting the shit. Somehow I manage to be present in the conversation and keep an eye on my sister and my... my McKenna. At least I want her to be mine. Corbin leaves to go to the bathroom, and I glance over at the girls. There are two guys hovering over their table.

"Not on my watch," I mumble, sliding out of the booth.

"What are you...." Colby's voice trails off when he sees what I'm going to break up. He makes it to Laramie. At the same time, I reach McKenna. "Hey, baby." He leans in and kisses his fiancée.

"Miss me?" I ask McKenna. I slide my arm around her waist. The perks of them sitting at a high-top table.

Her brown eyes peer up at me and are filled with relief. "Always," she replies.

"Hey, you with this guy?" the drunk ass asks McKenna.

"Yes. We told you we were taken," she tells him.

"Whatever." He looks over at his friend. "Let's go." They walk away from the table without a fight.

"Thanks," McKenna says.

Unable to stop my mouth, I lean in close, placing my lips next to her ear. "It gave me an excuse to hold you." Her quick intake of breath tells me that's not what she was expecting me to say. Good. I like the idea of surprising her.

"Our heroes," Laramie gushes dramatically. "You ready to go, Mac?"

"Yes. This was so much fun. I miss hanging out with you like this," McKenna replies.

"It's almost over, and then you'll be working one job and living a normal life again. No more studying."

"Can't come fast enough."

"You going to Colby's?" I ask my sister.

"Yeah, after I drop Mac off."

"I can take her." I turn to McKenna. "I can take you."

"You sure?"

"Yes." *Hell yes.* Any chance to have her all to myself, I'm going to take it like the selfish bastard I am when it comes to her.

"What are you doing this weekend? We need to get together and do some planning." My sister's eyes are bright with excitement.

"I'm all yours," McKenna tells her. "As long as I get a few hours of studying in. I take the test next Wednesday."

"I'll call you." My sister hops off her chair and comes around to hug McKenna and Colby. I then give my sister a hug and shake Colby's hand. "You make sure she gets home." Laramie points at me, then laces her arm through Colby's and leaves.

"Hey, you all heading out?" Corbin asks, appearing at our table.

"Yeah. I'm going to drop McKenna off. Colby and Lara just left."

"I'm heading out too. I have to be up at the supply house early in the morning. See you all later." Corbin waves.

"Ready?" I ask McKenna.

"Yes."

She stands from her chair, and with my hand on the small of her back, I lead her out to my truck. The ride to her place is short and quiet. Not uncomfortably so. For me, I'm just relishing having her in my truck next to me.

"I really missed it here," she says, resting her head on my shoulder.

"Yeah. You've been gone a long time."

"Five long years," she sighs.

"You're home now, Kenna."

"Sometimes, I feel as though life is passing me by. Laramie and Colby are getting married, and I'm still single and just getting ready to start my career."

"It's your dream, right? I know I've asked you that, but are you sure this is what you want?"

"More than anything. It's just hard to watch everyone growing and building their lives and feel like I'm just standing still."

Pulling into the driveway of her grandparents' house, I put the truck in Park, letting the engine run. I turn in my seat to face her. "What do you want, Kenna?"

She turns to face me. "I want to be a lawyer. I want to take over the practice that Gramps built. I want to live in this town, raise my kids here." She hesitates before saying, "Sorry. I'm rambling."

I take her hand in mine. "You have nothing to be sorry for. You have the job and your home. The kids, well, we'll have to work on that one." My tone is teasing, but the image of her carrying my baby has my cock pressing against the zipper of my jeans.

"I know. I just hate that I'm missing so much. I feel so disconnected. Laramie and I always said our kids would grow up together."

"Is there something my sister and Colby are keeping from me?"

"No." She laughs. "I'm just thinking about how life doesn't always turn out the way we think it will."

"You're right. But sometimes it's better. There have been a lot of changes, but do you know what won't?" I wait for her to shake her head. "You, and how you fit into our lives. No matter how much time passes, you're still our Kenna." My lips tilt in a smile.

"You're a good man, Rip Callahan."

"Come on. Keep them coming." I motion for her to keep the compliments heading my way, making her laugh.

"Thank you. Sometimes I get in my own head."

"We still on for tomorrow?"

"Yes."

Leaning in close, I press my lips to hers in a soft caress. "I'm looking forward to it."

"Thanks for the ride," she says breathlessly, reaching for the handle. I watch her walk to the front porch and disappear behind the door before pulling out of the driveway.

Chapter Ten

MCKENNA

STANDING IN MY BEDROOM AFTER A QUICK SHOWER, I'M TRYING TO DECIDE WHAT TO WEAR. I don't know what tonight is. I don't know if it's just two old friends getting together, or if it's more. It feels like more. However, that could only be my perception of wanting it to be more.

Glancing at the clock, I see that I have exactly fifteen minutes before Rip is supposed to be here. If I know anything about him, even the younger version, he's always punctual. Reaching into my drawer, I pull out a lacey red bra and panty set. They're sexy, and they make me feel that way. It doesn't matter that no one gets to see them but me. They do their job of boosting my confidence. In the back of my mind, I can't help but wonder if maybe tonight someone will see them? If maybe Rip will see them. I quickly shake off the idea.

I don't want to look like I tried too hard, yet I don't want to look frumpy either. Gah! Why am I making this so damn difficult? Flipping through the hangers, I decide on a sundress. It's a dark brown with small white embroidered flowers on the bust and at the hem of the bottom. It hits just above my knees. Slipping it over my head, I look at my reflection, releasing my hair from the pin it's been held up in all day. I run my hands through my locks, pleased they look tousled and sexy. Perfect. At least my hair is cooperating.

The doorbell rings. Shit. "Mac!" Grams calls out. "Rip's here."

"I'll be right down!" I call back to her.

Grabbing my mascara, I add a quick coat before tossing it back onto my dresser. Next is a quick layer of shimmer gloss to my lips, and I call it good. I don't have time for more accessories. Instead, I grab a pair of white flip-flops from the bottom of my closet and slide my feet into them as I unplug my phone and grab my purse. This is as good as it gets. With a deep breath, I open my bedroom door and descend the stairs. I don't know if this is a date, but it sure feels like one.

"There she is," Gramps says.

All eyes turn to me. Rip's eyes turn to me. My body heats as he slowly takes his time looking over every inch of me. When his eyes finally meet mine, a slow sexy smile tilts his lips. "Kenna, you look beautiful." He steps forward and offers me his hand, assisting me with the final step. Not that I needed the help, but I'm not going to turn down a chance to touch him. "These are for you." He presents me with a small bouquet of wildflowers I hadn't noticed.

"Thank you. You didn't have to do that."

"Let the man buy you flowers," Gramps says with a wink.

"I'll just put them in some water," I tell him.

"I've got that." Gram steps forward and takes the flowers from my hands.

"I guess I'll see you two in a little while," I tell my grandparents.

"Make sure she relaxes. She works too hard," Gramps tells Rip. "Just let us know if you're not coming home."

"I'll be h—" I start when Rip talks over me.

"I'll be sure to have her let you know. She's safe with me," he tells them.

"Oh, we know that," Gram says. Her smile is blinding. "You two kids have fun."

"I guess that's our cue to leave," I say with a nervous chuckle.

"After you." Rip places his hand on the small of my back and leads me to the front door and out to his truck.

"How was your day?" I ask once he's behind the wheel and we're headed to his place. It's not even a two-minute drive, but I need the distraction of conversation. I can still feel the heat of his touch on my back.

"Better now," he says, pulling into his driveway.

I ignore his confession, but my heart is doing this splutter thing in my chest. "What are we having?" I ask as I reach for the door handle.

"Stay there." He points his index finger at me as he jumps out of the truck and jogs to my door. He offers me his hand and helps me out. Instead of releasing his grip, he laces his fingers through mine as we make our way up the steps of the wraparound porch.

"I love this house. I love this porch."

He nods. "You've always loved wraparound porches."

I turn to look at him, but his eyes are focused on guiding us into his house. I don't know how he knows that about me. Well, I mean, he's known me for years. What's more unbelievable is that he remembered something that simple about me.

When we reach the kitchen, he turns to look at me, a sheepish smile on his handsome face. "I don't know if it's still your favorite, but I made chicken alfredo."

"Yum. I'm starving," I admit as my belly growls at the thought of a nice warm plate of chicken alfredo. "And yes, it's still my favorite." This, too, is not something I ever expected Rip to remember about me. Sure, we're friends, but I'm his sister's best friend.

"I made it. Now, come sit." He gives my hand a small tug and leads me into the dining room. It's set up with two place settings, fresh flowers, and a candle that's unlit in the middle.

"Kenna," he says, his voice husky as he drops my hand and pulls a seat out for me.

I smile at him but don't reply. I can't seem to form words. I don't know what's happening here.

Am I dreaming?

I watch as he grabs one of those lighters that you use to light candles and smiles when the candle is lit.

"I have sweet tea, wine, beer, water, milk," he rattles off all of my drink choices.

"Beer."

He grins. "Good choice. I'll be right back."

"Do you need some help?" I call out to him, craning my neck to see into the kitchen.

"No. I'm all set." He appears in the doorway with two bottles of beer. He hands me one and sets the other in front of his plate. He dashes back to the kitchen and comes back with a bubbling-hot casserole dish, filled with my favorite meal.

"You made this?" I ask in awe. It smells delicious.

"Yep," he says proudly.

"Where did you learn how to make it? It smells just like Gram's."

"That's because it's her recipe. She taught me," he confesses.

"What? What do you mean she taught you?"

"I might have mentioned a couple of weeks ago when we were talking about you coming home that I was thinking about making you dinner. I told her I wanted to make your favorite, and she offered to help me."

"Am I living in the twilight zone?" I question.

His head tilts back as his deep rumble of laughter fills the room around us. "No. You're not living in the twilight zone." He takes a minute to get his laughter under control before grabbing my plate and adding a huge helping of the creamy alfredo. "Dig in." He places my plate in front of me and gives himself double what he gave me.

After grabbing my fork, I take a bite and can't stop the moan that escapes my lips. "Rip." I sigh. "This is so good. Are you sure Gram didn't make this?" I ask, going in for another bite.

"All me." He smiles affectionately. "How is studying going?" he asks.

"Good. My brain is working overtime." I laugh. "I'll be glad to never have to pick up another textbook or take another test in my lifetime."

"I'm sure." He smiles.

"Your home is beautiful. I can't believe you did all of this on your own."

"It kept me busy. Feels like home, though, you know? I love that it has my personal touch, and that's it on the family farm. I'm close to Mom and Dad, yet still far enough away to have my privacy."

"You should be proud. You did an amazing job."

"Thank you." He takes a drink of beer. "How are you feeling about the test?"

"Terrified," I confess.

"What?" There's blatant surprise in his voice.

"I've wanted this for so long, and it's right there within my reach. There's nothing but this stupid exam in my way."

"McKenna, you're brilliant. You're going to ace this thing and be the best damn lawyer this town has ever seen. No offense to Harold, of course." He laughs.

"I don't know about brilliant, but I have put everything I am into this."

"That's all that matters. You're going to do great." He reaches over and places his hand over mine, giving it a gentle squeeze before picking his fork back up and continuing to eat.

"How are things with you? With the farm?" I ask, moving the conversation along. It's not that I don't want this sexy man to tell me he thinks I'm brilliant, but I need to steer the conversation to something that will make my heart flutter less. He doesn't even know how his words affect me.

"The farm is good. Dad and I are still splitting duties. He wants to retire, but I think he'd be bored, and I know he would drive Mom crazy."

"You're probably right," I agree. "Are Laramie and Colby going to build here on the farm too?" I ask him.

"I don't really know. Hell, I'm not sure they know," he comments. "Lara has nothing but wedding on the brain."

"I'm sure they'll figure it out. And yes, she's so excited. I'm happy for them."

"Yeah," he agrees.

"You said you did all the work yourself. Anything you would change? On the house, I mean?" I'm fumbling for safe conversation topics.

"Nah, I thought long and hard about every room, every step of the renovation."

"And what if your future wife doesn't approve?" I don't know why I ask the question. I guess spending time with him has me wishing that things were different, and that this home might be ours one day. That maybe one day, he might choose me for real.

He sits back in his chair and crosses his arms over his chest. His eyes bore into mine. "As I recall, we're married," he says. He's not teasing. His face is stone-serious.

"Come on now." I laugh.

"Tell me, McKenna. As my wife, what do you think about living here?" He swallows hard, almost as if he's afraid of what my answer will be.

"Rip—" I start, but he interrupts me.

"Humor me."

"Fine." I heave out a sigh, reaching for my beer and taking a long pull. "If I… if I were your wife, I would love nothing more than to live here. I love this house and everything you've done to it. The kitchen is incredible, one I've always dreamed of, and you know I love the wraparound porch. However, I've always loved this farm. It feels as much like home to me as Gram and Gramps' place.

"I spent a lot of time running these fields with you and your sister, and this place holds special memories for me. Life, before I came here, was grim, and meeting your sister, and by association you, that was one of the best highlights of my childhood." I clamp my mouth closed. I didn't mean to say all of that, but once I parted my lips, words just started spewing out of me.

I keep my eyes on my lap. I can't believe I just said all of that.

"Kenna." His voice is soft. I know he wants me to look at him, but I can't. It's not until I feel his index finger under my chin that I give in and lift my gaze to his. His brown eyes flash to my mouth, and I lick my lips.

I think he's going to kiss me. I really want him to kiss me.

He leans in a little closer. "I really want to kiss you," he says, his voice gravelly.

"Yes, please," I reply, breathless with anticipation.

He moves in closer. He's so close yet so far away. I've missed him and his kisses. His lips molded to mine for longer than I can even remember. I lean in, and he curses under his breath before pressing his lips to mine. They're soft and tentative. I'm about to reach out and hold him to me when a knock at the door has us pulling apart.

He gives me a smoldering look before pushing back in his chair and standing. I watch his every move so I don't miss it when he adjusts his hard length before making his way to the door. "What's up?" I hear him ask.

"Let's go grab dinner," Corbin says. "I was passing by on my way home," he says, explaining why he's here.

"Can't. I'm in the middle of something."

"Well, finish up, and we can go."

"Nah, I already ate."

"Then come with me. We can catch up."

"I have a lot of paperwork to finish."

"What's going on, Rip?" Corbin asks.

"Nothing. I have company," he confesses. "We'll grab dinner at the Silver Star tomorrow. First round's on me."

"Fine. See you then, old man." Corbin chuckles. I listen for the door to close and stand to start clearing the table. I don't know why, but I wanted him to tell Corbin he was with me. I know that our friends would be fine with it. Hell, Laramie already suspects, and she's happy for me. For us. But that's just it. If "us" is really what Rip wants, then why wouldn't he tell Corbin? Maybe he isn't as sure about us as he wants me to believe. Maybe I'm jumping into this too fast because it's what I've always wanted. I definitely need to slow down and protect my heart. He's just proven that. He was caught up in the moment. He's being nice by making me dinner, and it's a romantic setting. We both got lost in the moment. That's on me. I wanted him to kiss me—more than I've ever wanted anything.

"You don't have to do that," Rip says, taking our now empty plates out of my hand.

"Of course, I do. You made dinner. I clean up. It's the least that I can do."

"No, Kenna. That's not how this is going to go." He places the dishes in the sink. Turning, he rests against the counter, his hands braced on either side of him. "The dishes can wait. You're taking the night off, remember?"

I nod. "Thank you for dinner." Turning on my heels, I head for the door. A walk home is exactly what I need to clear my head. I'm so focused on leaving, on my foolish heart for thinking that this was something that it wasn't, I don't hear him until he has his arms around my waist, pulling my body into his.

"Stay." One word whispered into my ear, and I'm putty in his hands. A single nod and he releases me, but not fully. His hand on the small of my back guides me to the couch. We sit, with him pulling me into his arms and handing me the remote. "You pick."

"It's your house."

"Your choice, Kenna."

I don't care what we watch. I won't be able to pay attention anyway with his arms around me, holding me close. I settle on *Law and Order*, and he chuckles when he takes the remote and sets it on the table next to us.

Pulling my bare feet up on the couch, I'm careful to cover my legs with my dress. Once I'm settled, he pulls me a little further into him. "Better," he murmurs, kissing my temple.

I try to focus on the television, but I can feel my eyes getting heavy. I barely slept last night, so excited for dinner with him, and now, here in his arms, with a full belly, I don't ever remember a time I felt more content.

Chapter Eleven

RIP

"WHAT CRAWLED UP YOUR ASS?" CORBIN ASKS, POINTING A FRY AT ME BEFORE SHOVING IT in his mouth.

"Nothing." I pick up my burger and take a bite. "It's just been a long week." That's not entirely untrue. It has been a long week of me waiting for more time with McKenna. Last night was the best night I've had in, well, ever. I had her all to myself, and got to spend time kissing her, which is now my favorite pastime. She dozed off in my arms, and I wanted nothing more than to carry her upstairs to my bed. I would have, too, had it not been for my sister calling her phone and waking her up. I wanted to hold McKenna and wake up with her. I wanted to be able to compare it to the first time I held her all night. Compare the two and dissect this crazy intense need I have for her.

"I hear you." He nods, eating another bite.

Shaking out of my thoughts, I pull my head back into the present. "The homeowner still giving you shit about the budget?"

"Every damn day," he sighs. "How hard of a concept is it? You change the design, the materials change, which means the price changes."

"You think any more about hiring someone to deal with them?"

"Yeah. Colby and I talked to Dad about Laramie taking over the office, and he and Mom agree that it's a great idea."

"Have you talked to her about it?" My sister is strong-willed. Always has been. When she graduated, my parents and I offered her a job working for the family farm. She refused and said she wanted to forge her own path. I personally think it had something to do with her best friend leaving for college, leaving her behind. That was five years ago, and I have a feeling she's going to be joining James Construction. It might take some persuasion, but I think she'll take it. That's fine, as long as she's happy. There will always be a spot for her at Callahan Farm, and she knows that.

"Mom's having us all over for dinner tomorrow night, and the four of us are going to gang up on her." He laughs.

"Ah, so your brother knows his future wife pretty well then." It's going to take some convincing for Laramie to believe that she's needed, and the job isn't just being handed to her.

"No offense, but we all know that your sister is bull-headed." He shrugs.

"True story."

"What are you two gossiping about?" my sister asks, appearing beside our booth.

"Nothing much. What are you doing here?" I look around the bar for McKenna. They're supposed to be hanging out tonight.

"Stopped to grab some wings to go. We're having a girls' night at Mac's."

I nod. I guess she doesn't know that I already knew that information. I texted McKenna today and asked her if she had plans. I had no qualms canceling on Corbin to see her.

"What's my brother doing?" Corbin asks her.

"When I left the house, he was ready to fall asleep on the couch," she says with a smile. "He works too hard."

"We need help," Corbin says. This conversation couldn't have played into his hand better if he tried.

"Yeah, I hate seeing him drained like this. Oh, not to change the subject, but have you seen the forecast? Thunderstorms all day tomorrow."

My stomach falls. We were supposed to spend another day at the lake. "No. I hadn't heard." I try not to let the disappointment show. At the same time, my mind is racing with ideas to see McKenna. "We should just get together at my place anyway." Normally, I'd keep up on the weather for my job, but all I can seem to focus on is McKenna. Thankfully we have excellent farmhands to keep the place in line while I'm distracted.

"You sure?"

I shrug as if I'm indifferent when I'm anything but. "Why not? I have the spare bedroom, and the couch in the living room, and the recliner. I can even dig the air mattress out if we need it."

My little sister gives me a knowing grin. "Sounds like a plan. I'll spread the word. You two be safe. Call me if I need to give either of you a ride home." With a side hug for each of us, she's out the door.

Corbin grins. "She didn't even know I was planting the seed." His smirk tells me that he's proud of himself. It's good that he mentioned them needing help without coming out and suggesting she do it.

I just shake my head. "That's what it's going to take. At least she sees Colby exhausted, and I'm sure he's complained about the office work. You all might just get lucky. It might not be as hard as I originally thought to get her to work for you."

Corbin nods. "She's family. She belongs there as much as Colbs and I do."

Call me sentimental, or maybe it's all of these feelings seeing McKenna and spending time with her has brought to the surface, but his words pull at the strings of my heart. I love my little sister, and my best friend, and his brother. They're family to me too. Knowing my sister is marrying into a family who's going to be good to her and treat her right is comforting.

We finish eating and shoot the shit for another half an hour or so before we both head home. Alone. I want to call McKenna just to hear her voice, but I refrain. Instead, I curl up in bed and drift off to sleep, thinking about her.

"WELL, GANG, IT'S BEEN FUN, BUT I GOTTA BOUNCE," CORBIN SAYS, STANDING FROM HIS spot at the dining room table.

"Where are you headed?" Colby asks.

A glance at the clock on the wall tells me it's just after ten on Saturday night. The forecast was correct, and it's been pouring rain since early this afternoon. Everyone arrived a little before six. My sister and McKenna made a ton of snack food, and it looks more like we're having a Super Bowl party rather than a casual get-together. Every surface of my kitchen is covered with food.

"Hot date." He wags his eyebrows.

"Come on now," Colby gives him shit. "Let's call a spade a spade."

"Fine. I might be meeting up with Sara to keep her company."

"Is that what the kids are calling it these days?" McKenna teases.

Corbin aims his index finger at her. "You're lucky I've missed you," he says with an easy smile. "Besides, everyone is coupled up." He motions to where Laramie and Colby are snuggled on the love seat, and McKenna and I are on the couch. We're not cuddled up, but we are sitting closer than two people need to on this big couch. "Now, unless you need me to perform another wedding...." He glances around the room, wearing a cocky grin.

"We're working on that," Colby replies.

"I'm only getting married once," I tell him. It's true. I want to settle down and do it right.

"Well, you've already fucked that up. You married Mac twice now."

"Hey! Are you saying I'm a mistake?" McKenna asks, barely holding in her laughter.

"No, but you could have chosen the better-looking of the two of us." He taps his hand to his chest.

"And what would Sara think?" McKenna teases.

"Well-played, Mac. Well-played." He winks at her. "Anyway, Russ bowed out. He's working on his truck, and Josh is out with Stephanie at her sister's wedding. So, yeah, fifth wheel." He points at his himself. "I'm out." He waves to all of us as he turns for the door.

"You good to drive?" I call after him.

"Yeah. Only had two beers, and that was hours ago, and a whole hell of a lot of food later."

"Call me if you need a ride."

"Oh, I think Sara can handle that." He wags his eyebrows, and then he's out the door.

"Well now, since it's just the four of us, why don't we play some cards?" Colby suggests.

"I suck at cards," Laramie complains.

"Let's just watch a movie," this from McKenna.

"That. Let's do that." My sister nods and points at her best friend as if the idea is the best one she's heard in her entire life. "I'll grab some more wine, and you pick," she tells McKenna, tossing her the remote.

"Me? I don't care what we watch." She then tosses the remote into my lap.

"No," Laramie whines dramatically. "They're going to make us watch some thriller or shoot-'em-up movie."

"Come on, it won't be that bad," McKenna says.

"Yes, it will!" she calls over her shoulder from the kitchen.

"Choose wisely, my friend," McKenna says with a smile for me.

"Please, choose wisely," Colby pleads. "You know she's more opinionated when she's been drinking." While he says the words, there's a soft smile playing at his lips that's always there whenever my sister is involved.

Laramie comes back with her hands full. She passes me a beer and then does the same with Colby. She tops off McKenna's wineglass, which is almost running over, and does the same to hers before setting the empty wine bottle on the table, taking a hefty drink, and then sitting on Colby's lap.

Lifting my arm in the air, I'm ready to launch the remote to the love seat my sister and Colby are sitting on. A loud crack of thunder so loud it feels as though it rattles the house strikes, and then the lights go out.

"Shit."

"Well, that makes the decision for us." McKenna laughs.

"I'll dig out some flashlights, candles, and a lighter." I stand to go searching for what we need. "I have a couple of oil lamps too," I tell whoever happens to be listening to me ramble on in the darkness of my living room.

"I'll help," comes from Colby as he turns on the flashlight of his cell phone and follows me into the kitchen. Using my phone light as well, I rummage around in the drawers until I find the lighter I used to light the candles for my dinner with McKenna's Thursday night. Then I make my way to the dining room and snag them from the table.

"When did you get those?" my sister asks once the candles are lit and sitting on the coffee table.

"I've had them." It's a lie, and we both know it, but she doesn't call me out on it either. "I have a few more. I just need to dig them out."

"Where are the lamps?" Laramie asks.

"On the mantel." I turn around and, with the light of my cell phone flashlight, grab them and light both, which fills the room with a soft glow.

"It's either ghost stories or bed," Laramie suggests.

"Ugh. I vote bed if those are our only options," McKenna groans.

"Fine. Party-pooper. You guys keep a lamp, and we'll keep one."

"I should probably go home and check on my grandparents," McKenna says just as her cell phone rings. With the dim lighting, I watch as she pulls it out of her pocket and answers. "Hello." She listens quietly. "Yes, the power just went out." More listening. "Oh, okay. That makes sense. All right, I'll see you tomorrow." She taps her screen and lays her phone on the couch next to her. "That was Gram. I guess the alarm system on the house alerted them to a power failure. She called the electric company, and they're saying five to six hours before power is restored."

"We should go get them and bring them here," I say immediately.

"Oh, they're still in Jasper. They're just going to grab a hotel room and make a night of it."

"Well, you can't go stay there by yourself." My sister speaks up, and I make a mental note to buy her a really good Christmas present.

"I'm a big girl, Lara," McKenna says gently. "I've been living on my own for five years now."

"I don't care. I hate the thought of you staying there all alone with no power."

"I'll be fine."

"Kenna," I say, moving to stand next to where she's sitting on the couch. "We're not debating the topic of you taking care of yourself. However, you're already here, and we're all staying. You should stay." My tone is gentle, despite a storm very similar to the one raging outside roaring inside me. I want her to stay. I want her in my bed, in my arms. I just… I need her to stay. I won't sleep knowing she's staying at her grandparents' place all alone without power. Yes, she's an adult, but damn it. I want her here.

"Fine," she concedes.

"I'm going to go change." Laramie stands from the couch on wobbly legs.

"I've got her. I doubt we'll be back down," Colby says, grabbing one of the oil lamps and leading my sister upstairs to the guest room.

"Come on. I'll give you something to sleep in." I hold my hand out for McKenna, and without hesitation, she takes it. I pull her with a little too much force, causing her to fall into my arms. That's my cue to wrap her in my arms and hold her close. "I'm glad you're staying."

Tilting her head back, she peers up at me. "You sure you don't mind me sleeping on your couch?"

Gently, I push her hair back out of her eyes. "You're not sleeping on the couch, Kenna. You're sleeping with me." I press a kiss to the tip of her nose. Releasing my hold on her, I blow out the candles and lock up the house. I turn off the light switches so that the house won't be bright when the power does come on. Grabbing the oil lamp, I place my hand on the small of her back and lead her upstairs to my room.

She doesn't protest, and part of me thinks I've rendered her speechless. The other larger part hopes it's because she wants to sleep next to me just as badly as I want her in my bed.

In my room, I dig out a T-shirt and boxer shorts for her to change into. "I'll turn my head," I say, handing them to her. "We only have the one light. I promise I won't look."

"It's not like it's not something you've never seen before," she replies with a nervous laugh.

That's where she's wrong. I've never seen her before. And I know without a shadow of a doubt that woman... no, McKenna, would make all the difference. Swallowing hard, I fist my hands at my sides and will myself to stand with my back to her as I hear her changing.

"Okay," she whispers.

Slowly, I turn to find her in my T-shirt. The boxers are still in her hands. "All set?" I croak.

"Yeah. This is long enough, so I don't need these." She hands me back the boxers. "Can I set my clothes here?" She points to the top of the dresser.

I want to tell her that she can clean herself out a drawer. Hell, I'll buy McKenna her own dresser, but I refrain. "Sure."

"Your turn," she says, turning her back to me.

"I'm sure it's not something you've never seen before," I volley her words back to her.

"Something tells me this would be different." She speaks my earlier thoughts aloud, and it takes every ounce of restraint that I have not to kiss the hell out of her.

Chapter Twelve

MCKENNA

I'M NOT DRUNK. I AM, HOWEVER, TIPSY ENOUGH TO BE A LITTLE BOLD WHEN IT COMES TO Rip. I haven't been able to think of anything but him since our dinner Thursday night. Then, when Laramie called telling me that we were getting together at his place tonight, well, I might have shaved and moisturized every inch of my body in anticipation. Not that I expect anything to happen between us. However, just the fact that there would be a small chance, I wasn't going to risk it because I was too lazy to shave my legs or my lady bits.

"I'm good," he says. His voice is thick and husky, and it's making me want things that I know I can't have—namely, him. Slowly, I turn to face him.

"Are you sure you want to share your bed? I can sleep on the couch," I offer half-heartedly. We both know that I don't want to sleep on the couch, and he said he wanted me here in his bed, but I still feel as though the right thing to do is to offer to take the couch again. You know, just to be certain. I'm going to be an attorney, after all. If I'm anything, I'm thorough. At least I should be. When I'm working, I'm confident and assertive, but when it comes to Rip, I revert back to that same little girl who was told she was a mistake and ruined everything. He doesn't remind me of my father, not even close. Maggie tells me it's because I want him to want me. Well, she said it's because I want him to love me. Just like I wanted my father to love me. I won't confirm or deny her theory.

"It's not big enough for both of us." His eyes bore into mine, and my body heats from not only his gaze but his words. There is no misunderstanding that he wants me close.

"Okay." It's a lame reply, but I don't really know what else to say. I could ask him what's going on. I could ask him why all of a sudden, now that I'm home, he's lavishing me with attention. I could ask him if this is just a game. If I'm someone to just pass the time with, like a shiny new toy. I won't ask any of those things for fear of the answer.

Instead, I'm going to soak up his time and attention so that when he does decide that whatever this is, is over, I'll have the memories to keep me warm at night. Rip's never been what some would call a player, but I've watched every girl in our high school practically throw themselves at him. He's one of the good ones. The type of man that if you have the chance, you want to hold on tight and never let go. He's going to realize that he can do better than a twenty-four-year-old attorney who is still in therapy from the shit her parents put her through. Granted, it's every three or four months that I see her, but still. He can do better.

He deserves better.

"I'm going to set the lamp on the bathroom counter but leave the door open. That way, we can see to get to the restroom if we need to," Rip explains as he walks to the bathroom, pushing open the door and setting the lamp on the counter.

"Do you have a side?" I ask.

"Doesn't matter when I plan to hold you." He shrugs and walks to the opposite side of the bed I'm standing on and climbs in.

He has no idea what his words do to me. Then again, maybe he does. Rip Callahan is a man's man. He's rugged, and basically the definition of masculine. He works hard, and it shows. He didn't get those washboard abs from a gym. He got them from hard work and dedication to his family's farm.

"Kenna." His deep, gruff voice calls to me as he pulls the blankets back and motions for me to join him.

My knees wobble as I climb into bed and lie on my side to face him. It's dark, only a tiny glow from the bathroom giving us light. It's not enough to make out his features or his gorgeous brown eyes. That's okay. I have them memorized.

"Are you tired?" he whispers.

"A little," I confess. However, it's probably going to take me some time to fall asleep with him next to me.

"Rollover, Kenna," he instructs.

I do as he asks, resting my hands beneath my cheek. There's a dip in the mattress, and then I'm surrounded by warmth and the smell of sandalwood, along with something uniquely Rip. He slides his arm under my head, and I adjust my position. Not knowing what to do with my hands, I'm relieved when he takes the decision away from me and laces his fingers through mine.

We lie in silence for what seems like hours. I try to keep my focus on his breathing to match mine instead of focusing on the fact that the man I've always wanted is holding me in his arms. In his bed. For the second time in a matter of weeks. I've heard the saying that you never really get over your first crush, your first love. Rip is that person for me.

Do I love him? Yes. He's been a part of my life since I was six years old.

Am I in love with him? No. I'm not in love with him, but I know without a shadow of a doubt that if there are many more nights like this one, that could change. It would take very little effort for my heart to be twisted with his. Hell, the way mine is racing in my chest by just being near him, it may have already started to take root.

"I've missed you." His husky whisper causes goose bumps to break out against my skin.

I feel his lips press against my shoulder, and my mind immediately goes to our kiss. Just a peck, but I wanted more. I still want more. Maybe it's the alcohol making me brave. Maybe it's just him, and maybe it's that I've missed him too. Whatever the reason, I turn in his arms, placing my hand against his cheek.

"Rip?" My voice is barely a whisper.

"Yeah, baby?" His voice is velvety soft.

"Kiss me?"

No more words are said as he leans in and molds his lips to mine. He's not in a hurry as he nibbles at my bottom lip, soothing the ache with his tongue. His large, calloused hand slides under my T-shirt and presses against my back, moving me impossibly closer to him and his warmth. I release a moan that I can't hold in, and he takes the opportunity to slide his tongue past my lips. I expect him to move things along, but he does anything but. Instead, his tongue lazily explores my mouth while his hand traces up and down my spine. It's the slowest, most sensual kiss I've ever received in my entire life.

I never want it to end.

He kisses me until we're both breathless. I want more. I want all of him. I'm just about to make my move when he pulls back and guides my head to rest on his chest. He wraps his arms around me and presses his lips to the top of my head.

I try not to think of this as a rejection, but it's hard not to. Neither of us is drunk, so I can't blame it on the alcohol. I want to ask him why he stopped. I want to move to straddle his hips while his hands roam over my body. Then I remember this is Rip Callahan. My best friend's older brother. He can have any woman he wants, and I'm sure the way I was kissing him back, he knows that he could have me. Yet, he stopped us.

Hot tears prick my eyes, but I will them not to fall. The teenage girl in me just can't seem to let him go.

I don't say a word, lying still until his breathing evens out, and I know he's asleep. As carefully as I can, I slide out from under his arm and crawl out of bed. I want nothing more than to wake up next to him, but this is a foolish game I'm playing. I was lying to myself when I said I wasn't in love with him.

I've always been in love with Rip Callahan.

But I'm a grown woman who deserves more than just a few stolen kisses in the dark of night. If he wants me, he needs to be all in, and that's not Rip. I've never known him to be serious about anyone. His love is for the land that his family will one day pass on to him. That's a truth that I need to learn to face.

As quietly as I can, I grab my clothes and change back into them. Folding his T-shirt neatly, I place it on top of his dresser. Blindly, I make my way back downstairs to the living room and settle on the couch. Pulling the throw over me, I silently let my tears fall.

THE SUDDEN HUM OF THE REFRIGERATOR WAKES ME UP. GLANCING AROUND, I SEE THE SUN starting to rise through the window as memories of last night rush back to me. I should get up and leave. My car is here and facing Rip, and his rejection, doesn't really sound like a good time. Sitting up, I stretch my arms above my head, then stand to fold the blanket and return it to the back of the couch. That's when I feel someone watching me. Turning my head, I see Rip. His hair is tousled, and there are still sleep marks against his cheek. He's wearing the same low-hung basketball shorts, and with no shirt, his chiseled upper body is on display.

"You okay?" His voice is laced with sleep and so damn sexy.

"Yeah. I'm uh... just going to head home." I mess with the pillows, rearranging them to have something to do with my hands. That's why I don't see him approach.

"Come back to bed, Kenna."

"I should really go."

"Please?"

I want to. More than anything, I want to go back to his warm, cozy bed and let him hold me, but I need to preserve my heart here. "I'm not sure that's a good idea."

"Are you mad at me? Is this about last night?" He places his hands on my hips and turns me to face him. With one hand cupping my cheek, he uses the index finger of the other to wipe the tears under my eyes, he then lifts my chin so that we are face-to-face. "I'm sorry if I went too far, but damn it, McKenna, a man is only so strong. You were drinking... and damn it, I'm sorry. Please come back to bed."

"Wh-What?" I ask as my brain tries to comprehend what he's saying.

"Come on. It's still early." He laces his fingers through mine, and I follow him back upstairs and into his room. He closes the door, and the audible sound of the lock clicking in place has my heart skipping a beat.

Without saying a word, he leads me to the bed and pulls the covers back with a nod for me to climb in. Like the fool that I am for him, I do as he asks. I watch as he rounds the bed and climbs in, tugging me into his arms.

"Rip... I-I don't understand this."

"I want to hold you, McKenna. That's what this is. Now go back to sleep."

A little piece of my heart shatters. I'm falling hard and fast, and I don't know what to do. I know this is going to lead to my heart being torn to shreds, but I can't seem to stop whatever this is. Rip is a good friend, my best friend's brother, and that's all he'll ever be.

Eventually, I fall back to sleep, only to wake a few hours later alone. Making a stop in the bathroom, I take care of business and head downstairs, where I find Colby and Rip in the kitchen. Colby's sitting at the island watching Rip scramble eggs.

"Sleep well?" Rip asks.

"Yeah. Where's Laramie?"

"Still sleeping," Colby tells me.

I feel awkward just standing here, so I take one of the barstools and sit next to Colby. I'm barely seated before Rip is pushing a cup of coffee toward me. "Black," he says by way of explanation.

"Thanks."

"How's studying going? You excited to get this test over with?" Colby asks.

"Excited, but ready for it all to be over if that makes any sense. I'm glad to be home for good. Missed all of you." I make sure that I keep my eyes on him and not on Rip. Last night told me all that I need to know where Rip is concerned. He wants me, but he's not willing to take me. I get it. We have history. Now I know. He regrets the kisses we shared. However, he still held me like I was precious to him. I'm so confused by his actions.

"You barely made it home the last five years. You think you can adjust to country living?" he asks.

"You can take the girl out of the country, but you can't take the county out of the girl," I say with a laugh. "I'm not going to have a problem," I tell him.

"Well, I'm glad you're home and will be here for the wedding."

"Is that why you waited to ask her?"

"Partially. I also only plan to get married once. We were young when we started dating, and I wanted to give us both some time to grow up and be certain this is what we want. I want this to be for life. And yes, while I'm aware that's the plan in regard to marriage, I feel many take it too lightly, and that's not me."

"You two have always known what you want."

He nods. "Yeah, I have. So has she. But the thought of us getting married so young and it not working out, I couldn't survive losing her as my wife."

"You—" I point at him, fighting back the tears. "—you and Laramie are couple goals. The epitome of what a relationship should look like. I'd give anything to have a man love me half as much as you love her." Surprising us both, I lean over and give him a hug. "Thank you for loving my best friend and treating her like the queen that she is."

"She's my heart, Mac." Four words, a simple declaration of love, and I know those words come from deep within his soul.

"Morning," Laramie says as she drags her feet into the room. She goes to Colby immediately, who has his arms open for her.

"Hey, babe," he whispers.

"What are we talking about?" she asks, taking his cup of coffee and slurping down a huge drink.

"McKenna being home and her test. We're going to have to celebrate once she takes this exam."

"That's not necessary."

"Of course it is," Laramie replies, more alert with some caffeine running through her veins.

"Let's see if I pass it."

"You're going to pass," all three of them say at once. My eyes find Rip's, and he nods as if his words are the gospel.

"Fine," I concede. "Just a bonfire and friends is enough for me. You know I don't like all of the attention."

"Tell that to my future wife."

"You're marrying her. Can't you control her?" I tease.

"We all know there is no controlling Laramie Callahan." He chuckles.

"Hey, I'm right here," Laramie chimes in.

"Are you really going to dispute this, little sister?" Rip laughs.

"Nope." She grins, taking another sip of coffee.

"I don't know, maybe when you change her last name and have a couple of kids, that might do it." I smirk. Laramie has already told me that Colby is eager to start a family. He says he wants to be young enough to keep up with his kids, not old and gray. At his twenty-five and her twenty-four, they are both a far cry away from being old and gray.

"A man can dream," Colby remarks.

"Eat up," Rip says, placing a plate of scrambled eggs and toast in front of each of us.

"Thank you." I smile at him, and he nods. I can't read the expression on his face, so I don't even try. Instead, I turn my attention to my breakfast and chat with Colby and Laramie about plans they've already made for the wedding.

Chapter Thirteen

RIP

TODAY IS THE BIG DAY. MCKENNA HAD TO GO TO DALLAS TO SIT FOR THE BAR EXAM. SHE left on Tuesday afternoon for the four-hour drive. My sister went with her. They're going to do some wedding dress shopping while they're there. I've been up since early this morning. Earlier than normal. I wanted to get a head start on things here so I can stop and call her, wishing her luck on her final day of testing. I also want to hear her voice.

"Morning," she answers.

"Hey, beautiful. You ready? This is your last day, just a few hours, right?"

"I feel sick," she confesses. "And yes, today is the final day."

"Hey, now, none of that. You know this information. Your gramps has quizzed you. You've aced all of the practice tests. You're going to ace it. I know it." I wish I was there to hold her, to look into her eyes, and will her to believe me. I want to be the one to help calm her fears.

"I just want to pass." She laughs. "I don't care about acing it. Well, I mean, that would be nice, but I just want to pass. I want to start the next chapter in my life. The next six to twelve weeks is going to be torture just waiting in limbo."

"You're going to start helping out at the firm, though, right?"

"Yeah, but I can't do anything. I can do research and type briefs, etc., but I can't practice law. I busted my ass in high school to get a college degree at the same time as a high school diploma, then the rest of the undergrad and law school I did, the same to be where I am. I'm just ready to put this dream of mine to work." She chuckles.

"McKenna, you've got this. Go do your thing. Be amazing, then relax. I have a surprise for you, but you don't get it until after the test. Laramie will give you all of the details."

"What did you do?"

"You'll see. Go kick ass, baby. Call me after?"

"Yeah. I will. Thanks for calling. You actually helped calm my nerves."

"Good. I'll talk to you soon." Quickly, I pull the phone from my ear and end the call. I would sit here and listen to her voice all day long, but we both know today is not that day. She's going to go pass this test, and in six to twelve weeks, all of her hard work and dedication will have been worth it. And when she comes home to me, McKenna Dawson is who I want. When I think about my future, it's always been McKenna standing next to me. Now all I have to do is make that happen.

Standing, I slide my phone into my pocket. I'm too distracted to get any actual office work done. No, today is definitely a day to be spent doing manual labor. I won't be able to think straight until I hear from her. From the way my stomach is churning, you would think that I'm the one taking the test. I had this same feeling the day she left for college. If that's not a telltale sign that we're meant to be, I don't know what is.

"Hey, boss," Cliff, one of our farmhands, greets me. "What are you doing out here?"

"Couldn't focus."

"Thought getting your hands dirty might help?" he teases. Cliff and I went to school together. He's one of my oldest friends, and he knows me too well.

"Something like that," I reply vaguely.

"Well, I'm ready to ride out and check the fence. You want to ride along?"

"Definitely." Together we load up the tools into the back of the UTV, double-checking we have what we need before riding out and checking the fence. We have cattle that we raise and sell, as well as horses that we breed here at Callahan Farm. Grandpa started the farm with just cattle. When my parents got married, Dad expanded to breeding horses too. The two together have made the family farm lucrative. It's provided for my family for years, and it will do the same for my family, and hopefully the next generation too.

I hope that my kids, at least one of them, one day want to take over. If not, well, it was good while it lasted. I would never force them or make them feel guilty for following their dreams. I won't shame them for not wanting the family business, but I hope that they do—at least one of them. I laugh out loud when I realize the conversation I've been having in my mind. When have I ever daydreamed about kids and the next generation of Callahan?

Since McKenna came home.

The answer is easy and enlightening at the same time. Those kids I'm thinking about, she's their momma. I just need to get her on board with this elaborate plan I have in my head. Easy-peasy, right?

"What's so funny?" Cliff asks.

"Nothing. Just thinking. Up ahead." I point to a spot in the fence that needs to be mended. "These damn cows are rowdy fuckers," I say, shaking my head.

"Always looking for an escape," Cliff agrees.

We work side by side for the next few hours. We talk about what's on the agenda for the coming weeks, and McKenna is never far from my mind. I know today is a short day for her, and it's finally over. After two and a half long days of testing, she's finally done and gets a break, which is why I planned my surprise for her. I get to spoil her and my little sister at the same time. It's a win-win situation for me. I might have told Laramie that I didn't need her help where McKenna is concerned, but it doesn't hurt to butter her up a little just in case. Not that I need to. My sister wants to see us be together almost as much as I do. Almost.

"You expecting an important call?" Cliff asks, nodding at the phone in my hand. "I'm surprised the damn thing still has any battery left as many times as you've checked it."

"Something like that," I mutter. I'm not ready to get into it with him. The only person I want to talk to right now is McKenna. I'm starting to get worried. I thought I would have heard from her by now. Before I can check my phone again, the shrill ring sounds, and I grin when I see her name on the screen. "Gotta take this," I tell Cliff, my feet rapidly carrying me away for privacy. "Hey, baby."

"Rip! You bought us a spa day?" McKenna asks excitedly.

The tension that was wrapped around my chest like a fist loosens at the sound of her voice. "You deserve it. How did it go?" I make my way inside the barn and close myself into my small office. Taking a seat in my chair, I prop my feet up on the desk, and I know if I were able to see my reflection, I'd look like a fool from the smile stretching across my face.

"Today was much easier," she admits.

"Good. You're coming home tomorrow, right?" I ask her.

"I think so. Laramie and I are going to finish up here at the spa and do some dress shopping. We haven't got to do that yet. I've been too exhausted each night."

"It's all over, Kenna. You're going to be practicing law side by side with your grandfather in a matter of weeks." I leave no room for her to argue. I'll be her confidence if I have to. My girl is smart as hell. There's no way she didn't pass the exam.

"Thank you." Her voice is soft.

"Enjoy your spa day, Kenna. You deserve it. Be safe, and call me later. Let me know you all are back at your hotel safe."

"Don't worry, Colby has already given us strict orders to do the same. We'll be sure to call one of you."

I'm glad Colby is there for my sister, and by association, McKenna, but letting one of us know isn't going to work for me. "Call me, Kenna."

"Okay. Sheesh. We'll call and check-in. You do realize we're both adults, right?"

"Have fun," I say, ending the call. I can't get into this with her over the phone. I know McKenna. She's going to need to see my face, see my emotions, read it in my eyes when I tell her I want more from her. Now that the stress of the test is over, it's time.

I'm coming for you, McKenna Dawson.

IT'S SUNDAY AFTERNOON, AND I'M PACING MY LIVING ROOM FLOOR. THE GIRLS ARE ALMOST home. They decided to stay another night. Apparently, there were a lot of dress shops they needed to take in, and with the spa day I sprung on them, they didn't have enough time. They both sounded so excited Friday night when they called to tell me all about it. I'm glad that the two of them got to spend some quality time together, but I'm ready for them to be home. I miss McKenna. How I went five years without her while she was away at college is beyond me. In a matter of weeks, the girl has me under her spell.

Laramie called me about thirty minutes ago and said they were almost home. She also informed me that they were coming to my place. I didn't ask why because I don't care. I get to see McKenna. I don't have to make up an excuse to call her or drop by her grandparents' place. Not that I need an excuse, but it would be pretty out of the blue, considering she has no idea how I feel about her. Sure, I've dropped a few hints, but I know McKenna needs the facts. That attorney in her can't seem to help it. That's fine with me. I'm perfectly happy laying out the facts for her as soon as I get the chance.

Hearing a car pull up, I peek out the window and see Colby's truck. I watch as he and Corbin climb out. I meet them at the front door. "What are you two getting into?" I ask, stepping back to let them in.

"Not sure. Lara called and asked for me to meet her here. She told me to bring Corbin. We were hoping that you knew what was going on."

"Not a clue. She called me too and told me they were about half an hour away and that they were coming here."

"You think everything's okay?" Colby asks. I can hear the concern in his voice.

"Yes. Laramie would have told one of us. Of that, I'm certain." I know my sister, and if there was something wrong, something *really* wrong, she would have told me. Wouldn't she? I'm starting to second-guess myself when I hear another car pull in. All three of us move to the front door and step out on the front porch.

My eyes trail over my sister and McKenna as they climb out of my sister's SUV. They look fine, and both are wearing smiles a mile wide. Now it's clear that they're both safe, I lock my eyes on McKenna. She looks more relaxed, and even though I know that it's more than likely because the exams are over and she's had time with her best friend, I still puff out my chest a little, hoping my spa surprise helped that relaxed smile find its way to her lips.

"Colby James," my sister calls out.

Not that she needed to. Colby's feet are already hitting the steps, making his way to my sister. I watch as he pulls her into his arms, lifting her feet off the ground. They whisper to one another, and my heart squeezes. McKenna ascends the stairs and stops next to me. I can't seem to help it. I put my arm around her, pulling her into my chest.

"Miss you, Kenna," I say. My voice is husky as I whisper the greeting just for her.

"Let's go inside. I have some news," Laramie announces. Colby releases her but still keeps one hand on the small of her back as we all file back into my house and find seats in the living room. I lead McKenna to the love seat and pull her down next to me. Corbin takes the recliner while my sister points to the couch, nodding for Colby to sit, even though she remains standing.

"Thank you all for coming." She looks at Corbin, then back to Colby. "Mac and I had such a good time in Dallas." Her eyes flash to McKenna, who gives her a subtle nod. "I've missed my best friend," Laramie says, her voice cracking. "Anyway, Rip sent us to an afternoon at the spa... thank you, big brother." She smiles, and I nod. "We went to several bridal shops and just spent time together. I didn't realize that this trip was exactly what I needed for clarity."

"Lara, babe, what's going on?"

"Corbin, can you go sit by your brother?" She must see the panic on his face. "It's nothing bad, I promise. At least I hope not. I just... this will be easier if you two are sitting closer."

"Sure thing, Lara," Corbin says. He stands and moves to sit next to his brother on the couch.

"Babe?" Colby says again. There is a slight quiver of worry in his voice.

Laramie looks to McKenna again. "You've got this," McKenna tells her softly.

"Guys, I've thought a lot about life and the future, and if the offer still stands, I'd love to come and work for you at James Construction."

"What?" Colby jumps up from the couch. "Are you for real? You'll do it?"

Laramie nods, tears shimmering in her eyes. Colby embraces her again before passing her off to Corbin, who is now standing next to them. They hug it out before I stand and take her into my arms as well.

"Love you, little sister," I murmur.

"I love you too." She pulls away and wipes at her eyes. "Okay." She laughs. "I'm not done yet." She looks over at McKenna. "Which part should I do next?" she asks with a nervous laugh.

"Definitely the wedding." McKenna grins at my sister.

"Right, the wedding," Laramie repeats. "About that." She turns and locks eyes with her fiancé. Colby sits up straighter, and the fear is evident in his expression. "McKenna and I went to a dozen different dress shops. I tried on some gorgeous dresses, and so did she." My sister winks at McKenna, and she shrugs.

"You tried on wedding dresses?" I ask, not bothering to keep my voice quiet.

"She needed moral support," she says with another shrug.

My mind pulls up images of her in a white gown, and I shake off the thought as my sister commands me to focus. I nod, letting Laramie know that I'm listening, and she turns back to face Colby.

"I love you, Colby James. I don't care about the dress, or the venue, or flowers, or invitations. I just don't." She shrugs.

"Fuck, Lara, you scared the hell out of me." He stands and goes to her, wrapping her in his arms.

"I'm sorry." She kisses him quickly before pulling away. "I just want to be your wife."

"Whatever you want, babe, you know that," Colby tells her.

"I was hoping you would say that." She gives him a smile, then turns her head to wink at McKenna. What are these two hiding? "I was thinking we could get married here, on the farm."

"Done."

"In two weeks."

My mouth falls open. Two weeks? I turn to look at McKenna, and she has tears in her eyes. What in the hell am I missing?

"Two weeks?" Colby clarifies.

"Yes."

"You sure this is what you want?" he asks her.

"I don't want to wait."

"Then we have a wedding to plan." He picks her up and spins her in a circle, both of them laughing.

"Oh, one more thing."

"Anything," he says, and I know he's willing to give her the world.

"I think we should all take a trip."

"Where to?"

"Well, McKenna could use a break from all the college and studying, and we could also say it's our bachelor and bachelorette parties."

"Vegas, baby!" Corbin shouts. He's been quiet, which is unlike him.

"You read my mind, brother-in-law." Laramie grins at him.

"What?" McKenna asks.

"Did I forget to mention that part?" Laramie asks her.

"You kinda did," McKenna replies, smiling with a shake of her head.

"When?" Colby asks, only having eyes for my sister.

"A few days." She shrugs. "I wasn't sure if you, Corbin, and Rip could get the time off work."

"We'll make it work," Corbin assures her.

"What he said," Colby agrees.

"What do you say, big brother? You coming to Vegas?"

I look at McKenna. "You coming?"

"She's my best friend. Of course, I'll be there."

"I'm in," I tell the room, only my eyes stay on McKenna.

"Oh, and, Corbin, you can invite Sara," Laramie says nonchalantly.

"We're not—"

My sister cuts him off. "You are. Invite her. Everyone look at their schedules, and I'll make it happen."

Just like that, my baby sister is getting married a hell of a lot sooner than we thought, and we're headed to Vegas. Normally the unexpected trip would irritate me, but I have to admit, getting to spend some time with McKenna in Sin City sounds like a fun time to me.

Chapter Fourteen

MCKENNA

"DO WE REALLY HAVE TO SPLIT UP? I DIDN'T EVEN WANT A BACHELOR PARTY. WE SHOULD all just hang out," Colby suggests. There's tension in his voice.

We're all sitting in Colby and Laramie's suite in Vegas, making plans for our first night here. Our plane landed two hours ago, and we came straight to the hotel to check in. Currently, Colby is in freak-out mode that we girls are going to be walking around by ourselves. It's sweet, but we're big girls, and none of us plan on getting completely trashed. Well, maybe Laramie, this is her bachelorette party after all. Sara and I talked about it on the plane, and she needs to have a good time.

Speaking of Sara, I really like her. I need to find time to pull Corbin aside and let him know that he better hang onto her. Although, since she's here, I'm thinking that's something he already knows.

"Colbs, we'll be fine. We're big girls," Laramie says soothingly.

"I agree," Rip speaks up. His eyes find mine. "I don't think I'll be able to have a good time worrying about you ladies." He includes all of us, but his eyes are locked on mine.

The intensity of his gaze causes goose bumps to travel down my arms. One day I'm going to be brave and ask him why he's been giving me all the sexy looks, soft touches, and kisses. God, that man can kiss.

"We're three adult women who can handle ourselves. Besides, Sara and

I already talked about it. We're not going to get wasted. This is Laramie's weekend. We'll keep an eye on her."

"Is that supposed to make me feel better about this?" Colby asks.

"How about we all do our own thing, then meet up later?" Sara suggests.

I turn to look at her and tell her that I agree with the plan. Colby can take over watching Laramie, and she and I can have some fun. Only I stop when I see Corbin pull her into his arms and whisper in her ear. Oh, yeah, he's got it bad. I'm happy for him. Corbin is goofy as hell, but he's a good guy.

"That's a good idea," I agree with her, turning back to Colby and Laramie.

"That's perfect. You go do manly things. We're going to do girly things and meet up later." Laramie kisses Colby on the cheek and stands from the couch. "Now, we need to get ready." She glances at the clock on the wall. "Ladies, let's meet back here at seven. That gives us an hour to change and get spruced up for the night."

"Spruced up? Babe, why do you need to get spruced up?" Colby sounds panicked. He should be. I helped my best friend pack. I know that arsenal she has in her suitcase by way of wardrobe.

"It's Vegas, baby!" Laramie cheers and rushes off to the bedroom.

"Colby, Sara and I will watch out for her. You guys go have fun. We'll meet back here at seven, and then what, again at eleven or so?"

"That long?" he asks, sounding defeated.

"We'll start with eleven and see how the night goes," I tell him gently.

"Why in the fuck did I agree to this?" Colby asks, tilting his head back, resting it on the couch.

"Kenna?" Rip speaks up. I turn to look at him. There's something in his gaze that I can't name. He opens his mouth to speak, but I beat him to it.

"Rip, we're going to be fine. I'll keep my phone on all night. Check in with us as much as you want. I promise I'll keep your sister safe." He gives me a curt nod and leaves it at that.

"Well, we're going to go get ready. See you all in an hour," Corbin announces, waving over his shoulder as they exit the suite.

"I should go too. I'll see you both soon." I wave and turn to walk away when I hear Rip tell Colby he's going to walk with me.

He doesn't say a word as he falls in step beside me while I make my way to my suite at the other end of the hall. We decided to go all out for this trip, and the rooms are huge and breathtaking. Stopping at my door, I tap my room key, waiting for the light to turn green. Turning the handle, I push open the door and then face Rip. He's standing so close that I bump into him.

"I'll see you soon," I say, knowing I should step back, but I like being this close to him.

"Kenna." The way he says my name sends tingles down my spine. He lifts his hand to my face, and the warmth of his skin does nothing to cool my desire for him.

I'm not exactly sure how it happens, but we end up walking into my room, the door closing with an audible click behind us. "I-I need to get ready," I say, stumbling over my words. I can't decipher his expression, but it's hot as fuck, and I do not want to be all worked up over Rip before a night out on the town.

"I know. But I need something from you first."

"Okay?"

He wraps his arms around my waist and pulls me close. He gives me no warning when his lips mold with mine. The kiss is more urgent than any that we've shared before, and like the others, it leaves me completely breathless. I should pull back. I should stop this, whatever it is, but I can't. I'm not strong enough to resist him. Instead, I grip his shirt, holding him close to me.

Eventually, he slows the kiss, resting his forehead against mine. "I don't like the idea of you being in this city alone."

"I won't be alone."

"You know what I mean." His voice is soft and sweet when he says, "Can you do me a favor?"

"What?" I'm ready to tell him I'd do anything for him, which is true, but this is Laramie's bachelorette party, and no way am I giving him permission to come with us.

"Let me come with you," he suggests.

"No can do, buddy." I pat my hands against his chest.

He pulls back and grins at me. "I thought that you might say that. So, instead, how about you keep me in the loop, yeah? Let me know where you guys are?"

"Sure, I can do that. As long as you promise not to barge in on us until our agreed upon time."

"Deal."

I smile up at him. "Should we shake on it?" I ask awkwardly, holding my hand between us, even though he's still holding my body close to his.

"No, baby, you and I don't shake on it. There's only one thing that can seal this deal," he says huskily.

"And what's that?" I ask breathlessly.

He doesn't answer, not with words. Instead, he lowers his head and kisses me slow and deep. His tongue invades my mouth, and all I can do is tighten my grip on his shirt and enjoy the ride.

"You better get ready." He pulls away and moves further inside the room, taking a seat on the small couch.

I suck in a few deep breaths before I feel as though I can speak. "What are you doing?" I ask.

"Waiting for you to get ready."

"I don't need help."

His heated gaze trails over me, making me feel open and exposed. "You might need me to zip your dress or something," he finally says when his eyes find mine.

"I can manage."

"I'm not leaving. Time's wasting," he says with a smirk.

I don't have it in me to argue with him for multiple reasons. The two biggest are the fact that he just kissed me stupid, and I know I'm in no shape mentally to go to battle with him. And two, I'll take all the time he's willing to give me. I'm secretly thrilled that he wants to be here, so instead of arguing, I make my way to my bedroom, shutting the door behind me to get ready to go out on the town to help my best friend celebrate the last few days of being single before she marries the love of her life.

"NO."

That's the first word out of Rip's mouth when I walk back into the small living area of my suite. "What do you mean, no?" I tilt my head to the side.

"You can't wear that, Kenna."

I look down at the purple sundress I'm wearing. It's low cut with spaghetti straps and stops about midthigh. I've paired it with my cowboy boots. Sara and Laramie are going to be wearing the same thing. When we learned Sara was coming on the trip, we wanted her to feel included, so we reached out, and the three of us went shopping. It was Laramie's idea that we dress alike, and Sara and I readily agreed. She chose these, and we tried to argue that she should be the only one wearing white. She then told us that these were the exact outfits she wanted us to wear to the wedding when we both stood up with her. There were lots of tears, and of course, we bought the dresses.

"You don't get to decide that," I counter.

"McKenna," he says. His voice is a low growl. "You can't wear that. How in the fuck am I supposed to let you walk around Vegas looking like a wet dream?" He runs his fingers through his long hair.

I can't explain what his words make me feel. I'm all gushy inside and speaking of wet.... I shake out of that train of thought and focus on the fact that although he looks pained, his eyes haven't stopped taking me in. Almost as if he's trying to catalog the exact image in his memory for a later date.

"I'm sorry to break it to you, buddy, but your sister picked this outfit. All three of us are wearing the exact same thing, so you're just going to have to deal." Not only that, but he doesn't have a say so, regardless of what he thinks. He's not mine. I'm not his. Even if I want to be.

He stands from the couch and doesn't hide the fact that he grabs his crotch and adjusts before stalking toward me. "And this," he says, gliding his fingers over the hair of my side ponytail. "How am I supposed to resist you like this?" He leans in and presses a kiss to the corner of my mouth. He blows out a heavy breath, closing his eyes. "Are you ready to go?" he asks.

"Yes. Do you need to change or anything?"

"You think I should?" he asks.

I take in his black fitted T-shirt, worn jeans, and cowboy boots. "No." I shake my head. "You look fine." I step away from him, needing a little space. I grab my small crossbody, making sure I have my ID, cash, room key, and cell phone.

He grins wickedly. "Come on, let's get this night over with." With his hand on the small of my back, he leads me to the door. We don't speak as we make our way down the hall to Laramie and Colby's room. We reach their door, and I raise my hand to knock, but I'm frozen when his lips find their way next to my ear.

"You look beautiful, McKenna. I didn't get the chance to say it, but you take my breath away," he says softly. My hand drops to my side, and he chuckles, reaching around me to knock on the door. His hands land on my hips as we wait.

A few seconds later, Colby answers the door. He sees me and shakes his head. "Not you too," he groans.

"Right?" Rip asks, guiding us into the suite.

"I'm so excited!" Laramie exclaims when she sees me.

"It's not a good idea." I hear from behind us.

Turning to look, all I see is Rip's chest, so I lean to the side to look around him. Corbin and Sara are standing in the doorway, and he's not looking thrilled.

"What the bride wants, the bride gets." Sara shrugs.

"Change of plans," Colby announces. "We're all going out. One big party," he informs us.

"Good," Rip agrees.

"Perfect," Corbin says.

"No. No, we're not. This is not how it's supposed to work. The girls are going out, and you guys are going out, and we're going to meet up here in the hotel lobby at eleven." Laramie kisses Colby quickly before grabbing her purse. She looks inside, and I know she's going through the same mental checklist that I went through. "Ladies?" she says, heading toward the door.

I pull away from Rip or try to; his grip on my hips is tight. "Keep me posted," he says, his lips next to my ear, causing a shiver to race down my spine.

"Promise." I smile up at him, trying to reassure him. It's nice to know that he cares. That all three of them care.

He leans in close and kisses me. Just a soft peck on the lips, but it's the first time he's done this in front of our friends, other than the bonfire at our own fake wedding. Well, our second fake wedding. "Be safe. You call me if you need me."

"Okay." It's lame as far as replies go, but that's all that I've got. He releases me, and I follow Laramie and Sara out of the suite. I assume they had their own goodbyes and were too busy to see mine.

"What was that?" Laramie asks.

"That was hot," Sara replies.

"It was a peck on the lips." I downplay their comments.

"It might have just been a peck, but he looked like he wanted to eat you alive." This from Sara, with Laramie nodding her agreement.

I wanted him too. "Nah, just nervous about us going out on our own."

"I know my brother. He wants you," Laramie says, adamant that she's correct.

I wish she was. "Enough about Rip. This is your bachelorette party. Let's do this." Luckily all conversation about Rip and me halts, and we make our way to the hotel bar to get this night started.

Chapter Fifteen

RIP

THE GUYS AND I FOLLOWED THE LADIES DOWN TO THE HOTEL BAR. WE STAYED BACK, SO they didn't think we were spying on them. I've heard stories of Sin City, and the thought of something happening to any of them has me on edge. When they left the hotel to explore the strip, it took every ounce of willpower I could muster not to trail along behind them. Since then, I've checked my phone what feels like a million times waiting for a text from McKenna.

The three of us decided to stay here. We thought it made more sense to let the ladies know where we would be if they needed us. The bar at our hotel made the most sense. Besides, this is the place where we're meeting up with them to finish the night out as a group.

"It's been twenty minutes," I say, taking a drink of my lukewarm beer. It's only my second of the night. I'm taking it slow until the girls are with us again. The last thing I need is to be sloppy drunk, and McKenna or my sister to call and need me. Not on my watch. Not until they're with me.

"They're still at the casino down the street," Colby says, staring at his phone.

"That"—I point to his phone—"is genius."

"Yeah, and it was Lara's idea. She read an article that this app saved a guy working on a ranch a few towns over. He wasn't answering, and his wife was worried, so she pulled up the app and located him. She was able to go to his exact location and call for help. He'd fallen and broken his leg or something. I don't really remember the details, but Laramie was insistent that we get the app."

"We're getting that," I mutter to myself.

"We're?" Corbin asks.

"Kenna."

"What's up with that?" Colby asks. "Are the two of you together?"

"We will be."

"What does that mean?" Corbin laughs.

"It means I'm working on it," I say as my phone vibrates in my hand.

McKenna: We're still at the casino

It's followed by a picture of the three of them. Laramie is wearing a crown of some sort on her head with a sash that says *Bride*. McKenna and Sara are wearing sashes as well that say *Bride Tribe*. I can't help but smile. All three of them are lookers, their eyes glassy, and their smiles are wide. They definitely look like they're having a good time.

"What are you smiling at over there?" Corbin asks.

I turn my phone to show him, and then Colby. "They're living it up." I chuckle.

"I'm glad she's having fun, but I'm ready for them to come back," Corbin says, taking a drink of his beer.

"What about you?" I ask Corbin. "You missing your girl?"

"I'm not obsessing like the two of you, but I wouldn't mind sharing a drink or two with her." He's trying to act cool and nonchalant, but he's been my best friend my entire life. I know better.

"You can admit it. You're into her."

"Yeah, I mean, I like her, but I'm not ready to propose marriage like this guy." He motions toward his brother. "Or make her install an app so I can track her like you." He points at me.

"Hey, don't judge. I just want to keep her safe. It was his idea." I lift my chin toward Colby.

"No. It was your sister's idea, and to be honest, I've not really used it. I did a couple of times planning a surprise dinner for her at the house, so I could see how close she was. Tonight is really the first time I've used it to track her location."

"Y'all sound like creepers."

"Love will do that to you," Colby replies.

"That what this is, man? With Mac? Are you in love with her?"

"I could be." That's a lie. I'm pretty sure the way my heart races when she's close, or even if I just hear her name, and the way my palms itch to touch her, or maybe the way she's the first and last thought I have every single day says I'm well on my way to love, if not already there. I've known her for years, and this... crush that I have isn't new. I've just been biding my time, and that time is now.

I'm going all in to get the girl.

"Come on, man, you've always had a thing for her," Corbin reminds me.

"Yep." There's no use in denying it.

"Are we talking marriage and babies and all that?" Corbin inquires.

A picture of McKenna walking toward me in white with her belly swollen with our child pops in my head, and it's an image I very much want to see in real life. "If she'll have me."

"What happened to all this 'I'm only getting married once' bullshit? It's not going to be a snap decision?" Colby asks.

"This isn't a snap decision." Not by a long shot.

"Do you realize what you're saying, Rip? That you're ready to marry this girl. As in, she's it for you for the rest of your life."

"Yep."

"Wow," Colby breathes. "Your sister is going to be ecstatic."

"It's not happening next week or anything," I remind them. "Kenna and I are still working things out. We'll get to be where you are," I tell him.

"You sure you're ready for this, man? One woman for the rest of your life?" Corbin asks his brother.

I don't take offense to it. It's not a dig toward me or my sister, just a question in general, one that's asked more times than not, I would assume, by the friends of the groom.

"I'm ready."

"You're already acting like a married man," Corbin teases.

"And you're not?" Colby challenges.

"Well, I'm not single so...." He lets that little slither of information hang between us.

"It's official?" I ask.

"Yep. As of a few days ago. I really like her."

"Happy for you." I slap a hand on his shoulder, and Colby does the same from the other side of the table.

"Here we are, our women out living the high life, and we've barely consumed a six-pack between us the entire night." Colby shakes his head.

"Rather be with her," I mumble under my breath while I type a message back to McKenna.

Me: You're beautiful.

McKenna: Are you trying to flatter me, Rip Callahan?

Me: Depends. Is it working?

McKenna: **I don't know. You're all I can think about. What do you think?**

I grip my phone tightly in my fist as I shift in my seat. I want to race down the street to where she is and pull her into my arms, kiss the hell out of her, and drag her back to my room, or hell even hers. I'm not picky. I just… need her.

Me: **Glad it's not just me.**

McKenna: **You think about me?**

Me: **Every second of every day.**

I have no idea how much alcohol she's consumed by this point, so she might not remember this. There will, however, be our chat that she can go back and read when she's sober.

McKenna: **That's a lot.**

I chuckle out loud.

"Who are you texting?" Corbin asks.

"McKenna. They're still at the casino."

Me: **It is.**

McKenna: **We're headed back now, so we don't break curfew.**

Her text is followed by an emoji with its tongue sticking out.

Me: **See you soon, beautiful.**

"They're on their way back," I tell my friends, draining my warm beer. They both look up from their phones and nod. We're all wearing matching grins. It's telling that three guys can't have fun in the one city that's known for exactly that without the women in our lives.

Without a word, the three of us stand and make our way to the lobby.

My heart kicks up its pace in my chest, just like it always does when I know that I'm going to get to see her.

McKenna.

I've waited so long for a chance with her, and I'm taking it. I need to tell her exactly what I'm thinking. I need to tell her that I want to give us a real shot. I've been teasing her, dropping hints, stealing touches and kisses, but it's not enough.

I need more.

Standing shoulder to shoulder, the three of us wait in the lobby, our eyes glued to the door. When I see them, when I see her, my body reacts, something I'm used to at this point when it comes to McKenna. Laramie rushes to Colby, jumping in his arms, and Corbin doesn't give Sara the chance as he scoops her up and spins her around. And my girl? She saunters toward me, killing me in that sundress and those cowboy boots.

"Hey, handsome." She stops just out of reach, and that just won't do.

I take one stride so that we're toe to toe and wrap my arms around her. I pull her into a hug so fierce I'm sure she's struggling to breathe, but damn it, I just need to hold her. "Hey," I finally say, easing up on the hug.

"Rip Callahan, did you miss me?" She giggles, her eyes glassy from her buzz, and I can't help but think she looks cute as hell.

"So much," I murmur as I press my lips to hers.

"Hey, you're not drinking?" she asks when I pull back.

"I've had a couple," I admit.

"Oh, no, that won't do. We're celebrating." With her hand laced in mine, she starts to tug me toward the bar. "Let's go, ladies. We have to get some drinks into these fuddy-duddies," she calls over her shoulder.

I hear my sister squeal and then Sara's laughter as they encourage Colby and Corbin to follow us. I don't have to look back to know my friends are following along behind their girls just like I am. There isn't anything we wouldn't do for them.

An hour or so later, we're all sitting around a table at the hotel bar, trying to decide where to go next. It's just after midnight, but this city doesn't seem to ever sleep, and we're here to celebrate so that's what we're going to do.

"Oh! I love this song," my sister says, pulling Colby from his chair next to her and out to the dance floor.

My hand that's resting under the table on McKenna's thigh gives her a gentle squeeze when she does a little shimmy in her chair. I open my mouth to ask her if she wants to dance when she pushes her chair back.

McKenna stands and reaches for my hand. "Dance with me."

She's a little wobbly on her feet, and I'm feeling my buzz pretty heavy. That doesn't stop me from sliding my arm around her waist and pulling her into the middle of the bar, wrapping my arms around her.

"Rip, this is a fast song," she says, smiling up at me.

"I want to hold you."

"Yeah, but this song is sexy." She sways her hips, turning in my arms, pressing her back to my front. Reaching back, her hands clamp around my neck, and I bend my head, kissing her neck. "Oh." I hear her say when she grinds against my hard cock.

"That's all you, Kenna," I whisper in her ear. My hands grip her hips, and I pull her close, making sure there's no question as to what I'm referring to.

I can't tell you the name of the song or even the words. What I can tell you is that McKenna sways her hips to the beat, and she's driving me wild. I wrap my arms around her waist, holding her close.

Damn this woman.

I allow myself to get lost in her. We're the only two people in the room. Just me and McKenna savoring the feel of our bodies pressed close. My lips trail up her neck, and the taste of her skin explodes on my tongue. Drink after drink, song after song, we dance the night away. I lose track of time as the six of us hop from bar to bar and club to club. I don't take my hands off of her the entire night. Part of me has to be touching her. I crave the feel of her skin. Even with the buzz of alcohol thrumming through my veins, I know this will forever be the best night of my life. The night I finally got to treat her like she was mine. Not behind closed doors. Out for the world to see.

There is no coming back from this. I no longer have to pretend, and that's freeing. Tonight marks the night that McKenna Dawson becomes mine.

Chapter Sixteen

MCKENNA

THE SHRILL SOUND OF A CELL PHONE HAS ME PEELING MY EYES OPEN, ONLY TO SHIELD them from the sun. Damn, I should have thought to shut the blinds last night. While that sounds like a grand plan, I'm not even sure how I ended up back in my room.

Wait. Am I in my room?

Squinting, I survey the room and see my suitcase next to the closet door. I sigh in relief as the phone stops ringing.

I'm not much of a drinker, so last night was not only out of character for me, but I'm miserable today. My phone rings again, and I groan. I'm never drinking again. Never.

"I'll get it," a deep voice says from beside me.

I freeze. I know that voice. What the hell did I do last night?

Cautiously, I look over my shoulder to see Rip in nothing. Holy shit, he's buck-ass naked as he climbs out of bed to go in search of my cell phone. My head is fuzzy. What the hell is going on? He comes back with the phone to his ear. And lord have mercy, the full-frontal view, even with my brain not firing on all cylinders, is better than the back view. I know I'm staring, but I can't seem to stop. Rip is... wow.

"She's right here, Agnes. We'll catch the next flight. I'm going to grab us tickets now." He pulls the phone away from his ear and sits on the bed next to me. "Babe, it's your grams," he says, handing me the phone. I blink at him a few times, taking him in. There's worry in his features, and my heart drops to my stomach.

Something's wrong.

There are so many questions floating through my mind. What's he worried about, why's Gram calling, and why is he here sleeping with me, and why is he naked? I don't have to ask any of them as the phone is thrust into my hands. I peek under the covers to see if I'm clothed. "Hey, Gram," I say as I try not to cringe at the fact that I, too, am naked under the sheets. Oh, God. What did we do?

"Mac," Gram says, her voice cracking, pulling me out of my mental fog. Something's seriously wrong. That's when it registers that Rip told her when he was walking back into the room that we would be on the next flight out.

I sit up straighter, not bothering to hold the sheet over my chest, letting it pool at my waist at the broken sound of her voice. "What's wrong?" I can barely think over the pounding in my head, and at this point, I'm not sure if it's last night's alcohol consumption or the fear and sadness in Gram's voice.

"It's your grandfather. We had to call the ambulance. We're at Mercy General. He's had a heart attack."

"W-What?" I croak. I want to say more, but I can't seem to form the words. I feel Rip's hand on my naked back as he pulls the phone from my grasp.

"Agnes, how is he?" he asks. I sit here as the words she just uttered to me bounce around in my head.

Not Gramps. No, this can't be happening.

"McKenna and I are on the next flight home. We'll see you soon." Rip ends the call by dropping my phone on the bed, only to put his to his ear. "Mom, hey, can you do me a favor?" I listen as he explains the situation, asking his parents to go be with Gram until I can get there. No, until *we* can get there. Ending the call, he pulls me into his lap. "I'm going to get you home, baby. We need to get dressed and get to the airport."

There's so much going through my head right now—my worry for Gramps, the fear that we could lose him. Then there's the fact that I'm naked, sitting on Rip's lap who is also naked. I'd be lying if I said the feel of his skin against mine and the way his arms hold me tight was uncomfortable. It's anything but.

I nod, wrapping my arms around him as the tears begin to fall. Naked bodies be dammed. I need this. I need the comfort he's offering. I was gone to college for so long. So much time was missed with my grandparents, with Gramps, and now I might lose him. That's not how this was supposed to happen. We were supposed to work together, at least for a little while, until he retired and spent his days doing whatever he and Gram wanted to do. This isn't how it was supposed to go.

"Kenna, baby, I'm so sorry." Rip holds me tighter, and I'm grateful for him at this moment. His strong arms give me a sense of security, and that's a feat considering my world just tilted on its axis. The fact that we're naked is never too far from my mind, and I know we need to talk about it. And we will, but not this minute.

"We have to go," I say, crawling off his lap. I rush around the room, picking up my clothes from last night, I swallow hard, and I need to brush my teeth. I could really use a shower, but there's no time. "I'm never drinking again," I mutter under my breath.

"Hey, it's me." I hear Rip say into the phone. I'm sure he's talking to Laramie or Colby. "We're heading back today. Harold had a heart attack. Agnes just called. No, I got us on the next flight out. She's... as good as can be expected. Yeah, I'll let you know." He hangs up the phone and comes to me, wrapping his arms around me once again. "What can I do?"

God, he feels good with his arms wrapped around me, skin to skin.

"Nothing. I—" I stop and look up at him. "I don't know why we're naked in my hotel suite, but I don't have time to dissect that right now. Thank you for getting me on a flight home. You don't have to come with me. I don't want to cut your trip short too." I'm rambling as my mind races to catch up with what's happened since the shrill ringing of my phone woke me.

"Hey." He places his index finger under my chin so that we're eye to eye. "I want to be where you are, McKenna. Lean on me. Let me help you and your family through this."

"I'm scared," I confess.

"I know, baby. I know." He pulls me into his chest. I want him to tell me that everything is going to be okay, but I'm glad he's not. I don't need false assurances, and I know that neither of us knows how this is going to turn out. I just pray that Gramps makes it through this. He has fight in him. I know it. I just hope it shines through at this moment.

Moving from Rip's arms, I continue to get dressed. I glance over my shoulder to see him doing the same. He has a large white envelope in his hand, and a sad smile is tilting his lips. I don't have time to ask him what's in that envelope that would make him smile. I have to finish packing. "Thank you for this," I tell him.

"Don't ever thank me for taking care of you, McKenna." His tone is soothing, but there's an undercurrent of scolding to his tone.

It's not his job to take care of me, but I'm grateful he's doing so.

Running my hands over my face, I try to regroup. I don't know how we ended up here together, and my brain is too foggy to recall much of the latter part of the night. Slowly, I turn to face Rip. "What did we do?"

"The details are fuzzy, but from what I remember, we spent an incredible night together."

"W-What?" I whisper.

"I made love to you, McKenna."

I close my eyes, trying to remember last night, and all I can remember is Rip and me dancing, getting closer as the night wore on. I don't recall coming back to my room. This isn't real.

"Tell me you're joking."

His brown eyes bore into mine. "No. I'm not joking. Making love to you is not a joking matter." His voice is tight, yet his eyes are still soft as they take me in.

"I'm sorry. I—" I don't know what to say. What does one say to the man she's always wanted when she finds out that they finally slept together after a drunken night in Vegas?

"Stop." His voice is firm. "We can talk about this on the plane or after we land and see your grandfather. Right now, you need to get moving. We still have to stop at my suite and grab my bags before we head to the airport."

"Rip—" I try again but stop when he advances, his long legs carrying him toward me.

"Baby, we can talk about this, about us later. Right now, all that matters is us making that flight. I promised you and your gram that I would get you home, and that's exactly what I'm going to do." He surprises me when he bends and places a kiss on the corner of my mouth. "Finish doing what you need to do. I'm going to call downstairs and order a cab." He walks back to the bed, slides into his shirt, picks up his phone and the white envelope, and walks out of the room.

What's in that envelope? Wait... *I slept with Rip!*

Shaking out of my stupor, I rush to the bathroom to freshen up quickly before pulling on some clothes and throwing everything into my suitcase haphazardly. I make a quick sweep of the room to ensure I didn't miss anything and turn for the door to find Rip with his hand held out for me.

"I'll take that." He grabs my suitcase handle. "You all set?"

"I think so." My head is still fuzzy from last night, from hearing that Gramps had a heart attack, and the thought that this man, this handsome, kind, caring man, my best friend's older brother, was inside me last night. If I had more time, I'm sure I'd be freaking the hell out, but there's no time. My grandparents need me.

SETTLING INTO FIRST CLASS BACK TO TEXAS, I SIGH WITH RELIEF AS THE PLANE TAXIS down the runway. We'll be home in a few hours. I hate we'll be out of touch during that time. I called Gram before we boarded the plane, and she said he was in surgery. Closing my eyes, I send up a silent prayer that he's okay. *Please let him be okay.*

"Ma'am." I hear Rip say softly. "Can I have a blanket for my girlfriend?" he asks.

My girlfriend.

I want to open my eyes and tell her he's joking, but I decide to pretend to sleep instead. We had sex last night. When we were waiting to board, I'd asked to see what was inside the envelope. He handed it to me without complaint. Inside were pictures of us standing outside of our hotel in front of the fountain. Neither one of us are looking at the camera. Instead, our eyes are locked on one another. There was also a picture of our entire group with Elvis, standing outside of a wedding chapel. My heart rate kicked up thinking about marrying him for real.

The seven-year-old me would be giddy with excitement to be married to

Rip Callahan. Who am I kidding? He's everything, including my best friend's brother. Just because we slept together doesn't mean I can fantasize about forever with him. I'm an adult. We had sex, that's it. This too shall pass and all that.

I feel the heaviness of the blanket as warmth surrounds me. His lips press against my temple. "Sleep, beautiful," he says softly. Unable to hide any longer, I open my eyes to find him with his head resting against the seat, turned to face me. "Sorry if I woke you."

"You called me your girlfriend."

His hand reaches out and rests against my cheek. "You caught that, did you?"

"Do drunken hookups really count as a relationship?" I ask.

Something flashes in his eyes. "It wasn't just a hookup." There's no room in his tone for arguments.

"We should, you know, just pretend it never happened. Just let it pass."

"Let it pass?" He raises his eyebrows in question.

"Yes, in a few days, life will be back to normal. We were both under the influence of alcohol. It happens. No reason for either of us to feel guilty. You definitely don't need to feel as though we need to be in a relationship because of it."

"There's no going back for me, Kenna. I was inside you last night. That means something to me."

My heart leaps into my throat. "Rip?"

He leans in close. His mouth's a breath from mine. "I made love to you last night, McKenna. The details are a little fuzzy, but I remember enough. I remember feeling like I was finally home." His eyes are soft. "I hate that I can't remember every single second of our first time together."

"It was a thing, but now it's over. No harm done." Except maybe to my heart. The way it's beating frantically in my chest, it seems as though that forgetting won't be an option for me. Not for a while, if not ever. I can't believe we spent the night together and I can't remember it.

"No."

"What do you mean no?"

"I don't want it to be over."

"Rip." I sigh. "If this is some kind of weird sense of responsibility thing you have going on in that head of yours, you can drop it. We don't have to make this a thing."

"We do."

"No, we don't."

"We'll see," he says, crossing his arms over his chest.

I don't have the energy to argue with him, and I certainly don't need every damn person on this plane involved in our private life. He's not thinking clearly. I never want him to feel trapped like my father. I'll give him some time to think about it, and once I see that Gramps is going to be fine, I'll figure out how to navigate being friends who have seen each other naked.

Chapter Seventeen

RIP

AS WE APPROACH THE ENTRANCE TO THE HOSPITAL, MY HAND ON HER THIGH GIVES A SOFT tap, letting her know I'm here for her. Guiding our rental into the parking lot, I rush to grab the keys and my phone and catch up with her as she power walks her way to the main entrance. When we landed, we called to check on Harold. Agnes had informed us that the surgery went well, and they were admitting him to the cardiac floor.

Catching up to McKenna, I entwine my fingers with hers just as we're entering the hospital. I wish there was something else I could do other than hold her hand and drive her to the hospital. I know her heart is aching at the thought of losing her grandfather. Her dream has always been to work side by side with him before he retires. She's busted her ass to finish college early, only to be faced with the uncertainty of her grandfather's future.

"Harold Dawson," she says when we reach the reception desk.

"Are you family?" the lady behind the desk asks.

"She's his granddaughter," I answer for McKenna.

"And you are?"

"Her husband." There's no way I'm letting her go back there alone, and if they don't think I'm family, they won't let me. Boyfriend isn't a good enough title in these kinds of situations.

"He's on the fifth floor, the cardiac until. I'm not sure if he's been assigned a room yet. Take that elevator"—she points to our right—"and the nurse at the desk will be able to help you."

"Thank you," I say, my feet already moving, guiding McKenna to the elevators. Once the doors close, I hit the number five on the wall and wrap her in my arms. She feels right.

"I'm so scared," she murmurs into my neck.

"I know, I am too, but I'm going to be right beside you the entire time. Your gram said the surgery went well. He's going to be okay." She doesn't say anything. Instead, she snuggles closer to me, soaking up the comfort I'm so desperately trying to give her.

We exit the elevator hand in hand, and when we approach the desk, I speak for her... for us. "Hi, we're looking for Harold Dawson."

"Are you family?"

"Yes, my wife is his granddaughter." I can feel McKenna's eyes on me when I once again refer to her as my wife. That's something that I could definitely get used to.

"They just brought him up. I need to check on him again. Why don't I show you to his room?" she offers. "Follow me? We have a two-visitor rule, but as long as you don't upset him and let him rest, it will be fine." She gives me a flirty wink. I'm ready to chastise her for flirting with me in front of my wife when McKenna demands her attention.

"Thank you," McKenna says, pulling the nurse's attention.

"Of course." The nurse must see the look on McKenna's face because all hints of flirtation are gone as she leads us to Harold's room.

"Mr. Dawson, you have visitors," the nurse says after knocking lightly on the door.

"Mac." Harold holds his hand out for McKenna, and she drops mine, racing to him.

"Hey, Gramps," she whispers through her tears.

I make my way to them and place my palm on the small of her back, letting her silently know I'm here for her. "You gave us a scare," I tell Harold.

"Oh, I'm fine now. Right as rain, in fact. The doc fixed up my ticker, and Agnes is already talking about taking all the good food away from me. I'm going to be just fine." He chuckles, and although he's a little pale, he sounds like himself.

McKenna's lip quivers. "I was so scared," she tells him, her voice cracking.

"My sweet girl," he says but stops and looks at where her other hand is clasped tightly in mine. "What's this?" He looks up, and the grin on his ashen face is not something I expected.

"Oh my word, is that what I think it is?" Agnes says from her post on the opposite side of the bed. "Rip?" she asks since McKenna seems to be struck speechless.

"I'm working on convincing McKenna to be my girlfriend," I tell them.

"Congratulations, you two." Harold smiles at us.

"Gram, Gramps, this is a mis—" McKenna starts, but Harold talks over her.

"I couldn't think of a better man for you," he tells her. There's nothing but honesty and acceptance in his gaze. "I'd say this news turned a bad day into a great day." He looks at his wife.

"Yes," Agnes says, wiping at her eyes. "I'm so happy for both of you. I always hoped this would be how the two of you ended up. Come here." She walks to our side of the bed, wrapping us both in a hug.

"Grams—" McKenna starts. This time it's me who's talking over her.

"Thank you. I'll make her happy. I promise you."

"Oh, Rip, we know that you will."

Bending, I place a kiss on McKenna's temple. She stares up at me like

I've lost my mind. That's okay. We've yet to really talk about us and our night together, other than me telling her I wanted her to be mine. We will. I needed her to see her family. I needed her to be able to see with her own eyes that Harold was going to be okay. At least, I hoped that was the outcome we would find when we arrived. Luck happened to be on our side, and he's going to be fine. He'll struggle through some diet modifications, but I know for a fact he'll do whatever Agnes tells him. That's what you do for the woman you love, no matter if it's to save your life or not.

"Tell us about your trip," Agnes insists. The heaviness and sadness that was in her eyes when we walked in are now masked by her happiness for us.

"It was fun," McKenna says, glancing up at me.

"Best trip I've ever taken," I say, keeping my eyes on McKenna. I need her to know that my words are true. I might not remember every detail of our night together, but I do remember going back to her room and her asking me to stay. I remember us falling into bed, and after that, it's a fog, but the condom wrapper on the floor and the condom in the bathroom trash tell me the ending of our night at least. I hate that I can't remember, but that's okay. I plan to repeat that night, sans alcohol, very soon.

"We're going to have to celebrate. Dinner," Harold says, looking at his wife.

"As long as they have heart-healthy options on the menu. Or I could make us a family dinner at the house," she offers.

"As long as we get to celebrate these kids and their future, I'm fine with it," Harold tells her. I'd expected him to be at least grumpy from being in the hospital, but he's always been a happy guy.

"He was whining about staying here, so this news comes at a great time. It gave me a break from all the fussing." Agnes rubs her hands over her husband's affectionately.

We spend the next thirty minutes or so catching up. Agnes tells us about the ride here in the ambulance. Apparently, they didn't want her to ride along, but she wasn't taking no for an answer. McKenna gets so much of her fire from her, and I wouldn't have it any other way. When Harold yawns, McKenna tells him that we're going so he can get some rest but promises to come back in a few hours before visiting hours are over.

"Can you stay with Rip tonight? I know you two are an item now, and well, I'd feel better if you weren't staying at the house alone," Harold says.

"Gramps, I'm a big girl."

"I know you are, sweetheart, but let your boyfriend take care of you. That's his job." He reaches for Agnes's hand.

"She's staying with me," I tell Harold. I can feel McKenna's stare, but I don't meet it. I'm not having this conversation with her here. She gives both of her grandparents a hug goodbye, and we're back on the elevator. I tug her back into my arms, and she comes willingly, which I take as a good sign.

"Are you hungry?" I ask once we're on the road.

"Starving," she says, turning her head that's resting against the back of the seat to look at me.

"How's a drive-through sound? We can take it back to your grandparents' and eat while we grab some of your things."

"Food, sleep, and then we can deal with everything else. We've made a mess."

"What mess?" I ask, knowing damn well what she's talking about.

"This." She holds up her hand, motioning between the two of us. "They think we're together now."

"We are together now."

"Rip," she sighs. "You're off the hook."

"We are," I insist. At least I hope we are. I'll do everything in my power to make her mine.

"This is crazy. Do you hear yourself right now?"

I pull up to the drive-through speaker and order my meal and then hers before turning to look at her. "Want to add anything else?"

"How did you—? No." She shakes her head. "That's good."

"That will be all," I tell the speaker. The server gives me my total, and I pull forward.

"How did you know what I wanted?"

"I pay attention, McKenna. This isn't something new for me. I've been attracted to you for years, but I refused to hold you back. I was afraid if we started something, you wouldn't follow through with school. I wanted to make sure you followed your dreams." Grabbing my wallet out of my back pocket, I pass my card through the window. When the girl hands it back, I hand McKenna my card and my wallet. "You mind putting that back in for me?" I ask, pulling up to grab our food.

"What-What is this?" she asks.

I set the bag of food on the back seat floorboard and pull forward so I don't clog up the line. Glancing over, I see a picture of McKenna at the lake. It was the summer she graduated from high school, about a week or so before she left for college. "A picture," I reply, looking both ways before pulling out onto the road.

"It's a picture of me."

"I know."

"Why do you have it?"

"I missed you." Never again will I hide what I want with her. I've waited long enough. A picture of her is the last thing she expected to find. I know that she's battling with her feelings, and it's taking her a little longer to be on board with us, but we've crossed that line, and going backward seems silly when I know there will never be anyone else like McKenna in my life. She's it.

"Are you feeling okay? Are you still hungover from last night? Should you be driving?" she rattles off.

"I'm feeling great, happy about us, sad about Harold. I'm not still hungover, and I'm fine to drive."

"Rip, I've been home for a few weeks, we spend one night together, and suddenly we're in a relationship, and you want us to stay that way? Do you not hear how crazy that sounds?"

"It sounds crazier to me not to be."

"I need sleep," she mutters.

"Why don't we go straight to my place so you can eat and take a nap? We'll go to yours after."

"Your place is fine," she says with a sigh.

Glancing over, her eyes are closed. I know today has been a lot, waking up to hear that her grandfather was in the hospital, finding out that we slept together last night, and cutting our trip short... it's a lot to process. I just hope I can convince her to give this a shot. To give us a shot.

At the house, I grab the food and follow her up the steps to the front door. She kicks off her shoes and goes straight to the kitchen island, where we eat in silence. This is the first thing we've had other than some snacks on the plane, so we both devour our food. Standing, I don't bother with the trash, leaving it on the counter. I offer her my hand, and to my surprise, she takes it. "Let's go sleep."

She follows me, exhaustion setting in as I guide her upstairs to my room. I quickly strip out of my clothes, offering her my T-shirt to sleep in. I watch as she disappears into the bathroom to change. Sliding under the covers, I wait for her. My arms itch to hold her. I just need to be able to show her this is what I want. I know she wants it too. I know she does. I see it in the way that she looks at me. The way her breathing accelerates whenever I'm close. She wants this, but she's afraid to want it. I just need her to give me time to prove to her that we can go the distance. I need her to know that the two of us are going to be forever.

When she slides under the covers, I pull her into my arms, and she comes willingly. Her body shakes with silent tears, and it breaks me in two. I know our night together is putting pressure on her when she's already stressed and worried about her grandfather.

I hold her tight, kissing the top of her head. "I'm right here," I tell her. "I've got you, and I'm not going anywhere." Eventually, her tears subside, and her breathing evens out. Once I know she's resting peacefully, I allow myself to drift off to sleep.

Chapter Eighteen

MCKENNA

MY EYES OPEN AT THE SOUND OF THE SHOWER SHUTTING OFF. I DON'T BOTHER TO GET OUT of bed. Instead, I just lie here staring up at the ceiling as I try to process what's happened in the last twenty-four hours. Gramps had a heart attack, and I slept with my best friend's brother, who just also happens to be one of my best friends.

"Hey, you feeling better?" Rip's deep voice pulls my attention.

He's standing just in the doorway of the bathroom. There's a white towel tucked around his narrow waist, water dripping down the planes and valleys of his abs, and another towel in his hand as he dries his hair. He's all tanned and toned, and my every fantasy. "Yeah. Food and sleep do wonders for a person."

He chuckles softly. "I talked to Agnes. He's doing well. I told her we were coming back. She's going to leave when we get there and go home and get some rest."

My heart swells in my chest, so much so, it makes it hard to swallow. He's such a good man. "Thank you," I croak.

He gives me a nod as his cell phone rings. I watch his every move as he makes his way across the room and to the opposite side of the bed to pull it off the charger. "Hey, Lara," he greets his sister.

"Yeah, he's going to be okay." He gives me a small smile. "She is too. She just woke up from a nap. We're going to head back to the hospital in a little while." He's quiet as he listens, and then his smile broadens. "Of course I'm taking care of her. She's my girl."

"What?!" I hear Laramie scream.

He listens, the smile still pulling at his lips. "No, little sister, it wasn't just a really good dream. We're together." His voice is lower, husky even as he says those two words. His big brown eyes bore into mine, and I fight the urge to stick my head under the covers and hide. I can't though. His gaze is like a magnet, and I can't look away.

We're together.

"Okay. We'll see you all tomorrow." He ends the call and walks toward the bed. He bends his head and presses his lips to mine. "I'm going to go make us something to eat. After you shower, we'll head back to the hospital."

"Rip?"

"Yeah, baby?"

"We have to talk about this."

He links his left hand with mine. "I know we do, but right now, all you need to worry about is your grandfather. I'm not going anywhere." He kisses the back of my hand.

"We can't just ignore this."

"Go shower, so we can go see your gramps." He kisses me quickly, just a peck, and disappears into his closet. He comes out wearing a pair of cargo shorts and a Callahan Farm T-shirt. He smiles at me softly, points to the bathroom, and disappears.

I lie here in his bed, listening as his footsteps carry him down the stairs. I feel as though I'm in a different universe. He can't seriously think that us being together because of one night is a good idea. My parents were together for months and when I came along, it all came crashing down. We can't rush into this. Ugh. Tossing off the covers, I see my suitcase at the end of the bed and dig out some clothes.

In the bathroom, the hot spray does wonders for my aching shoulders. I'm never drinking again. Ever. The pounding in my head is reason enough. However, if I needed one more, it would be that I slept with Rip and can't remember it. That's not something I would ever want to forget. I take my time in the shower, enjoying the spray of the jets and the massage they're providing. My mind goes to Rip and our night together. I hate to admit it, but I'm disappointed that I don't remember our first time. Not because of the meaning of the night. However, I do wish I could remember what it felt like to have him hover over me, all those muscles, my hands roaming his body as he pushes inside me. I shake out of the thought. My first time with him and my drunk ass can't remember it.

He's saying that we're together every chance he gets, and I want that. I want it more than anything, but I also don't want this to be rushed. I don't want either of us to have regrets in this, and I don't ever want to feel as though I'm his obligation. I know that I need to get out of my own head, and I know without a shadow of a doubt Maggie would tell me the same thing. I need to call her. Sure it's a thrill to hear him refer to me as his girlfriend. It would be even more so if it were true. If only I knew how to get through his thick skull that he has no obligation to me. We slept together, that doesn't mean he has to go all in. I know he thinks he's ready, but it's only been a few weeks. Things are happening at a rapid pace, and I just want to slow them down a little. I hate to admit it, but I might need Laramie's help. I'm going to have to call her as soon as she gets home. Her text told me they were flying home today, cutting their trip short as well. I hate that for them, but I love her for it all the same.

I need my best friend.

Realizing I've been in here way longer than necessary, I shut off the water and step out. I make quick work of drying off and getting dressed. I rummage under the sink to find a hairdryer and do a quick dry of my hair before pulling it back into a ponytail. I don't bother with makeup, knowing we're going to the hospital, and the way my emotions are all over the place with Gramps and now this thing with Rip, it's hard to tell when the tears will flow, but I'm pretty sure they will. That's just how the day feels it might pan out.

When I make it to the bottom of the steps, the smell of bacon fills my senses. *I love bacon!* Turning the corner, I see Rip standing at the counter, assembling what looks like bacon, lettuce, and tomato sandwiches. "Hey, babe. Feel better?" he asks.

"Much. That smells good."

He grins at me. "I know they're one of your favorites. I thought it might help you feel better."

I watch as he cuts the sandwich in half, adds some plain potato chips and a pickle spear to the paper plate, and slides it across the counter to me. "Thank you." I wait for him to finish his own plate and take the seat next to me before I start to eat. We eat in silence until Rip breaks the ice.

"Laramie thought she was dreaming."

"About?"

"Us being together. Apparently, she woke up telling Colby she could see the future, and she just knew we were destined to be a couple."

"For real?" I ask.

"Yep. Colby called while you were in the shower."

"So they know? I mean, that we got drunk and hooked up?"

"They know that we were all over each other." He nods. "They don't know that we're together officially. Not yet."

"What about Corbin and Sara?"

"I told them."

"What? When? Why?" I rapid-fire questions at him.

"I told them while you were in the shower, and why not? Should I not be excited to tell my best friend that I'm in a relationship?"

"We're not in a relationship, Rip." I sigh. Already I can feel a headache coming on.

"We can be."

Three words upturn my entire world. I take a deep breath and ignore my heart that seems to melt at his words. "Look, I know you have this sense of responsibility. I get it. You slept with your sister's best friend, a good friend to you as well, but you don't owe me anything."

"Eat, babe. I told your, Grams, we'd be there to relieve her soon."

With a roll of my eyes, I pick up my sandwich and take a healthy bite. He's avoiding the conversation. That's fine. He's not going to have a choice but to talk to me when about it when I tell everyone he was just joking, that we're not really together. That also means I have to tell my grandparents we're not really together.

My heart aches at the thought. I glance over at Rip, and he winks at me.

Infuriating sexy man.

"THERE THEY ARE, THE NEW COUPLE." GRAMPS' SMILE IS WIDE AS WE WALK INTO THE ROOM. "Come sit." He points to the two chairs on the side of his bed.

"Hey, Gramps." I go to him, giving him a kiss on the cheek. "You look like you're feeling better."

"Much. This old ticker"—he taps his chest—"is working just fine. And I have this pretty lady here to keep me company."

Grams smiles from her single seat on the opposite side of the bed. "Always the charmer," she says with so much adoration in her voice I have to swallow back the emotions welling in my throat.

The love they share is unlike anything I've ever seen. To think that she could have lost him, that we could have lost him, tears me up inside. I know he's okay. I'm sitting here with his hand in mine, watching as he smiles and winks at her, but the threat was real. I'm not ready for a world without either of them. They saved me, raised me, and gave me all the love a little girl could ever need. They are my world, and to think of this world without them... well, it's not a happy place. I know that it's going to happen—that's the circle of life—but I'm not ready. I'll never be ready.

"I could use a cup of coffee. McKenna, will you walk with me?" Grams asks.

"Uh, sure. I thought you were going to run home?"

"Shirley brought me some clothes and a nice lunch," she says, speaking of Rip's mom. "I was able to shower here in the room, and I feel so refreshed. I even took a little cat nap here in the chair."

"You should go home and get some proper rest," Gramps says.

"Oh, hush you. I'm just fine." Gram pats his leg.

I look over at Rip, and he shrugs. "That was nice of her," I say.

"Yes," Gram agrees. "She and Roger were here for a nice visit. Don't worry. We didn't tell them your news." Grams smiles.

"Well... I might have hinted that the two of you have some exciting news," Gramps confesses. "I didn't tell them what, but they'll be expecting to hear from you," he tells us.

"I'll call them when we leave here. We might just swing by their place. It's not like it's a far drive." Rip chuckles.

"Good plan, son." Gramps nods.

I give Rip a "what the hell are you talking about" look, but he just winks at me. I've got to get a handle on this before the entire damn town knows we got drunk in Vegas and I slept with him.

"Come on. I need to stretch my legs." Gram stands from her chair. "You two behave while we're gone." She points at Gramps and Rip.

I release Gramps' hand and move to walk past Rip. His arms snake around my waist as he pulls me into him, placing a kiss on my temple. He lets me go like nothing happened, and on shaking legs, I follow Grams out of the room.

Grams links her arms through mine as we make our way to the elevator. "I want all the details," she gushes.

Taking a deep breath, I open my mouth and let the words flow freely. "It's not real. We drank too much, and we woke up in bed together." Heat coats my cheeks as my embarrassment takes root.

"Pft, don't try to tell me that your relationship isn't real. Do you not see the way he looks at you?"

"I'm telling you. It's not real."

"Why?"

"What? I just told you why?"

"I'm not buying it. It was spontaneous, and alcohol was involved, but, McKenna, I'm telling you neither one of you would have gone through with that night had you both not wanted it. Think about that. Really think about it and then tell me your connection and relationship isn't real."

We step out of the elevator, and the cafeteria is packed. I don't need the town in my private business, so I don't respond. Instead, I follow her through the line as she orders two black coffees, one for her and one for Gramps. I decide a sweet tea sounds good, and at the last second, I order two instead of one. Grams grins. She knows it's for Rip without me having to tell her. It doesn't matter. We've been friends since we were kids. I'm just being nice.

That's my story, and I'm sticking to it.

Chapter Nineteen

RIP

"THAT DIDN'T TAKE LONG," HAROLD SAYS AS MCKENNA AND AGNES WALK BACK INTO THE room.

"We didn't want to give the two of you time for mischief." Agnes smiles, handing him a coffee. He takes a large drink and grimaces.

"Black?"

Agnes gives him a stern look, and he takes another drink, this time without complaint.

"I thought you might be thirsty," McKenna says, handing me a sweet tea.

"Thanks, babe." I drop a kiss to the top of her head and twist open my tea, taking a hefty drink.

"So, what did the two of you talk about while we were gone?" McKenna asks.

She looks worried, and to tell you the truth, I was worried that Harold was going to tear into me about dating his granddaughter and not hurting her. Instead, he thanked me for coming home early with McKenna and making sure she wasn't alone. To say I was shocked was an understatement.

I've known Harold and Agnes since I was little. They've been our neighbors for longer than I've been alive. The one thing I know about them is that McKenna is the apple of their eye. I was sure I was in for a lecture. Don't get me wrong. I was ready for it. I'm ready for anything anyone tosses my way. I'm not going to let anything get between us.

"Nothing much. Your gramps thanked me for coming home with you."

"You didn't have to do that, you know." She turns to look at me.

"I did."

"You don't owe me anything."

"I didn't do it because I felt like I owed you or because I felt obligated." I turn to face her. Reaching out, I tuck a loose strand of hair behind her ear. "I did it because I wanted to. I did it because I wanted to be there for you and because not being where you are didn't sound the least bit appealing to me."

"Awe," Agnes coos. "Hold on to this one, Mac." She smiles at us.

"Knock knock," a nurse says while knocking and pushing into the room. "Visiting hours are over," she tells us.

"I'm staying," Agnes tells her.

She nods. "That's fine, but I'm afraid only one of you, and it's the same deal as last night. If you get caught, I saw nothing."

"Deal." Agnes laughs.

"You kids head home and get some rest. They said I might be able to go home tomorrow."

"Maybe," the nurse reminds him.

"Maybe." Harold nods as if he's agreeing, but we can all see his desire and determination to convince the doctors to let him go home.

Quickly, we say our goodbyes and leave the hospital. The drive home is quiet until we turn on our road. "Will you stay with me tonight?"

"Do you think that's a good idea?"

"I think it's the best idea I've ever had. Besides, you promised Harold."

She contemplates her answer. As we are about five hundred feet from her grandparents' driveway, she says, "Yes. I'll stay with you."

I'm glad. I hadn't planned on stopping anyway. I was going to drive on past their place and pull into mine to see if I could sway her decision. Not that I would ever force her to stay with me. But I was hoping a few kisses might help persuade her. If she decided to go to her grandparents' place, I was good with taking the couch. Parking my truck in the driveway, I turn off the ignition and angle to look at her. "You hungry?"

"Starving, actually."

"Come on, let me feed you." Grabbing my phone and keys, I climb out of the truck and meet her at the bottom of the porch steps. With my hand on the small of her back, we climb the steps, and I give her the code to unlock the door.

"What if I come back and steal you blind?" she asks, pushing open the door.

"You won't. Besides, you don't have to steal anything. If it's mine, it's yours. I'll give you anything you want."

"Those are big declarations, Rip Callahan."

"They are," I agree. "That should tell you that this isn't a game to me, Kenna. I want you. I want you in my life, in my house, in my bed. I want anything and everything that you're willing to give me."

"That's... unexpected."

"Is it? I've been honest with you from the day you came home. When I kissed you that night at the bonfire, I knew I was tired of waiting."

"Tired of waiting?"

"Let me make us some dinner, and I'll tell you anything that you want to know."

"Can I help?" Hope blooms in my chest. Maybe we can finally talk, and she'll listen.

"You can. You can sit your fine ass at the island so I can see you while I'm making you something to eat."

"I know how to cook."

"I know you do, baby, but I want to take care of you. It's been an emotional day, and you just need to relax."

"What are we having?" she asks, ignoring my term of endearment. Well, she tries too. I saw the flash in her eyes, the one that tells me she's not immune to me.

"Omelets."

"Perfect. I always loved eating breakfast for dinner. Gram used to do it pretty often when I was growing up."

"I think I might have heard you mention that a time or two." I wink at her.

"Thank you for coming back with me today. It was nice to know I wasn't alone."

"McKenna." I stop what I'm doing and wait for her to set those big brown eyes on me. "As long as there's breath in my lungs, you will never be alone. Never."

She swallows hard, and tears once again mist her eyes. Dropping what I'm doing, I dry my hands and make my way around the counter to her.

"I don't know why I'm so emotional," she says as I wrap my arms around her.

"It's been a long, hard day, baby. You have to give yourself some grace."

"I'm sorry." She snuggles into my chest.

"You have nothing to be sorry for. Why don't you go stretch out on the couch? I'll bring you a glass of wine and dinner when it's ready."

"Omelets and wine?"

"We make our own rules, McKenna." I grin. "Go sit, and I'll bring you a glass while I'm cooking dinner."

"Thank you, Rip. For everything."

"Anything for my girl." I kiss her forehead and step away from her. I promised my girl a glass of wine, so that's what I'm going to do.

A FEW HOURS LATER, WE'RE SITTING ON THE COUCH. MCKENNA'S HEAD IS LEANING ON MY shoulder, and it's my idea of the perfect night. When she yawns, I know it's time to call it quits. "You ready for bed?"

"Yes." She sits up and stretches before standing from the couch.

"Go on upstairs. You know where my shirts are if you need something to sleep in. I'm going to lock up and turn out the lights."

"I have clothes to sleep in."

"Yeah, but I like you in mine." I grin before turning and walking away to lock up. It would be too easy to get lost in her down here, and if and when I make love to her again, it's going to be in a bed, and I'm going to memorize every fucking second of it.

"Bathroom's all yours," she says a few minutes later as I walk into my room.

"Nice shirt," I comment.

"Thanks, this really nice guy said I could wear it."

"Did he now?"

"He did. Something about liking me in his clothes."

I take slow, gradual steps toward her, which takes effort. All I want to do is run to her and hold her close. "I do like you in my clothes. Do you know what else I like?"

"What's that?" she whispers.

"I like that you're here with me." My hands land on her hips, and I move in, pressing her body to mine. "You know what else I like?"

"Tell me."

"You in my bed, in my arms." I kiss the tip of her nose and release her. "I'm going to change. I'll be right back." I disappear into the bathroom. After taking care of business, I strip down to my boxer briefs and brush my teeth. Turning out the light, I make my way blindly to the bed. I can see her form, lying on what I've come to refer to as her side. I waste no time sliding under the covers, moving over to the center, and wrapping my arms around her.

Her breathing evens out, and I think she's fallen asleep. I let my eyes drift closed when I hear her soft voice.

"Rip?"

"Yeah, baby?"

"Do you think we should talk about this? About last night?"

"Is that what you want? To talk about it?"

"I think we should," she counters.

"I'm listening."

"We had sex."

"Yes."

"Do you remember it?"

"Bits and pieces. I remember walking back to your suite and following you inside. I remember kisses. There were lots of kisses."

"I remember asking you to stay."

"Yeah, you asked me to stay."

"I don't remember the actual sex part," she admits.

"Me either."

"So, where do we go from here?"

"I'd say where we are is a damn good start."

"Here? In your bed?"

"Yep."

"What does that mean? How is me in your bed a good start?"

I'm quiet for a few minutes, processing how to handle this. She's had a rough day, but I swore I wasn't going to hide from this any longer. "The day you left for college tore me apart."

"What do you mean?" She rolls over in my arms to face me. I can't see her face, but I can feel her breath on my cheek. We're so close.

"I've wanted you for so long, McKenna. I can't tell you the exact day you stopped being my sister's best friend and more to me. Hell, I think you've always been more to me. You were my first kiss." I find her lips in the dark and give her a chaste kiss.

"Why didn't you ever tell me that?"

"You had big dreams, Kenna. I was afraid if we started something, you wouldn't go through with them. I wanted you to achieve everything in life you always dreamed of."

"I've always had a crush on you," she confesses.

"I had hoped."

"So, what now?"

Rolling over, I turn on the bedside lamp so we can see each other. Climbing out of bed, I walk to her side and drop to my knees. She sits up, moving her legs to hang over the side of the bed. There's confusion written all over her face. I know this is corny as fuck, but if she needs me to spell it out for her, I will.

"McKenna Dawson, I want you to be mine. I want to spend as much time with you as I can, and I want this relationship to grow. I don't want us to see other people, and I want to touch you and kiss you anytime that I want." I pause and bring our joined hands to my lips, pressing featherlight kisses against her knuckles. "I have something to ask you."

"O-kay?" She's curious yet hesitant.

"McKenna, will you be my girlfriend?" I ask. "And before you say yes, that title seems too insignificant with the way I feel about you. Full disclosure: I want you to be more than my girlfriend. I want to build a life with you."

"Are you…." Her voice trails off as she swallows hard.

"Not tonight. Not in this moment. Tonight, I just want confirmation that you're mine, and I'm yours, and we'll work on the 'forever after all' part together."

She smiles so big her face lights up. "You remember that?"

"I've never forgotten a single moment that I've shared with you."

"I was seven."

"And I was nine, but I still remember. One day, I hope that when we say our vows, it will be for real."

"Am I dreaming?"

"No, baby, you're not dreaming. This is real. This is us. If you'll have me."

She nods as a lone tear trails down her cheek. "I've always wanted you. I just… I thought you were just being nice and flirty the last few weeks."

"Oh, I have been. But not because you were my sister's best friend. It was all because I wanted you to be mine."

"You're mine?"

Dropping her hands, I stand and hold my arms out to my sides. "All of this is yours, McKenna."

She bites down on her bottom lip, and I would give anything to know what she is thinking. Before I get a chance to ask, her cell phone on the nightstand rings. Glancing down, I see my sister's name.

"It's Laramie."

"She's probably in town and wants an update." She reaches for her phone but doesn't move to answer it. "This, us, it's not a secret?"

"Fuck that. I want the world to know you're mine."

"What if this doesn't work out?"

"Do you want it to?"

"Yes." She nods. "More than anything." I don't want her to be a secret. I want her. I know I've been telling me this all along, but tonight it feels different. The way my heart squeezes when she looks at me. It feels real. It is real. This is us. It's finally our time.

"Me too. Relationships take work, and there's no one else I want to work at it with. Just you." Her phone stops ringing, only to start again. I take the phone from her hands, swipe the screen, and place it to my ear. "Hey, sis," I greet Laramie.

"Is everything okay? I've been calling."

"This is your second call, and we were in the middle of a conversation."

"Oh, no, is everything okay?"

I smile at McKenna. "Everything is perfect. My girlfriend and I just needed to discuss a few things."

"Girlfriend? Damnit, Rip, have the two of you been holding out on me?"

"No, we just made it officially official. Here, I'll let you talk to my girlfriend." I pull the phone from my ear and hand it to McKenna. "It's for you, baby." I kiss her softly before moving to my side of the bed.

I smile as I slide under the covers and listen to McKenna give Laramie an update on her grandfather. Then I hear her explain that she is indeed my girlfriend. My smile is wide, and I reach over and turn off the lamp, bathing the room in darkness. I snuggle up to McKenna, where she's resting back on the pillow talking to my sister—talking to her best friend about me. Her new boyfriend.

Our day might have started out rocky with the unease of what we shared last night and the news of her grandfather, but the ending, well, it's made a shitty day one of the best I've ever had.

She's finally mine.

Chapter Twenty

MCKENNA

IT'S BEEN A WEEK SINCE I GOT THE CALL WHILE IN VEGAS THAT GRAMPS WAS BEING rushed to the hospital having a heart attack. A week as a reminder that life is short. A week of sleeping every night in Rip's bed and in his arms. I'm not sure what happened in my former life to bring me such blessings, but I'm not going to kick a gift horse in the mouth.

Gramps is doing well. He's a little cranky about straight-up black coffee and decaf at that, but otherwise, he's healing from his surgery, and the doctor even cleared him to go back to the office a few hours a day next week. I've been holding down the fort, keeping the office running, and keeping in contact with his friend Mr. Morgan from the next town over. They cover for one another, and he's been taking all of Gramps' court dates. I've been making sure the files are thorough and complete, and it's been going well. I've checked the website for my bar exam results about ten times a day. It would be so much easier if I could just handle everything on my own.

As for Rip, well, this thing between us was unexpected. At least to me it was unexpected. To hear Laramie, my grandparents, and hell, even Sara, they all say they saw it coming. I guess I was too close and too guarded to see it. I never in a million years would have dreamed that Rip and I would end up in a relationship. Sure, it was something I thought a lot about growing up, but never did I think it would be my reality.

"Are we in for the night?" I ask Rip.

"You're staying, right?" he asks.

"Yeah, I put my bag in your room."

"Good. Then yes, I'm good with being in for the night."

It's Saturday night, and we've just finished dinner. Rip threw some steaks on the grill while I made us a salad. I'm about to ask him if he wants to call the guys for a beer or something when his phone rings.

"Hey, Corbin, what's up?" he greets his best friend. There's a pause. "Nah, Kenna and I just had dinner. We're just going to chill here." Rip laughs and shakes his head. "I'm not denying it. She's prettier to look at," he says, smiling down at me. "Later," he says, ending the call.

"What's Corbin into tonight?"

"Just going to the Silver Star to grab a bite to eat. Wanted me to come down and shoot a game of pool."

"You should go."

"I'm good right here."

"No, really. I was getting ready to tell you that you don't have to spend all of your time with me. I know you and the guys used to go out a lot, and well, I don't want that to change because we're dating."

"We're more than dating, and I want to spend every second of my time with you. I'll still hang out with the guys, but, Kenna, I just got you. I'm not ready to let you go just yet."

I'm not ready for you to let me go ever.

It's been a week, and I'm already hooked. He's charming and generous, and well, he's one of my best friends. I love spending time with him too.

My phone rings and he leans over, grabbing it from the table and handing it to me. "Hey, Laramie," I greet my best friend.

"Hey, you. What are you getting into tonight?"

"Nothing much. Rip and I just finished dinner."

"Cool, let's go down to the Silver Star for a drink."

"I think we're just going to stay in."

"No. Nope. Not going to happen. Is my brother there with you?"

"He is."

"Put this call on speaker."

I hit the button, transferring the call to the phone's speaker. "Okay," I tell Laramie.

"Rip?"

"Yes, little sister."

"I have a bone to pick with you."

"Let's hear it," he says, his voice laced with amusement.

"You're stealing my best friend. I haven't seen her all week. Every time I call, she's with you, which isn't going to work for me. I love the two of you together. Hell, it's something I've always wanted to happen, but you need to listen up. Stop being a McKenna hog."

Rip bites down on his fist to keep from laughing. "I'm sorry?" he says, only it's more like a question than a true apology.

"I'll accept if you bring her to the Silver Star. Colby is coming with me, and Sara and Corbin are going too."

"I just talked to Corbin. I told him I was out."

"Well, now I'm telling you that you're in. Come on, Rip," she whines. "I had her first."

"She's mine, Lara," he says. There is no teasing in his voice.

"I know, but you have to share. Don't make me call Mom."

This time he does laugh. He throws his head back, and the deep grumble is a welcome sound. "Babe, do you want to go to the Silver Star?" he asks me.

"Mac, you better say yes. You know if you do, he'll come."

"Sure, we can go."

"Yes!" Laramie cheers. "No backing out, you two. I mean it. Meet us there in twenty."

"We'll see you there," Rip assures her, ending the call. "Looks like we're going out after all."

"I just need to go upstairs and change."

"Good idea. You cannot go to the Silver Star wearing booty shorts and a tight tank top. I'll never make it out of there alive."

"Why's that?" I ask coyly.

"Because I'll have to beat the shit out of all of those nasty fuckers trying to move in on my girl."

"I'll be right down."

"Hey, will you grab me a clean shirt while you're up there?"

"Sure, which one?"

"I don't care. Just grab one. I've got no one to impress. I've already got the girl." He gives me a swift kiss on the lips and releases his hold on me so that I can run upstairs and change.

I admit I'm nervous. This is our first outing as a couple. We've stayed in every night this week. Today we cleaned the house, where he complained I was helping, but I stayed here all week, so that's the least that I could do. We went over to my grandparents' and had lunch, and I packed a few more things that I needed. We've been in a blissful Rip and McKenna bubble, and I don't know what's waiting for us outside of his house.

I guess I'm about to find out.

"FINALLY!" LARAMIE SIGHS DRAMATICALLY. "I DIDN'T THINK YOU'D EVER GET HERE." SHE

tugs on my arms, pulling me from Rip.

"Hey, she's mine." Rip reaches out for me, but Laramie moves to stand, blocking him.

"Nope. She was mine first. I need time with my best friend. You are not going to continue to hog her. Now, go away. Corbin and Colby are back at the pool table. I think Russ is there as well. Sara, Mac, and I are having a girls' night."

"That wasn't the plan." Rip glares at her, crossing his arms over his chest.

"I knew what I had to say to get you both here. Now go." She waves her hand in the air.

"Kenna." Just the sound of him saying my name sends fire through my veins. I step back and out of Laramie's reach and rush to him. He wraps his arms around me and holds me close. When he pulls back, he slides his hand behind my neck and presses his lips to mine. "Have fun. I'll be over there if you need me."

"We're at the Silver Star. What could happen?" I say, barely containing my smile.

"I just need you to know that you come first. You'll always come first."

"Go. Have a few beers, shoot some pool."

"Why do I miss you already?" he whines.

"Oh my God. McKenna, what have you done to my brother?" Laramie steps beside me and links her arm through mine.

Rip leans in and kisses me again. This time it's just a quick peck, but the effect it has on me is all the same. My knees are weak, and my smile is wide. "Have fun, beautiful," he says before bopping his sister on the nose and sauntering to the other side of the bar.

"Girl, you must have some magic going on downstairs," Sara says when we reach the table.

"What?" I ask, sputtering with laughter.

"I've never seen Rip like that before. Never."

"Um, we're not sleeping together," I confess.

"Do what now?" Laramie asks. "He's into you."

"I'm into him."

"Are the two of you official?" Sara asks.

"Yeah, we are." I fight the urge to glance over my shoulder to seek him out. "We slept together in Vegas, but neither one of us really remember it. Not the actual act, that is."

"All the more reason for a repeat," Sara insists.

"We'll get there." What I don't tell them is that our make-out sessions every night this week are a dead giveaway that we will indeed get there. Neither one of us has talked about the fact that we've yet to have sex. I think we're both silently on the same page that we needed some time to get used to this new dynamic of our relationship.

"Enough about me. One week. You're getting married in one week!" I say to Laramie.

"Finally," she sighs, sitting back in her chair. "I was good with us taking our time. We started dating when we were so young. We both wanted to make sure that this was it for us. I mean, we both knew, but we wanted to give it some time. From the moment he proposed, I can't stop this... urgency. I know it's crazy considering how long we dated, but I'm just ready to be his wife."

"You're glowing," Sara tells her.

"Love will do that to you." She points at me and then at Sara. "Don't think I haven't noticed a glow about the two of you." She grins, taking a sip of her beer.

"Corbin is... unexpected. I thought we were just having fun at first, but it's more than that."

"Have you guys talked about it?" Laramie asks.

"Yeah. He wanted to make sure I knew we were exclusive."

"I'm so excited for you. I knew that once that boy fell, it would be hard." I raise the beer that they had waiting for me at the table, and we all cheer.

"He's great," Sara says, blushing.

"I have a feeling it won't be long and the two of you will be right behind me."

"What do you mean?" Sara asks.

"Marriage."

"No one is talking about marriage," I tell her.

"Oh, come on. You've already married my brother twice." She chuckles. "They say the third time is a charm."

My heart rate kicks up. I'm still coming to terms with the fact that Rip is my boyfriend. The thought of being his wife? It sends a thrill through me. "Yeah, let's not go getting ahead of ourselves."

"Right? Corbin and I have been dating a hot minute," Sara chimes in. "Too early for that kind of talk."

"I'm telling you, ladies. I know these things." Laramie taps her index finger against her temple. "Case in point," she says, and I feel his hands on my shoulders.

"I'm going to grab a beer. Need anything?" he asks, kissing me just below my ear.

I tilt my head back, looking at him upside down. "I'm good."

He surprises me when he leans over and kisses me on the lips. "Sara? Sis?" he asks.

"We're good," they say at the same time.

"I'm not a fan of girls' night," Rip grumbles, not bothering to lower his voice. He leans in and kisses me again, this time straight on, not with my head tilted back.

"She's coming home with you," Laramie reminds him.

"You're damn right she is." He gives my shoulders a squeeze, and then he's gone.

"Girl, he's smitten." Sara laughs.

"He's not the only one," I tell her.

"I'm so freaking excited about this. I've always wanted the two of you together so that we could be family for real. It looks like I might be getting my wish."

She's not the only one, I think to myself. This is all happening so fast, and it's surreal, but Rip is all in. I was worried about how tonight would go, but he doesn't seem to mind one bit that people see him kissing me. Maybe Laramie's right. Perhaps the third time is the charm?

A girl can dream.

Chapter Twenty-One

RIP

IT'S JUST BEFORE MIDNIGHT, AND ALTHOUGH I'VE ENJOYED HANGING WITH THE GUYS, I'M ready to get McKenna home. I need to strip down out of these clothes and cuddle the shit out of her. Those were our original plans for the night, and I hope she's not too tired for us to follow through.

"I'm out," I say, finishing off my bottle of water and tossing it in a nearby trash can.

"Yeah, me too," Corbin agrees. His eyes flash to where the girls are sitting, and I know my best friend—he and I have the same thing on our minds.

"Yep." Colby tilts his water bottle back and drains in, tossing it in the trash.

We all stopped drinking after two beers. Tonight was girls' night, so we let them indulge, and as the dutiful boyfriends that we are, we'll see that they get home safe. And by home, I mean my home, at least for McKenna. Hell, I've been trying to think of ways all week to ask her to move in with me. Sure, this is new, but I've known her for years. It's not like we're strangers, and she's it for me. Why not move forward with our life together?

I'm sold, but I know getting McKenna on board will be a little more difficult. Although, I have managed to get her to spend every night with me since we've been home from Vegas. Maybe I'm wrong, and it won't be as difficult as I thought.

The three of us make our way to their table. I block everyone out but McKenna. "You about ready to head out?" I ask, leaning over her shoulder and pressing a kiss to her neck.

"Yes." She turns to look at me over her shoulder. "You good to drive?"

"I am. I had two beers when we first got here and nothing but water since."

She nods. "Take me home, cowboy."

I can't stop my chuckle at the nickname. We were making dinner earlier this week, and I called her lawyer girl as we were debating about the best way to slice vegetables for stir-fry. She countered with the name of cowboy. That's the thing with McKenna. She's fun. There's never a moment of unease or awkwardness between us. I don't know if it's because we were friends before or if it's the fact that my heart is already so invested.

"We'll see you all later," Corbin says as he tugs Sara's chair back from the table to help her stand. He's pulling out all the stops with this one. I've never seen him act this way with a woman.

"Drive safe," McKenna tells him as she scoots back and stands to give Sara, then Corbin a hug. Laramie is next, then she and McKenna share a hug. "One more week, Lara." McKenna smiles at her.

"Seven days too long," Colby says, pulling my sister into his arms.

"I can't believe it's finally happening," McKenna says as she leans into my embrace.

"Oh, it's happening," Colby assures her, making us all laugh.

"We'll see you later," I say, guiding my girl out of the bar. "You hungry?" I ask as I open the door of the truck.

"No, we snacked on pretzel bites and nachos."

"Home then?" I ask once she's settled.

"Yeah." She turns her head to look at me. "Take me home, cowboy."

Leaning in close, I press my lips to hers. There's nothing in this world like the feeling of kissing McKenna.

"Anything you want, lawyer girl." I tickle her side before quickly pulling away and shutting her door. Rushing around to my side of the truck, I'm quick to start the engine and pull out of the lot. The ride is silent, but not uncomfortably so. It's just the two of us being together, that feeling of being with the right person at any given moment. She's that person for me, no matter where we are.

She's my McKenna.

NOT FIFTEEN MINUTES AFTER WE'RE HOME, WE'RE LYING IN MY BED, SNUGGLED UNDER THE covers, making out like teenagers. My cock is hard, as always, when I'm anywhere near her. However, I've not pushed us to take this further. I know we already had sex, and bits of pieces of that night come back to me at random times, but I still can't remember everything.

I know I've come on strong, and I'm making this her choice. I'm not just with her to get my dick wet, don't misunderstand. I want that very much, but having McKenna know that I'm with her for more than sex is important. Especially for how fast we've progressed since she's been home. In just a month, I'm calling her mine, she's calling me hers, and she's in my bed in my arms every night. That's a win for me.

"Where are you going?" I ask when she pulls away from me. I reach for her, snagging the hem of my shirt, trying to pull her back to me, making her giggle.

"B-Bathroom," she stutters with laughter.

"Fine," I sigh dramatically. "I'll miss you."

"You're crazy," she says, pulling away and climbing out of bed. In the darkness of my bedroom, she makes her way to the bathroom. When the door clicks closed, the light comes on.

Lying back on the pillow, I can't help but smile. I've been doing that a lot lately. Not that I was unhappy before McKenna came home, but I am definitely happier with her here. Not just here in my house and in my bed, but back home in Texas.

I see the light click off, so I pull the covers back to welcome her back to bed. She climbs back in, and I pull the covers up over us before reaching for her. Expecting to find my T-shirt, I'm surprised when it is silky smooth skin that my fingertips slide over. "Kenna?"

"I think you're wearing too many clothes, cowboy."

"Fuck," I mutter as I slide my boxer briefs over my hips, using my feet to pull them down my legs and kick them off somewhere under the covers. "Come here, baby," I say, my voice husky with need.

She moves in close, her hands resting on my abs. "There are eight of them. You're aware of that, right?" she asks playfully.

"I'm aware."

"Small memories of our night together are coming back to me."

"Me too."

"I remember us helping one another strip, and I remember you hugging me, your naked body pressed against mine. I remember lots of touching and kissing, but nothing else."

"I remember all of that, and I remember staring down at you. Your hair was spread out on the pillow, and you were beautiful." I run my lips over her neck as we let the details of our first night together, the ones we're slowly piecing together, settle in our minds. My lips travel to her naked breasts, and I pull one tight bud into my mouth.

"Rip," she breathes."Show me."

"Show you what, baby?"

"Show me what we can't remember. I want to remember. I want to know what it's like to have you inside me."

Her words are like fire coursing through my veins—hot, scorching flames of desire for her. "You sure about this?"

"Do you want me?"

"More than my next breath."

"Then show me."

"My fucking pleasure," I growl.

In one swift move, I'm resting on the bed between her spread thighs. The blanket pools around my waist, which causes her to shiver with nothing to protect her naked skin from the cold air of the air-conditioned room. "Sorry, baby." Reaching for the cover, I pull it over my head and over her body. Sure, I'd rather see her, all of her for this, but we have a lifetime for that.

Her hands under the covers find their way to my hair. I wiggle my shoulders between her legs, bringing my face close to her pussy. I can smell her arousal, and my dick is so hard I'm surprised there's not a hole in the mattress. Moving her legs over my shoulders and holding her open with my hands, my tongue caresses her clit. Just a few soft strokes to give us both our first taste.

Her hands tighten in my hair, and her hips lift off the bed. My mouth goes to work, licking, sucking, and tasting her. Her legs begin to tremble, and I want her there. I need her to come because I'm not so sure I won't shoot off like a damn rocket as soon as I'm surrounded by her heat. Adjusting my position, I slide one finger inside, making a come-hither motion, and that sets her off. She's full-on pulling my hair as her moans of pleasure greet me, even under the covers. I lazily stroke my fingerin and out of her as I softly kiss her clit.

It's not until her hands release their hold on me and the covers fly over my head do I pull my mouth away. "You okay, lawyer girl?"

"Can't move," she pants.

Gently placing McKenna's legs on the bed, I kiss my way up her body until I'm smiling down at her. I can't make out her features, but the light glow of the moonlight tells me her eyes are closed. "Kenna," I whisper. My voice is gravelly, and my heart is pounding in my chest. I go to move beside her, but she stops me with her hands on my arms.

"What are you doing?"

"Giving you some time."

"No. No. No, I don't want time, Rip. I want you. I can't tell you how many times I've wondered what it would be like to be with you. To know that we shared a night together that we can't remember, well, that sucks," she says, making me laugh. "I want you, Rip Callahan. I want my boyfriend to fuck me."

"I can't fuck you, Kenna, but I can make love to you. Will you let me do that, baby? Will you let me make love to you?"

"Is there a difference? However you say it, you inside me is the end game, so yeah, whatever play on words you want to use, I'm ready for more. More of you."

Moving off her, I reach into the nightstand and grab the new, unopened box of condoms I stored there just a week ago. Ripping open the box, I pull out a foil packet and cover my dick. Then, I'm back where I belong, hovering over my girl, the warmth of her body calling to me like a beacon in the night.

"There's a difference, Kenna. You see, saying that you're fucking someone has no feelings involved. Making love, whether it's sweet—" I press a tender kiss to her lips. "—or dirty," I say, pushing inside her in one swift thrust. "...

when your heart is involved, it's always making love. No matter what we do in this bed, I'll never be fucking you. Understand?"

"I-Is your heart involved?"

I pull out almost all the way and push back in. "My heart's involved, Kenna. My heart, my mind, my body. Everything I am is yours."

"Rip—" She shudders, and I find a rhythm, rocking my hips into hers.

"You're mine, McKenna. I want you for a lifetime. I want to make love to you for years to come. Fuck me. I want to make love to you for the rest of my life. You're made for me. Your pussy loves my cock," I say when I feel her pulsing around me. "You own me, all of me," I say, kissing her slow and deep. Her nails dig into my back, and I welcome the pain. Finally, we're where we're supposed to be.

While I've always cared for her, over the last month spending time together, and then after this week, all the time we've spent together, her agreeing to be my girlfriend, I know how this ends.

Mrs. McKenna Callahan.

I've given her my heart.

I want to give her my name.

I want to give her my babies.

I want her future.

"More," she gasps. I rest my head on her shoulder and let loose. I give her everything I have. "R-Rip, Oh, I'm close. Don't stop. Please, don't stop."

"Come for me, Kenna. I'm close, baby, and I need you to come again. Let me have it," I growl.

Over and over again, I bring our hips together until she cries out my name. With one final thrust, I still as I spill over inside her.

Chapter Twenty-Two

MCKENNA

"HOW AM I SUPPOSED TO SLEEP WITHOUT YOU?" RIP ASKS. HE'S CURRENTLY LYING ON HIS bed, propped up on one arm with the bedsheet pooling at his waist as he watches me get dressed.

"You've slept years without me. I think you'll be fine."

"No. I won't. That's before I knew what it was like to fall asleep with you in my arms. I'm telling you, baby. I won't be okay."

He's being so serious. There's no hint of amusement on his face. Call me crazy, but I believe him. I'm also wondering how I'm going to sleep without his arms around me, but I guess we're about to find out.

"Come on, Kenna. We can go visit them. We'll stay the entire day and then come back here to sleep."

"Rip." I sigh. He's making this hard for me. "I've been here every night since we came home from Vegas. It's Sunday, Gramps is home, and even though I've been checking on him, I feel like I need to be there."

"Fine." He stands and quickly pulls on his jeans from last night, sans underwear.

"What are you doing?"

"I'm going with you. I'll just pack a bag."

"We can't do that. Not in my grandparents' house." My eyes widen at the thought.

"Kenna, do you really believe they that think we're sleeping in separate beds while you're here?"

"No, I don't think that, but we can't do that there. That's all kinds of wrong."

He walks toward me and places his index finger under my chin so that our eyes meet. "I'm not saying I'm going to make love to you there. I just need you close when I go to sleep. I'll talk to Harold."

"No. No, you are not going to talk to Harold about anything. He just had a heart attack. He doesn't need this stress."

"I know." He nods, wrapping me in his warm embrace. "I just can't handle the thought of you not being here."

"That's what dating is, Rip. We see each other, maybe have a sleepover or two, and we go home to our own places."

"Then we're not dating. We're more than dating. I don't give a fuck what you label it, but that's what we are."

I smile up at him. "You're going to be okay, cowboy."

"Last night..." He swallows hard. "Kenna, tell me this isn't you running away from me. From us. Tell me I didn't scare you away."

My hand lands on his cheek. "You didn't scare me away. Was it intense? Yes. Was it more of a declaration than I was expecting? Definitely, it's soon, and I just... I want you to be sure, you know? I know that you're a fixer, Rip. At least when it comes to your sister and me, that's what you've always done. Even if it meant marrying me when we were kids." I kiss underneath his chin. "A lot has happened, and maybe, just maybe, it's because you knew I was upset about Gramps."

"No. Fuck that. McKenna, you know better." He steps back and hits his hands against his bare chest. "I'm standing right here, right now telling you that everything between us is real." He moves until the back of his knees hits the bed, and he sits, pulling me between his legs. His forehead rests against my belly, and his arms are wrapped tightly around me.

I give him the time that he needs. Running my hands through his hair, I do my best to soothe him. It's not my intention to upset him, but I'm gone for this man. And I never want him to feel trapped. That's what happened to my parents, and it didn't end well for them. I never want to live that kind of life again. I was little, but I have the scars as memories.

When Rip finally lifts his head, his eyes are bright and full of so much emotion. "McKenna, what I feel for you is real. I promise you." He links his hands with mine and places them over his heart. "You're right here. When I tell you I can't sleep without you, it's not to make you feel better. It's because I don't ever want to be without you. It doesn't matter if I'm asleep or if I'm awake."

"I can't just keep staying here like I live here, Rip."

"Then move in with me."

"What?" I try to take a step back, but he's faster and locks his arms around my waist, holding me to him.

"Move in with me. Make this your home. Our home together."

"That's a big step just to not have to sleep alone."

"That's not what this is," he growls.

I know that it's not. It's hard for me when there are so many worries racing through my mind. "I'll think about it."

He nods. "That's all I ask." Sliding his hand behind my neck, he pulls me closer and kisses me softly. "I'm still going with you. Maybe there are some things around the house I can take care of while you visit with them."

"You sure you don't have things to do here?"

"I'm sure. You come first, McKenna."

"I need to finish getting ready."

"Me too." Another quick kiss and he releases me.

We finish getting ready for the day. I don't bother with my hair. I went to bed with it wet after our shower last night, and it's a mess. Instead, I tie it up in a knot on top of my head and call it good.

Once we're in the truck driving the short distance to my grandparents' place, I'm suddenly nervous. Are we moving too fast? Has he really had the time he needs to think about this? About us? Will he have regrets?

Shaking out of my thoughts when we pull into their driveway, I push it all to the back of my mind. Today, I just want to spend the day with my family.

"AGNES, DINNER WAS DELICIOUS," RIP SAYS. "THANK YOU."

"You're welcome. I'm glad you enjoyed it."

"It was good, dear, but your fried chicken is better than this grilled." Gramps glares at his now-empty plate.

"Deal with it," Grams tells him. "We have to keep that heart of yours healthy. Now, how about some dessert?"

"Yes!" Gramps says emphatically.

I stifle my laughter, knowing Grams as I do. She's not about to put a slice of chocolate cake in front of him. Gramps, the poor guy, he knows it too. Maybe it's wishful thinking.

"You need some help?" I ask her.

"Sure."

I stand and help clear the table. Rip tries to as well, but Grams tells him to sit. We carry the empty dishes to the kitchen, and I begin to load the dishwasher while she serves up fresh fruit with fat-free Cool Whip. "He's going to be so disappointed," I tell her.

"I know." She laughs. "But he's had years of eating whatever he wants. I'm not ready to let him go, so he's going to have to suck it up."

"He might whine, but he's not going to fight you on it."

"I know. And he will get used to it. It's been a week. Speaking of a week, how are things with you and Rip?"

"Good. We're together now." I shrug, placing the final plate into the dishwasher.

"Are you not happy about that?"

"No. I am. I mean, it's Rip, and he's wonderful. I just… I don't want him to have any regrets. This is all kind of fast."

"Is it, though? Maybe it's easier for me to see because I've been watching the Rip and McKenna show for years. When you left for college, he spent more time here than at his place."

"Really?"

"Yep. Always stopping by to see if we needed anything. How do you think he started helping me pack in my supplies? He missed you. I think being here around us, in this house, made him feel closer to you." She gives me a minute to process. "He blew it off as being a good neighbor, and he is the best, but Harold and I both knew there was more. There wasn't a single time he was here, or we would run into him in town, that he didn't ask about you. He was starving for any little morsel of information we could give him."

"I wish he would have told me." I can't believe he wanted me all that time. I mean, I know he told me, but to hear it from Gram somehow makes it more real. Don't get me wrong. I don't think Rip is lying to me, not at all. But this is my grandmother. She's never held back punches when telling me what I need to hear, good or bad. She and my grandfather saved me from my parents, and we've had many hard conversations in my lifetime. So, yeah, coming from her, it's definitely more real.

"Do you, though? Would you have been able to leave him?"

I think about how I'm dreading going to sleep tonight without him, and I know there's a really good chance I would have stayed. "Probably not, but we'll never know for sure."

"He wanted you to follow your dream, McKenna. You've done that, and now you can think about what comes next. Marriage and a family."

"Hey now, who said anything about marriage and a family?"

"Do you not want to be married? Not have a family of your own? Has that changed since you've been away at college?"

"No."

"That's what I thought," she says smugly. "Now, let's get this dessert delivered." She sniggers, and I know she's enjoying this. I'm glad to see that both of them are doing well and moving forward with a healthier lifestyle.

"What is this?" Gramps asks. He's looking down at his bowl of fresh fruit and whipped cream like he might cry.

"It's healthy and just the right amount of sweet." Grams tells him with a tilt in her lips. "This is your new dessert."

"You're enjoying this?"

"I am. You're acting like a toddler when I'm trying to save your life."

Gramps nods. "Love you, Aggie," he says softly.

"I love you too. Now dig in."

LATER THAT NIGHT, I'M IN BED AND HAVE BEEN STARING AT THE CEILING FOR WHAT FEELS like hours. I miss Rip. What's worse is that it's my own stubbornness as to why he's not here holding me now. When my phone vibrates on the nightstand,

I know it's him.

Rip: I miss you.

The text is followed by a picture of my side of his big king-size bed.

Rip: This bed is too empty.

I type out a message but decide to call him instead. I need to hear his voice. Backing out of the message, I hit his contact.

"Kenna."

"Hey."

"Can't sleep?"

"No."

"Me either."

"Want me to come and get you?"

I glance at the alarm clock. It's already one in the morning. "No. You have to be up in a few hours." He gets up at five every day to start the chores on the farm.

"Well, that's a few hours of sleep I'll get compared to none."

"No, I don't want to wake my grandparents."

"I hate this."

"How is it that I've been home for a little over a month, and I'm already so attached to you?"

"Because we're meant to be, Kenna."

"It's hard to resist you when you say things like that."

"Good." He chuckles softly.

"I should let you go. I just wanted to hear your voice."

"Pretend like I'm there with my arms around you. Holding you close."

"Yeah," I say, feeling my eyes getting heavy. How can just talking to this man put me so at ease?

"Sweet dreams, baby."

"Night, Rip." I end the call, place my phone back on the nightstand, and drift off to sleep with his voice in my head.

Chapter Twenty-Three

RIP

TODAY MY LITTLE SISTER MARRIES THE LOVE OF HER LIFE, AND I'M A GRUMPY BASTARD. Why, you ask? My best friend gets to walk down the aisle with my girl while I'm walking with his girlfriend. As maid of honor and best man, that's the order of things, but I don't have to like it. It's not just me. I'm not the only one. Corbin is a little grouchy himself.

"What's up with the two of you?" Colby asks.

"Nothing," Corbin and I mumble at the same time.

"Fuck that. This is my wedding day. You know how long I've waited to marry Lara. You two surly bastards aren't going to ruin in. Start talking."

I look at Corbin and shrug. "Fine, I'm irritated I don't get to walk in with Sara."

Colby rolls his eyes. "And you?" he asks me.

"What he said, with Kenna," I confess.

"Seriously? Are the two of you so pussy-whipped that you're whining that you can't walk in with your girlfriends at my wedding?"

Corbin and I share another look. "Yes," we say at the same time.

Colby surprises me when he throws his head back in laughter. Reaching into the pocket of his blue jeans, he pulls out his cell and dials. The phone rings out in the room, letting us know he has it on speaker.

"Hey, handsome, you ready for this?" Laramie asks him.

"I've been ready. However, our brothers are not feeling the same way."

"What?" Laramie asks with panic in her voice.

"Yeah, they're both sulking because they can't walk in with their girlfriends."

"Colby!" Lara scolds him. "You gave me a heart attack. Is that all? They're sulking?"

"Pretty much," he says smugly, knowing damn well Lara is going to put us in our place.

"Whatever, I don't care about the order. They can just take their right places when they reach the archway that Corbin, Colby, and their father built for today. All I care about is that everyone who is important to me is there to watch us get married. The rest is just details."

"Who are you, and what have you done with my sister?" I ask, loud enough that she can hear.

Laramie laughs "I'm getting married today, big brother. It's going to take a whole hell of a lot more than you and my brother-in-law bitching about not walking down the aisle with your women. Besides, I'm sure the four of you aren't far behind us."

"Right." Corbin laughs. "How long did the two of you date before taking the plunge?" he asks.

"That's us. We started out young. The two of you aren't getting any younger." She sniggers.

"Bye, sis. Love you," I call out.

"Bye, sis. Love you," Corbin mimics me.

"You two got lucky," Colby says. "Love you, baby. I'll see you soon."

"You're damn right, you will. Love you too," Laramie says, ending their call.

"That is not how I expected that call to go," I admit, running my hands through my hair.

"I was ready to have my ass handed to me," Corbin admits.

"Yeah, well, my wife is a badass like that." Colby flashes us a cheesy grin. "Looks like the lineup is changed. Just take your correct places at the altar. Now can the two of you stop sulking?"

"Sorry, man." I feel a little bad, but not enough to go back to the original plan.

There's a knock on the door, and Colby and Corbin's dad, Sam, walks in. "You ready for this?" he asks Colby.

"I've been ready."

"That you have. We're ready for all of you. Colby, head on down to the archway, and these two will be right behind you with the ladies, and then Laramie and Roger will follow."

"Let's do this," Colby says, pulling his dad into a tight hug. Corbin and I take our turns as well before the four of us head out of my old bedroom and downstairs.

The wedding is being held in the backyard of my parents' farmhouse. Colby made an arch and covered it with wildflowers, which is where they will stand to say their vows. Laramie wanted a simple country wedding, and she's pulled it off. Colby heads outside while Corbin and I gather in the kitchen, waiting for the women to join us.

"You two clean up nice."

A smile instantly graces my face. I turn to see McKenna. She's wearing a purple sundress and brown cowboy boots. Her hair is in a braid and hanging over one shoulder. She takes my breath away.

"Thank you," I say, my eyes only for her.

"Hey, none of that," Sara scolds when I lean in for a kiss. "We don't want to ruin our makeup."

That's when I look over at Sara. She's wearing the same dress as McKenna and similar boots, and her long blonde hair is styled the same as McKenna's as well.

"Babe, come on." Corbin leans in and kisses the corner of her mouth as she swats him away.

"If he gets a kiss, so do I," I say, kissing the corner of Kenna's mouth.

"You two are on a roll today." McKenna laughs.

Instead of commenting, because she's right, I pull her into a hug. "You look beautiful," I whisper, just for her.

"And you're handsome," she tells me, glancing over her shoulder at me.

"All right, are we ready?" Dad asks, joining us. Laramie has her arm through his, and I'm man enough to admit I get a little choked up seeing my baby sister ready to get married to her best friend.

"Lara." Releasing McKenna, I go to my sister and place a kiss on her cheek. "You're beautiful."

"Thank you." Her smile is blinding. "You in a better mood?"

"I am. Thank you."

She shrugs. "You love her. There's nothing wrong with that."

I glance back at McKenna, who is talking to Sara, and thankfully didn't hear her. "I do," I say when I turn back to face my sister and my dad.

"Son, you plan on doing something about that?" he asks me.

"I don't want to scare her off."

"She loves you too," Laramie announces.

"Yeah, I think she does." I swallow the emotions rising in my throat. I don't know if it's that my little sister is getting married or the fact that I just told my family, well, other than Mom, that I'm in love with McKenna. Not that I needed to tell them; it sounds like they already know. "Let's do this, little sis." I give her hand that's not gripping Dad's arm a soft squeeze and go back to McKenna.

"So, how are we doing this?" Sara asks.

"McKenna and Corbin were supposed to be first."

"Since Colby is already down there, how about you and Corbin go first?" McKenna suggests. "He's been standing out there all by himself while we've all had each other. He might need his best man, his brother."

"Done." Corbin offers Sara his arm, and they wait for their cue to begin their walk down the aisle.

I stand with McKenna, her arm linked with mine, my hand resting on her arm. I can't seem to stop touching her, no matter where we are. "You ever think about your wedding day?"

"I have."

"And?"

"And what?"

"Are you going to tell me about it?"

"That's a conversation I should have with my future husband."

"So tell me."

She stiffens, then turns to look at me. "Rip?"

"When I think about my wedding day, it's you walking toward me."

"You're up," Dad says, tapping me on the shoulder.

I wink at a speechless McKenna as we begin our trek down the makeshift aisle. I know that I've come on strong, and I know I told myself I wasn't going to push for more from her, but damn, the emotions of the day got to me.

I want Laramie to be right. I want us to be next. I'm more than ready to start my life with her. I know I need to slow down, but I'm ready for our forever.

"CAN THE WEDDING PARTY PLEASE MAKE THEIR WAY TO THE DANCE FLOOR?" THE DEEJAY announces.

"Finally," I say, pushing back from the table and walking to the center of the barn, or in this case, the dance floor for the night. I've been sitting at the opposite end of the table as McKenna all night. I get it. That's how my sister wanted it. Her girls on her side, his guys on his, but I've been itching to get my hands on my girl.

"If I didn't know better, I'd say your sister is trying to torture us," Corbin comments.

"Hey, cowboy." I hear from beside me.

McKenna.

I pull her into my arms and twirl us around. "Have I told you how beautiful you are?"

"A time or two."

"Well, it deserves to be said again. And again, and again," I say, kissing the tip of her nose.

"Everyone is watching."

"I don't care who's watching, Kenna. If I want to kiss my girlfriend, I'm going to kiss you. If they don't like it, they can look away."

"I guess it's still hard for me to get used to this. Being together in front of our families."

"You better get used to it. I'm not holding back. Like right now, I want to kiss you."

"Do you now?" she asks, looking up at me.

I don't answer her. Instead, I press my lips to hers. It's just a quick kiss, but it's more than that in meaning. She's right, all eyes are on us, as the only three couples on the dance floor, and I don't want to leave any room for questions. My actions are telling the entire room all that they need to know.

McKenna and I are together, and nothing is coming between us. Well, maybe not that last part, but they'll learn quickly enough. McKenna is my number one.

Over the next few hours, we tear up the dance floor. McKenna dances with my dad, her gramps, and I think every other man in attendance at the wedding. I hate it and love it at the same time. We're all glad to have her home, but I want her all to myself. That's fine. She's already agreed to come home with me. So, while she's dancing with them, I'm the one she's sleeping next to. It's not until after Colby slips my sister's garter off her that I'm able to get her back on the dance floor.

"We need all the single ladies," the deejay announces when I just finally got my arms back around my girl.

She tries to pull away from me. "Where are you going? You're not single," I remind her.

She throws her head back and laughs. "Rip, by single, he means those who aren't married."

"Fine, is the minister still here?" I ask, making her laugh harder. She thinks I'm kidding, but I'd marry her this minute without a second thought.

"Mac!" Laramie calls out for her. "Get out there."

"I'm trying," she calls back, still laughing.

"She's not single!" I yell out for my sister, and everyone in the room erupts with laughter.

"Let her go, brother," Laramie tells me.

"Fine," I grumble, fighting a grin. "Come back to me," I say, kissing McKenna quickly.

"Always," she assures me.

I watch as McKenna, Sara, and about a half dozen other single ladies, correction, unmarried women, gather in the center of the floor.

"Ready, ladies?" Laramie asks. She turns her back to them and counts to three. On three, she tosses her bouquet in the air.

I watch McKenna as she moves to the back of the pack. It doesn't matter, though. My sister tosses the bouquet with all of her might, and it lands right in my girl's hands. Everyone crowds around her, laughing and smiling while I stand here thinking about dropping to one knee right here and now and asking her to marry me.

"All right, fellas, your turn," the deejay announces.

I head straight for McKenna and intercept her as she's walking off the floor. "So, you caught the bouquet."

She holds it up. "Looks like it."

"Does that mean if I catch the garter, we're destined to be together?"

"It means that you catch the garter." She stands on her toes and presses a kiss to my lips. "Good luck, cowboy."

"Wait." I reach out for her arms, stopping her from walking away. "If I catch it, what do I get?"

"What do you want?"

"You."

She smiles. "I'm already yours, Rip Callahan."

I nod. That's not what I meant, but it will do for now. Making my way out to the floor, I follow McKenna's lead and situate myself in the back of the pack.

"Ready or not, here it comes," Colby says, tossing the garter into the air.

All I have to do is raise my hand over my head, and it falls into my palm. I couldn't have coordinated it better if I tried. Twirling the garter around my finger, I ignore the fact that it was just on my sister's thigh and that Colby stuck his head under her dress and removed it with his teeth. Instead, I make a motion for McKenna to come my way. Bouquet in hand, she comes to me, wearing a shy smile.

"Look what I found," I say, nodding toward the garter.

"Lucky you."

"Lucky me," I say, pulling her into my arms. I don't let her go the rest of the night. I keep my arms around her, and I must give off the "she's mine don't touch" vibe because no one else asks her to dance.

When the crowd finally dies down and the newlyweds disappear, I lead my girl to my house and spend the rest of the night making love to her, all while thinking about what it's going to be like when she's walking toward me in a white dress.

Chapter Twenty-Four

MCKENNA

IT'S HARD TO BELIEVE COLBY AND LARAMIE HAVE BEEN MARRIED FOR TWO WEEKS TODAY. They spent a week at the beach, celebrating their nuptials, and now the happy couple wants everyone at their place to celebrate. Never mind we were all at the wedding. It's an excuse for them to have us over, now that Laramie is actually living there.

She told me she didn't want to move in until they were married. She wanted to leave something sacred for marriage. I didn't point out that she spent most nights there anyway. Now, however, that's where she gets her mail, so it's official.

"You ready?" Rip asks from the doorway of his bathroom.

"Yes," I say, placing the wand back in my mascara.

"You don't need that stuff."

"What stuff?"

"Makeup. You're already beautiful."

"Are you setting yourself up to get lucky tonight, cowboy?" I ask, fluttering my mascara-coated lashes at him.

"Oh, I'm getting lucky, and by association, so are you." He winks, and my body flares to life.

I don't know if I'll ever not have this reaction to him. We've been dating for a month. Although it feels as though a lifetime has passed, every look, every touch, every sexual encounter feels like our first. To say that I'm madly in love with him would be an understatement. Not that I've told him. The thought of saying those words and him not feeling the same makes me sick to my stomach. Yeah, I'm not going there. Not yet.

"No time for that," I say, walking past him. I should have known he wouldn't let me off that easy. He snakes an arm around my waist and pulls me close.

"We can make time. You come first, remember? You need me to take care of the ache, Kenna?"

"You are so bad," I say breathlessly.

He chuckles. "Only for you, baby." He runs his hands over my breasts. Even covered in my tank top, I know he can feel my body's reaction to him. "Tell me what you want, baby."

"We have to go."

His lips find their way to my neck. "You sure about that?" He nips at my ear.

As if she knows that her brother is trying to seduce me, my cell rings, and a quick glance at the screen tells me I'm right. It's Laramie calling.

"Don't answer," Rip says as he continues trailing kisses down my neck. Like the hussy I am for him, I tilt my head to the side, giving him full access. "There's my girl," he whispers huskily. My phone stops ringing, only to start again.

"She's going to keep calling," I say as I pull away from him. Retrieving my phone from my back pocket, I answer. "Hey."

"Are you having sex?" she huffs out, and I sputter with laughter.

"No. We're not doing that," I tell her honestly. Not that we both don't want it to lead there.

"We could be," Rip calls out so that Laramie can hear him.

"You two better get your asses over here. You're late."

Pulling the phone from my ear, I see she's right. It's five minutes after six. "We're on our way. You need us to stop and pick anything up?"

"No. We have everything. Just waiting on you slowpokes." I can tell by the tone of her voice she's trying not to laugh. "I mean, we are the newlyweds," she teases.

"Hey, we were married years ago. We just haven't lost the spark," Rip says, again his voice is loud enough she can hear.

"Am I on speaker?"

"No, he's just… close."

"Damn right, I'm close," Rip says, patting my ass, making me yelp.

"Rip, hands off and get your ass over here," Laramie says so loud, I have to pull the phone from my ear.

"On our way, little sister," he replies. He then takes the phone from my hand and ends the call. "Killjoy," he mutters.

"Come on. I need to grab the brownies and cookies I made and the gift."

"Tell me again why we had to get them another gift?" We got them a wedding gift.

I smile, thinking about that conversation. He was insistent that we put both of our names on the gifts we bought separately. "We're together now, Kenna. This is what we do," he'd told me.

"What's got you all smiley?" he inquires.

"You, Rip Callahan. This smile is all for you."

"Good." He leans down and kisses me. "I want all your smiles."

"Come on, cowboy. We're already in trouble."

"We're taking my truck."

"What's wrong with my car?" I ask, even though I already know. Rip is tall at six four, and my little Honda isn't made for a man his size.

"Too damn small," he grumbles.

"Fine, you big baby." I roll my eyes playfully as he extends his arms out for me, but I'm able to jump back before he reaches me and race out of his room and down the steps.

"THAT TOOK FOREVER," LARAMIE SAYS WHEN SHE ANSWERS THE DOOR.

"I love the sign," I say, pointing to the gift I got them for their wedding. It's a welcome sign with their last name and wedding date.

"Me too. Thank you so much," she says, pulling me into the house.

"Nice to see you too, sis." Rip chuckles behind us.

"Hey, Rip." She waves a hand in the air, pulling me into the living room. "I've missed you," she says, plopping down on the couch, pulling me down with her.

"Hey, Sara," I say, looking over at our other friend, who's sitting on the other side of the couch.

"Hi." Sara waves and laughs.

"What's the urgency?"

"I missed you. I don't want to be one of those married women who loses all contact with her friends."

"Lara, that would never happen."

"Well, it's been two very long weeks, so yeah." She shrugs.

"Where are Colby and Corbin?" Rip asks.

"Basement," she tells him.

"Babe, I set everything on the kitchen counter. You need anything?"

"Thank you, and no, I'm good. Go see the guys." Rip bends his head to kiss me quickly before heading to the basement.

"How are things between the two of you?" Sara asks.

"Too good to be true."

"Impossible."

"Things are great. It kind of feels like I'm living a dream."

"We know you've had that dream," Laramie says, barely keeping a straight face.

"Hey, I'm not denying it. I've always had a thing for Rip. I just never in a million years thought we would be here. Enough about me, how was the honeymoon?"

"Yes. That." Sara points at me. "How's married life?" she adds.

"It's not much different, except he calls me wife, and he's my husband." Her face lights up. "That's going to be hard to get used to, but I'm up to the challenge." She laughs. "The honeymoon was perfect. We had great weather. We hung out on the beach, went on a dolphin tour, and spent a lot of time at the beach house we rented."

"I bet you did." I wag my eyebrows, and we all fall into a fit of laughter. "What about you?" I ask Sara once our laughter is under control. "How are things with Corbin?"

"I'm in love with him." Her eyes go wide, and she covers her face with her hands. "Shit. I didn't mean to say that."

"Hey." Laramie grabs her hand. "If you can't be honest with us, as your friends, we're not doing our job. There's nothing wrong with how you feel."

"I know, but it's so soon. We've only been seriously seeing each other a few weeks, but we've been, you know, hanging out or whatever for about three months in total, and I'm... smitten that sounds better."

"That's nothing. I've been with Rip officially for what? Five weeks now, and I'm head over heels in love with him." I freeze when I realize what I just said. Sara and Laramie are looking at me with wide eyes. "What? I've known him forever, and he's hard not to love. I never stood a chance."

"Kenna," Rip's deep, gruff voice calls from behind me.

"Oh, no." It's now my eyes that are wide as I stare at my two friends. "Please tell me he didn't hear me," I whisper. They both nod. "Shit. Shit. Shit," I mutter to myself.

Sara stands and walks to the other side of the room. The side that my back is to. The same side I refuse to look at because I know that Rip is standing there and heard what I confessed to my friends.

"Come on, babe." I hear Colby.

"I want to see how this plays out." Laramie smiles.

"Lara." Rip's tone is a warning, and we all know it.

"Fine." She puts her hand in Colby's and allows him to pull her up from the couch. She stops and places her hand on my shoulder. Leaning down, she whispers in my ear, "He loves you too. We all know it."

I don't say a word. I can't. I wasn't ready to tell him. It was supposed to be a confession among friends. It's too soon. He's going to feel like I'm trapping him into this. The pressure to say it back is going to be real. I'm his sister's best friend, after all. Closing my eyes, I focus on my breathing and pretend he's not standing behind me. I want to open my eyes and have this be a dream.

I feel the couch dip with his weight, and his arms are around me, pulling me into his chest. "Kenna," he says, his voice cracking. "Open your eyes for me, baby."

"I can't."

"Yes, you can."

"Can we just pretend that didn't happen?"

"No." The firmness to his voice is back.

"Please?" My voice is pleading. I'm not ready for this to be over. It's too soon.

"Kenna, baby, open your eyes for me." Knowing I'm not going to get out of this, I slowly open my eyes. He's watching me, an expression I can't name on his face. "There you are," he murmurs, resting his palm against my cheek. "I need you to do one more thing for me, okay?"

I nod, my stomach a knot of nerves. I don't know what he's going to ask of me, maybe to keep my feelings to myself for a while?

"I need you to say it again, McKenna."

He used my full name. He means business. "I don't understand?"

"Come on, lawyer girl." He smiles, his eyes soft. "You're the smartest woman I know. I know you know what I mean, but I'll say it again. I need to hear you say it again. Tell me," he says gently.

At this point, the damage is done. I might as well tell him. "I'm in love with you." I watch as his face transforms into a smile I've never seen.

"Fucking yes, you do." His lips find mine in a bruising kiss.

I don't know what's happening, but I kiss him back with just as much passion and need. When he tears his lips from mine, he's breathing heavy, and his eyes are hooded. Both of his hands cradle my face, and he stares into my eyes.

"I love the hell out of you, McKenna Dawson. Fuck, baby. I've wanted to say those words to you, but I was afraid you would run. I love you." He leans in and kisses me again. This time it's just a short peck, but it still makes my heart race.

"I didn't want to tell you. It's too soon."

"No. It's not. We've known each other our entire lives. This is real, and you can't take it back, babe. You already said it."

"I don't want to take it back," I confess.

"I thought that day you agreed to be mine was the best day of my life, then again when I made love to you, both times." He winks. "But this, this moment, it tops them both."

I don't know what to say, so I just hug him.

Everything I've ever dreamed about is happening, and it's a little surreal. How am I lucky enough to have all of my dreams come true?

Chapter Twenty-Five

RIP

MY HAIR IS DRENCHED WITH SWEAT, EVEN WITH THE COOL WIND THAT'S BLOWING IN A summer storm. It's Saturday, and I'm repairing the fence. I told McKenna I would be done early afternoon, but there were more spots that needed attention than I thought. So, not only am I hot, sweaty, and tired, I'm missing time with her.

Finally, the last bit of barbed wire is secure, and I'm done for the day. The sun is setting over the horizon as I tear off my T-shirt and wipe my face. That's when I hear it—the sound of a motor. I'm expecting it to be my dad to check on things. McKenna isn't the only one I told I would be done early afternoon. I did, however, text both of them and told them it was taking longer than anticipated, much to my dismay.

When the four-wheeler comes into view, it's not my dad. It's my girl, her long dark hair whipping in the wind as she makes her way to where I'm working. She turns off the engine, and I take the two small steps it takes to press my lips to hers.

"Hey, beautiful."

"Hi." She smiles. "I brought you a sandwich and some cold water. I know you packed lunch, but it's getting late."

"You spoil me," I say, pressing my lips to hers again.

"Can't a girl just be nice to her boyfriend?"

"Yes. You can." I step back, offering her my hand and helping her step off the machine.

"How much more do you have to go? Can I help?" She hands me a small brown bag and two bottles of water.

I look down at her blue jeans, cropped tank top, and flannel she has over top of her tank. The sleeves are rolled up to her elbows. This is one of the things I love most about her. She's just her. Just McKenna. She's a "jeans and tank top, with flannel and cowboy boots" kind of girl. Being at college in the city didn't change her.

"I just finished up, actually."

"I guess I'm a little late." She pouts.

"No. You're not too late. In fact, I think you're right on time." I point to the sunset, and she smiles.

"It's beautiful."

"It is." I'm not looking at the sky. I can't take my eyes off her. Setting the food and water on the four-wheeler, I place my hands on her hips and turn us so that we're facing the sunset. With my arms wrapped around her from behind, we watch as the sky changes in vibrant colors of oranges, pinks, and purples as the sun sets.

"Looks like a postcard," she murmurs and then pulls out of my arms. "You need to eat."

"I will. First, I need something from you?"

"Oh, yeah?" she asks, backing up.

"Yes."

"What's that?"

"It's impossible to watch that—" I nod toward the sunset "—with you and not kiss you."

"You want to kiss me, cowboy?" she asks, stepping closer. She lifts her hand, and I capture her wrist with one hand, sliding the other around her waist.

"I want to more than kiss you, Kenna." I lean in close, our mouths a breath apart.

"Show me."

That's exactly what I do.

I kiss her, taking my time tasting her lips, enjoying the hell out of the fact that this incredible woman is mine, and I can kiss her anytime I want. She breaks the connection and smiles up at me. I'm glad I'm holding onto her because that single look makes my knees weak. I want to drop to one knee right here, right this very moment, and ask her to marry me. I want all the sunsets and sunrises with her. I want everything.

There are two small things that are stopping me. One, the way she freaked out on me last weekend when I heard her tell my sister that she was head over heels in love with me. That, and I don't have a ring. Not yet. That's something I'm going to remedy soon. I don't want that to be the reason I miss the next perfect opportunity to give me her forever.

"I should pack up before the storm rolls in."

"What can I do to help?"

I kiss her forehead. "You being here is enough. Thank you for bringing me food."

"You didn't even get to eat it."

"I'll eat it on the way back to the barn. Let me get this packed up, and I'll follow you back to the house."

"I know the way."

"Yeah, but it looks as if it could pour at any minute, and I'd feel better knowing that I'm with you, just in case."

"Fine. Let me help you pack up."

Together we have the tools packed up in no time, and we're headed back to the house. I eat the sandwich she brought on the way. When I get to the house, I need a shower and my girl. Maybe I'll even convince her for both at the same time.

It doesn't take long for the clouds to build and darken. The sunset we just wanted is long since gone and replaced with dark clouds and the threat of storms.

"Go on inside," I tell McKenna when we get back to the barn. The rain is already sprinkling from the sky. It's only a matter of time before it unleashes.

"You sure you don't want help?"

"Nah. I'm going to close up, and I'll be right behind you."

"See you inside," she says, jogging off for the house. I watch her until she makes it to the porch just as the sky unleashes with what seems like buckets of rainfall from the sky.

Putting away all of the tools so I can easily find them the next time I need them, I throw away my empty water bottles from the cooler, and it's still pouring down rain. I refuse to waste more time out here in the barn when my girl is in the house. Locking up the barn, I make a run for it. By the time I make it to the porch, I'm soaked. I look like I took a dip in the pond. Not wanting to create a pool in the house, I strip down to my boxer briefs.

The front door opens, and McKenna hands me a towel. Before taking it from her hands, I pull my underwear down my legs, dropping them to the pile of wet clothes, before wrapping the towel around my waist.

"Come in here before someone sees you." She chuckles.

"Mom and Dad can't see me from their place, and all the farmhands are gone for the day."

"Still." She shakes her head.

"What? Are you jealous?"

"No. I mean, it's your bare ass. You can show it to whoever you want." She crosses her arms over her chest defiantly.

"You need to work on your poker face, lawyer girl," I tease. "That scowl gives you away."

"Fine. I'm not exactly thrilled that anyone could show up and see you in all of your glory."

"My glory?" I ask, fighting my laughter.

"Get in here." She tugs on my arm, pulling me into the house and shutting the door behind us.

"Well, you got me in here, now what are you going to do with me?" I ask. Grabbing the towel, I pull it from where I have it tucked around my waist and begin to dry my hair.

Her eyes travel to my dick, and she licks her lips. "Rip." She closes her mouth as she takes a step closer. When I feel her hand wrap around my dick, I drop the wet towel to the floor.

"I need a shower."

"You're all wet," she says huskily.

"Kenna?"

"Yeah?"

"Shower. Now."

"I'm good," she says as she strokes me from root to tip.

"Baby, I'm still dripping water all over the floor, and if you keep doing that, the mess is going to be even bigger."

"You think so?" she asks, running the pad of her thumb over the head of my dick.

"Fuck it."

She squeals when I bend to lift her into my arms. She lets go of my dick, and I lift her bridal style.

"What are you doing?" she asks, laughing.

"We're going to shower."

"Is that how this relationship is going to go? When you want something, you're just going to manhandle me to seeing things your way?"

"Baby, you can do whatever the hell you want with me once I get you in that shower. I've been working outside all day, and I'm a sweaty mess. Give me two minutes to soap up and rinse off, and then I'm all yours."

"All mine."

"All yours. Now strip," I say, entering the bathroom and placing her feet on the floor. Reaching into the shower, I turn on the water and don't wait for it to get warm. I step inside and get to work lathering up. By the time I'm ready to rinse, the water is warm, and McKenna is stepping inside. "Perfect timing," I say, spinning to make sure all the soap is off my body.

Turning back to face her, I spread my arms wide. "Do your worst," I tell her.

She grins and pushes on my chest, moving me backward until the backs of my legs hit the shower bench. "Sit."

"Yes, ma'am." She drops to her knees, and my dick throbs with need.

"Hands on the bench," she instructs. She takes it a step further and places my hands exactly where she wants them on the edge of the bench.

I can't take my eyes off her as her tongue peeks out past her full, plump lips and traces the tip of my dick. I open my mouth to tell her how good it feels when she takes me in her mouth. "Fuck, I wasn't ready," I pant, as the feeling of her wet hot mouth surrounding me crashes into me.

She releases me with an audible pop and looks me in the eye. "I want you to come. Tell me what you like so I can make that happen."

"You, Kenna." I lift my hand, and she shakes her head and points to the bench. "I need to touch you."

"No. You need to tell me what you like. What feels good so I can do that. To you," she adds.

"I already told you. It's you, baby. When it's the love of your life kneeling before you with your cock in her mouth, that's pretty much all it takes." Her eyes soften, and she nods just before she takes me back into her mouth.

My hands grip the bench so hard I'm not certain that I'm not leaving marks in the stone. I want to close my eyes and just feel, but the sight of her head bobbing up and down on my dick is something I can't look away from. She's working me with her hands and her mouth, and I feel the telltale sign of tingles racing up and down my spine.

She stares up at me with those big brown eyes, her mouth full of my cock, and gives a subtle shake of her head. "Kenna, I-I'm close," I say, barely holding on. Letting go of the bench, I tap her shoulder to get her attention. What she does next has me shooting my load down her throat, with her name falling from my lips.

She takes everything I give her before releasing me and wiping her mouth with the back of her arm. The warm water of the shower is still on, filling the room with steam. Pulling her into my lap, I kiss her with everything I am. I kiss her over and over, not giving a fuck that she just had my dick in her mouth. When I finally get feeling back in my legs, I stand and place her on the bench, dropping to my knees before her.

"That was for you," she says, pushing my hair out of my eyes.

"And this is for you." I put pressure on her thighs, spread her legs apart, and close my mouth over her clit. I eat at her like she's my last meal. Almost instantly, her hands burrow in my hair, and she's calling out my name. I don't move my mouth until her legs stop quivering, and she loosens her grip.

"Wow," she breathes.

"Wow is right," I say, standing.

"No, I mean that—" She points to my hard dick.

"Yeah, I'm not done with you." Stepping out of the shower, I grab a condom, and I'm back, sheathed and lifting her from the bench. She wraps her legs around my waist, and I slide inside her. "Perfect fit," I say, pressing her back against the shower wall.

"Show me."

"My pleasure." I pull back and slam home over and over and over again. I need her to come because I'm ready to, and I refuse to go again without her. Moving to the bench, I sit. "Spin around," I tell her.

Doing as I ask, she turns her back to me and slides her pussy over my cock. "Oh." She exhales.

"Come back to me," I say, and she doesn't hesitate to lean her back against my chest. Reaching around her, my hand finds her clit, and I stroke her while lifting my hips, giving her all of me.

"Rip, that's… so good," she puffs.

"Come for me, Kenna. I can't hold on any longer. Your pussy is going crazy. I need you to come for me."

"Faster," she pants.

I abandon her clit and place my hands on her hips. I lift her up and slam her back down over and over again. Her pussy convulses; she's close.

"There. Right. There," she says, tilting her head back.

Two more thrusts and I feel her coming, and I allow myself to spill over inside her. My entire body is spent but in the best possible way. We manage to clean up and dry off before falling into bed exhausted.

Chapter Twenty-Six

MCKENNA

"DAWSON LAW FIRM, THIS IS MCKENNA," I SAY INTO THE RECEIVER.

"Yes, I need to speak to McKenna Dawson," my best friend says. She's trying to disguise her voice, but it doesn't work. I know it's her.

"She's not here. She's having lunch with her best friend."

"What the hell, Mac?" Laramie laughs.

"Got ya. What's up?" I ask with a chuckle.

"We still on for girls' night tomorrow tonight?"

"Yep."

"Okay, well, how about we just hang out at my place? Colby said he would get Corbin and Rip to meet up at the Silver Star for dinner and a few beers."

"Sure. What can I bring?"

"I figured we'd just order pizza."

"Sure. Same time?"

"Yes, around seven. I think the guys are meeting at our place at seven, so I figured that's easiest if you and Sara want to ride with them."

"That works for me. I'll see you then."

"See you." I end the call and go back to the court brief I'm reading when the phone rings again.

I don't know how Gramps gets anything done when Mary's not here.

She went to high school with my mom and has worked for Gramps for years. She's on vacation with her family this week, and her absence is apparent.

"Dawson Law Firm," I greet the caller.

"Even your professional phone voice is sexy."

Rip.

"Hey," I say, feeling my face flush.

"Miss you."

"You do?"

"Always. Are you sure you want to do girls' night tomorrow tonight?"

"I am. Your sister just called. Change of plans. We're hanging out at their place."

"Perfect."

"I mean, the girls are hanging out at her place. Colby is supposed to call you and Corbin for dinner and beers at the Silver Star."

"I liked the first plan better," he confesses. "That must be why Colbs called."

"Did you not call him back?"

"No. I will. I was missing you and needed to hear your voice."

I sigh a happy sigh into the phone. "What am I going to do with you, Rip Callahan?"

"Love me, baby. That's all I want is for you to love me."

"Done."

"Good. You staying with me tonight?"

"I should probably stay at Gram and Gramps."

"We'll spend the day with them tomorrow before we have to leave, or Sunday. Just... please stay with me. It's been a long day, and I need to feel your skin next to mine."

How can I say no to that? "Okay."

"I guess I need to call Colby back. You want me to pick you up?"

"I think I can drive that quarter of a mile to get to your place on my own," I tease.

"Don't fault a man for wanting to take care of the woman he loves," he counters.

"I need to get back to work."

"Me too. See you soon," he says, and the line goes dead.

I have four more hours until this workweek is finished. Glancing at the calendar on my desk, I have it marked that my results from the bar exam could come in as early as next week. I've been checking the website for my grades religiously, even though I know it could take anywhere from eight to twelve weeks. Next week is eight weeks. I'm anxious to hear my results and hopefully begin working as an attorney.

Everything I've ever wanted seems to be falling into place. I can't help but be skeptical of when the other shoe is going to drop. I'm trying really hard to not let my insecurities come between me and what I want for my future. Surely, it can't be this easy to live your dream.

"WHERE ARE YOU GOING?" I ASK RIP WHEN I FEEL HIM CLIMB OUT OF BED.

"I'm going to go feed the animals. I gave Thomas the day off. I should be back around noon."

"You want me to make you some breakfast?" I ask, sitting up, making sure to hold the sheet over my naked breasts.

"No, baby. Go back to sleep. It's still early." He sits next to me on the bed.

I look to the window and see that it's still dark outside. "What time is it?"

"Five. Chores are never done on a farm," he says, pressing a kiss to my forehead. He stands and makes his way to the door.

"Be safe," I call after him.

He stops and turns to look at me over his shoulder. "Always, baby."

Dropping back to the bed, I snuggle under the blankets that smell like him and drift off to sleep. A few hours later, I wake to the sun high in the sky. The alarm clock tells me that it's just after eight. I debate on going over to visit my grandparents, and then I remember that Gramps said they were going to visit friends today. So, instead, I take my time in the shower and getting ready for the day.

Forty-five minutes later, I'm in the kitchen toasting a bagel when my cell rings. "Hello."

"Hey," Laramie greets me. "What are you getting into today?"

"Nothing. Rip is working. He gave Thomas the day off," I explain. "I was going to clean house a little since it's something we usually do on the weekends. I figured I could get it done while he's working, and we can spend the day together tomorrow. What about you?"

"Nothing much. Colbs is working. You want some company?"

"Sure. Are you okay?"

"Yeah. Of course. I'm fine. Why?" She's quick to ask.

"You just sound funny."

"Nope. I'm perfect. I'm going to head over now if that's okay. I need to run an errand, but I should be there in say, half an hour?"

"That works for me."

"Do you need anything?"

"Nope. We're all good. I'll see you soon."

Placing my phone back on the counter, I eat my bagel while unloading and reloading the dishwasher. We were both too tired to bother with doing it last night. By the time I'm finished, I've eaten the rest of my bagel and wiped down the counters. Next, I sweep the floor and move on to the living room. I've just finished dusting and sweeping the living room when Laramie knocks.

"Come in!" I call out, placing the cordless sweeper back on the charging stand in the closet.

"Hey, hey." She smiles.

"It's weird that I just invited you to enter your brother's house."

"Why? You might as well say you live here too."

"No." I shake my head. "No. I don't live here. I do stay here frequently at his request, but I don't live here."

"Why not?"

"It's too soon."

"You know that's bullshit, right?"

"Can we not talk about this?" I ask. "Come sit down, tell me what's up with you."

She follows me to the couch and takes a seat, turning to face me. "What's in the bag?" I ask, looking at the reusable shopping bag with our local pharmacy's logo on the side.

"That's part of why I'm here."

"Okay."

"I'm late."

"Did we set a definite time?" I ask, confused.

"No, Mac, I'm late. As in my period is late."

"Oh. Oh! How long?"

"A few days."

"That's not so bad."

"I stopped taking my birth control the day before the wedding. We decided we've wasted so much time that we're ready to move forward. That included marriage and babies."

"Really?" I ask, feeling hot tears well in my eyes. "I'm so happy for you, Lara." I lean into her, and she meets me in the middle for a tight hug.

"Anyway," she says, wiping at her eyes. "I wanted to take a test, but I didn't want to do it by myself. And Colby is so excited I didn't want him to be disappointed if it's negative."

"Isn't it too early to tell? I mean, don't you need some time before the home test can pick it up?"

"Yes, but there are some home kits that detect early. I bought one of every kind." She points to the bag.

"I can see that." I laugh, looking at the bag.

"How long will Rip be working?"

"He said he'd be home around noon."

"That gives us about an hour and a half, give or take, before he comes home."

"You sure you don't want Colby with you when you take them?"

She nods. "I'm sure. Mac, I wish you could have seen his face when we talked about starting a family. He lit up like a Christmas tree. I don't want to disappoint him. If I'm not, we'll continue to try, and he won't be disappointed. Besides, I really doubt that I am. I mean, it's been a month and a handful of days since I stopped my birth control pills. From what I've read, it could take some time."

"Okay, well, let's head up. We can use the spare bedroom, just in case Rip happens to come home early."

"Good idea." Laramie stands and grasps the bag. "Can you grab a couple of bottles of water? I drank two on the way here, but I might need more." She holds up the bag as proof.

"Sure, I'll be right up."

In the kitchen, I grab four bottles of water just in case. She's got several tests in the bag. Stepping into the bedroom, I see the tests spilled out on the bed, with one of the boxes open. "Laramie, I've got water."

"I'm good for now. I'm starting with one, and we'll go from there," she tells me through the bathroom door.

Placing the water bottles on the nightstand, I take a seat on the bed and pick up one of the tests, reading the box. My mind wanders to my last period, and I freeze. I can't remember. Wait, I do. It was the week before I took the bar exam. I remember being relieved that I wouldn't have to deal with Aunt Flo while testing. That was— "Oh, no."

"What?" Laramie asks, appearing beside me. I stare up at her, but I can't seem to form words. "McKenna, talk to me," she says, reaching for my hands.

All I can do is shake my head, over and over again. This can't be right. This can't be happening. I'm just starting my career, and then this thing with Rip is new. He's going to think I trapped him. *Just like my father.* It's too soon. I refuse to let him feel like he has no choice but to be with me because he got me pregnant. Oh. My. God. I might be pregnant.

"McKenna!" Laramie says forcefully. "Talk to me."

"Lara—" I start and swallow hard. "I'm late."

"What?"

I hold up a pregnancy test. "I… was thinking about you and how happy I was for you, and then I realized I couldn't remember my last period. I had to think, and it was the week before the bar exam."

"Okay. Well, that was stressful, as well as your gramps having a heart attack. You're worried about your results, and you're in a new-ish relationship. That's a lot going on. I'm sure your cycle is just thrown off."

"I can't be pregnant."

"Would it be that bad?" she asks. "I mean, you'd make me an aunt." She smiles.

"It's too soon. It's my parents all over again," I tell her, and her smile drops from her face. "I'm so stupid. Here I am trying to make something of myself, and instead, I let history repeat itself."

"First of all, I don't want you to refer to yourself as anything like your parents. You and I both know that you're nothing like either of them. Second of all, my brother isn't trapped. He's in love with you."

"We've been dating for like a minute, Laramie. This is what happened with my parents too. Dad felt trapped. He felt like his only option was to marry my mother. Only they never made it to the altar. He disappeared, and she slipped into a state of depression and got hooked on drugs after I was born. I caused that. It was me and my existence. I can't do that to him. I can't."

"Let's start with one of these." She holds up a pregnancy test. "Before you start jumping to conclusions, let's see what we're working with. And as far as your existence, he'd be lost without you, McKenna. I know your parents messed you up, but believe this when I tell you that Rip loves you. If the test is positive, he's going to love your baby too. Do you need to call Maggie?"

Laramie is the only person other than my grandparents who knows that I've seen a counselor since I was seven. It's not a frequent thing, usually two or three times a year, just to keep those insecurities that I live with at bay. "Okay." I wipe the tears from my cheeks. "I'm glad you're here. I couldn't do this on my own."

"Regardless of the results, you won't be alone. You have my brother, me, our friends, your grandparents, my parents. You have a huge support system."

"What did your test say?" I ask, realizing I've made this moment about me when it was supposed to be about her.

"I haven't checked yet."

"Go. Go look." I push on her arm, and she laughs.

"Come with me."

She grabs another pregnancy test, I'm assuming for her to take another, and one for me, and together we make our way into the bathroom. Together, we stare down at the test that's flashing the word pregnant.

"Oh my," she whispers. "I'm-I'm going to have a baby." Her arms wrap around me in a fierce hug, and her body shakes with her tears.

"I'm so happy for you," I tell her. I am. She and Colby have waited a long time to start their lives together. I understand they wanted to be older and make sure that the love they found as teenagers was real. It was a good plan not to rush into anything. So to see them starting the next phase of their life as a married couple and soon-to-be parents makes my heart swell for them. I couldn't be happier.

"I'm going to take another," she says, releasing me and wiping the tears from her cheeks. "And you need to take the first." She hands me a box. "I'm going to step out of the room. Let me know when you're ready."

"I don't know that I'll ever be ready," I tell her honestly. At least not right now. Not when I've been dating the guy for almost two months, and I'm already pregnant?

Yesterday I was wondering when the other shoe would drop. I guess I got my answer. I knew it was all too good to be true.

Chapter Twenty-Seven

RIP

I FINISH MUCKING THE LAST STALL SOONER THAN I ANTICIPATED. NOT THAT I'M COMPLAINING. I need a shower and some snuggle time with McKenna. I'm sure she's already up and moving. I wonder if I can convince her to lie back down with me for a few hours. I hated leaving her in bed this morning, but there was work to do. Saturdays are supposed to be the days that I get to snuggle and sleep in with her.

Closing up the barn, I head for the house, only to backtrack, deciding to check the mail first. I ordered McKenna a plaque for her office with her name and Attorney at Law underneath it. The last thing I need is for her to grab the mail and intercept the package before me. Not that she makes a habit of getting my mail, but she's a sweetheart and has stopped a few times on her way in to grab it for me. I got a shipping notification, so I'm expecting it any day now. In addition to that, she's yet to receive her grades for the bar exam. That means that technically she's not an Attorney at Law just yet. It's just a minor detail of her grade. McKenna is wicked smart, and I know she passed.

By the time I make it to the mailbox, I'm wishing I would have just brought my truck or one of the utility vehicles. It's hot as hell out here today, but that's expected for late summer in Texas.

On my way back to the house, I sift through the mail. The gift I ordered isn't here, which is good since she's at the house, and I don't have to worry about hiding it from her. I open the electric bill and notice it's about the same amount as last month. The rest is junk mail. Magazines, offers for credit cards, publishers clearing house, hell, I didn't even know that still existed. Stepping up on the porch, I look at the last envelope in the pile. I'm expecting it to be more trash. However, this one looks more official than the others. Looking at the return address, I see it's from the County Clerk of Nevada. Curious, I rip into the envelope.

Inside there is a certificate of marriage. Why in the hell am I getting a certificate of marriage? Skimming over the document, I get to the names, and my eyes widen. I blink hard, once, twice, three times, and every time the same names appear on the paper.

MARRIAGE CERTIFICATE
RIP ALAN CALLAHAN
MCKENNA GRACE DAWSON

"Holy fuck," I mutter. I stare down at my name and McKenna's, trying to decipher what I'm seeing. We're married? We got married in Vegas? How do I not remember that? I need a minute. Sitting on the top step, that's when I notice that my sister's car is here. Good, I need to process this before I tell McKenna. She's going to flip out on me. Not because she's mad, but I know her. She already thinks we're moving fast. Sure she loves me, but this... it's not just something we can tear up and be done with.

She's my wife.

McKenna Callahan.

Fuck me, but do I love the sound of that.

I can work with this. I was going to ask her to marry me anyway. I didn't know how or when, but I met with a jeweler yesterday. I was so pumped afterward I had to call her at the office just to hear her voice. Now, instead of planning to ask her to marry me, I need to convince her to stay married to me. Now that the idea is settling in my mind, I know that's what I have to do. If she wants another wedding for our families, we can do that too. But I don't want this to go away. I want her to be my wife.

Standing, I smile. I need to tell her. I need to show her that I'm not the least bit upset about this news. No. In fact, I'm elated. I wish I could remember that night. I hate that I don't remember marrying her or our first time together, but that's one night out of the rest of our lives. We can't dwell on the past. All we can do is move forward, and I want to move forward with her as McKenna Callahan.

"Here goes," I say before rushing into the house. I drop all the mail on the table as soon as I enter the front door, kick off my boots, and go in search of my wife. "Kenna!" I call out. She's not in the kitchen or the living room. I hear footsteps upstairs. Laramie must have wanted to get some of her things that she left here now that she's officially living with her husband.

Who would have thought we'd be married weeks apart? Or that I would be married first? Regardless, I know I'm in for a battle of wills with McKenna. She's going to go all sexy lawyer on me and tell me she'll handle it.

I don't want her to handle it.

"Kenna!" I call again, taking the stairs two at a time. I stop at the top and follow their voices into the spare bedroom. "Hey." I smile at my girl and my sister, who are sitting on the bed. The smile drops from my face when I see that they're both crying. "What is it? What's wrong?"

"Nothing." Laramie smiles at me. "Nothing is wrong."

I take her in, trying to see if she's lying, but she seems to be sincere. My eyes to go McKenna, and she's looking at her lap, wringing her hands together. "Baby?" Her head whips up, and there's shock written all over her face. "Kenna, baby, what's wrong?"

Her shoulders stiffen. "I'm fine. We're just… emotional."

"I call bullshit." Reaching out, I swipe my thumb across her cheek, wiping at her tears. I turn to look at Laramie, and that's when I see them. Pregnancy tests. Lots of and lots of pregnancy tests. My heart begins to race, and if this means what I think it means, my great day just turned fantastic.

"Those are mine," Laramie informs me.

My shoulders fall. Of course, I'm happy for my sister, but I really, really wanted them to be McKenna's. "Well?" I ask her.

She holds up a stick. "Pregnant." She smiles.

"No shit?"

"Yep. You're going to be an uncle."

It's not daddy, but I'll take it. "Congrats, Lara." I move to give her a hug, then turn back to McKenna. "You okay?"

"Yes." She nods and gives me a watery smile. I don't quite believe her, but she'll tell me in her own time. Maybe she wishes it was us too? Lucky for her, we're married, and we can start working on that tonight. Hell, we can start now. I have no issue with kicking my sister out and ravishing my girl for the next several hours. The urge to make love to her, with the knowledge that she's my wife, is strong.

"What had you rushing up here in a tizzy?" my sister asks. "Did you think I was stealing your girlfriend?" she teases.

"You mean my wife."

"You haven't earned that title yet, buddy." Laramie laughs.

"Actually, I have." Reaching into my back pocket, I pull out the envelope and hand it to McKenna. "I finished a little early and walked out to get the mail before coming inside. This was in the mailbox." I stand still, watching McKenna's every move as she pulls out the paperwork detailing that our marriage license was filed with the state of Nevada.

"Rip?" She looks up at me. "What is this?"

"From what I can tell, we got married while we were in Vegas."

"Oh, no." Laramie smacks her hand over her mouth. "I thought that was fake."

"What?" McKenna and I ask at the same time.

"The wedding. I remember bits and pieces of you two standing before Elvis, but I thought it was just from the pictures we have of you two and him."

"I asked Colby about it, and he said he couldn't remember either."

"What?" McKenna asks again.

I drop to my knees in front of her, where she's sitting on the edge of the bed, and take her hands in mine. "We're married, baby." I smile up at her.

"No. Rip. No. We can't be married. That's not how this works." She stands, stepping around me as she begins to pace the room.

"McKenna?" Laramie tries to get her attention, but she's in the zone as she paces back and forth across the plush carpet.

"I'll handle this. I mean, I can't practice in Nevada. Hell, I can't even practice in Texas yet, but I'll handle it. I know Gramps has connections. He can file the petition for dissolution."

"No." I stand up and face her, my arms crossed over my chest. "We've made love since then, Kenna. That's not going to work."

"Fine. A divorce then. I'll be sure it's discreet, and it will be quick."

"No."

"What now?" she asks, throwing her arms up in the air. She stops pacing and stares at me.

"No. I don't want you to handle it. No, I don't want a dissolution. No, I don't want a divorce."

"Then what do you want, Rip? We can't just ignore this. It's not going to go away."

"I don't want to ignore it either. I want you to be my wife." My eyes hold hers, and that's the only reason I see it. That's when I see her prepare for a fight. One I'm more than willing to give her. I'll fight for us.

"No."

"Yes."

"You don't want this. It was a drunken incident, and I'm going to get us out of this."

"McKenna, I need you to listen to me. I don't want out of this. I want you. I want you to be my wife."

She's shaking her head before I'm even finished talking. "If this is about the baby, you're off the hook there too. You don't owe me anything. I refuse to rope you into this life that you didn't ask for."

"Baby?"

Her eyes widen, and I turn to look at Laramie. She gives me a subtle nod. "You're pregnant?"

"I'll handle that too," she assures me.

"Excuse me? What the fuck does that mean?"

"Nothing. I'm not doing that. Just that I can do this on my own." I turn to look at my sister. "Are you really pregnant?"

"Yes."

"How long have you known?" I ask, turning my attention back to McKenna. She's clammed up, tears rolling down her cheeks, her arms tucked around herself.

"I thought I might be, so I came over. I didn't want to take a test alone. It turns out my suspicion triggered a suspicion for Mac. I convinced her to take one of the many tests that I stopped and bought on my way here."

I take a step toward McKenna, and she takes a step back, so I stop my movement. "What makes you think I would ever let you do this on your own? That baby is mine." That's when it hits me. What if it's not mine? No, that's not the kind of person she is. It's on the tip of my tongue to ask her, but I bite back the words.

"Yes. This is your baby, but you don't owe me anything. I have a good job lined up as soon as I get those stupid test results, and I can do this on my own. I refuse to let my child live in an environment like I grew up in. I don't want to trap you, and I won't. I won't keep you from the baby, but you have no obligation to me."

"McKenna, do you hear yourself? Baby, can we talk about this? I love you. I'm not standing here out of obligation. It's my fucking heart, the one that you and now our baby owns that's talking to you right now. I love you."

"I'm sorry. I can't do this." She backs away. "I need time. I just— I need to go." She turns and races from the room.

"Kenna!" I shout, moving to go after her when my sister's hand on my arm stops me.

"Let her go. She just needs time to process this. You know her history, Rip."

"I do. And she knows me. She knows that I love her. Fuck me, I love her, and I love that baby. I don't want a divorce, Lara. I want her. I want our family."

"Come here." Laramie pulls me into a hug, and I flinch when I hear the front door slam closed.

"Go with her. Please? I don't want her driving upset."

"Are you sure?"

"Please, Lara. She's pregnant. Don't let her drive upset."

"Okay." She turns to look at the bed.

"Leave them. Just go," I say, running my fingers through my hair. "Please, just stay with her."

"Okay. I'll text you in a little while."

"I love them."

"I know you do. She just needs some time."

"I'm going too." I move toward the door, but she stops me.

"No. Stay here. I have to go before she leaves."

I nod, dropping down to the bed. Resting my elbows on my knees, I cover my eyes with the palm of my hands and fight the urge to race after her. I don't understand what just happened. I came in here excited to tell her we were married. I knew I would have a fight on my hands, but I got a hell of a lot more than I bargained for.

I'm not just a husband. I'm going to be an uncle and a daddy.

Chapter Twenty-Eight

MCKENNA

I HOLD IT TOGETHER UNTIL I GET TO MY CAR. AS SOON AS THE DOOR SHUTS, I LOSE MY battle with my tears, and a sob rattles from my chest. My heart is shattering, and somewhere deep inside, I know it's my own doing. I know that I'm being irrational, but I can't seem to stop.

I might have been young, but I heard the fights. I heard the harsh words my father would scream and yell at my mother. I remember him looking me in the eye and telling me I was a mistake, that I ruined his life.

My rational brain knows Rip is not that man, that he would never, but the little girl in me who had to hear her father tell her over and over again that she was a mistake, she can't seem to take a deep breath.

I refuse to trap him.

It's too soon. He needs time to think about this. And we're married? Talk about adding to an already huge pile of shit.

"McKenna." Laramie scares the hell out of me when she beats on the passenger-side window. "Let me in."

"No."

"Come on, Mac. I told him to stay in the house. Open the door. It's just me."

I click the lock and she climbs in. I'm quick to lock us both back inside my car. "Tell me what you're thinking."

"History repeating itself."

"McKenna, you know Rip is better than that. He loves you."

"I know. I love him too, but my dad, he loved my mom. Once upon a time." I laugh humorlessly. "It was not a fairy-tale ending for them."

"Mac, I know you're upset and that a lot has been tossed at you in the last hour. I know you need time to process this. I'm here for that. Whatever you need. But as your best friend, not as his sister, but as your best friend, I want you to really think about this. Think about how he treats you."

"I know he loves me. I can feel it."

"If you trust in his love, trust him to make the best choice for him. I'm not sure if you saw him in there, but he was giddy with happiness. He wants you to be his wife, McKenna. Did you catch that part of the conversation?"

"I heard him."

"What do you want?"

I don't even have to think about my answer. "I want him to want to marry me, not because of a drunken mistake but because he chose to do so. That he made a conscious decision to ask me to be his forever, not that he was tricked into marrying me. We were drunk, Lara. Hell, we didn't even remember it. None of us did. How is that a good foundation for a marriage?"

"It's a good foundation when it's love. It doesn't matter how or when, but that the relationship is real."

"And this baby." I place my hands over my still-flat stomach. "This baby deserves better than two parents who stuck it out because it was the right thing to do."

"Is that what you think?"

"I don't know. Don't you see? How am I supposed to know? How is he supposed to know? He might think this is what he wants. He's caught up in the moment of finding out we were married while too drunk to remember and walking in on me after just taking a pregnancy test. A *positive* pregnancy test. It doesn't seem like he has much of a choice to me."

"He has a choice, McKenna. He's choosing you and the baby you created out of love."

"We were drunk."

"Does that mean you don't love your baby?"

My hands fly to my belly, and I can't explain the feeling inside me. It's warmth, and light, and hope. "No. I love this baby." It's the truth. It's a surprise, and it wasn't how I thought this moment would go, but I could never not want a part of Rip and me.

"He loves both of you."

"Lara." My voice cracks. "How did we get here? How did I end up pregnant and married to the man I've always loved, and I can't remember the night that gave me both him and this baby?"

"I can't explain it, McKenna. I can tell you it sounds a hell of a lot like fate."

"Fate? Do you believe that?"

"I know you're close to this." She taps her chest. "And everything is right here, but I'm telling you he's not with you out of obligation or duty. I know my brother, McKenna, and he loves you."

I nod. "Sometimes love isn't enough. I lived it, Laramie. I know what happens when the unexpected is thrust upon you. I know the loss, and the pain, the shame." I look down at my lap. "It took me a long time to push his hateful words out of my head, and as I got older, hers as well. I struggle with insecurities. If I'm being honest, their words aren't gone. I still hear them every single day. It drove them to drugs, Laramie. They couldn't deal with me. I caused that. I don't want that for this baby. I want his or her life to be full of love and to always feel safe."

There's a knock on my window, and I turn to see Rip standing there, shoving his hands in his jeans pockets. He's still dirty from his morning working the farm. I want to tear open this door and jump into his arms and let him tell me this is all going to work out. I imagine that's exactly how it started with my parents too. There is no happy ending in this situation. He didn't get to choose.

"Talk to him." Laramie reaches over the console and hugs me. I watch as she unlocks the door and climbs out, only for Rip to take her place.

He closes the door, and how, I'm not sure, but he manages to turn his tall form to face me as he sits sideways in the seat. "Kenna." His voice cracks.

I keep my eyes straight ahead. I can't look at him. I can't face the hurt in his eyes when I'm doing this for him. I would never want him to turn out like my father. "What do you want, Rip?"

I jump when I feel his hand on my belly. "You, McKenna. I want you, and I want our baby."

I try hard not to let him see how his words affect me, but a sob rips from my throat. "I'm sorry," I mumble through my tears.

"What exactly are you apologizing for, McKenna? Are you apologizing for making me a husband? Or are you apologizing for making me a father? Which is it, baby, so I can work on showing you those aren't things to be sorry about? Baby, look at me."

I shake my head. I can't look at him. "I'm sorry," I say again. It's all I can think to say, and I'm not sure I could form more than those two words right now anyway.

His hand gently cups my chin as he turns my head to look at him. "I love you, McKenna. I love our baby. Sure, we didn't do this the traditional way. We didn't plan our wedding, but we did get married, and then made a baby. That's pretty damn traditional. However, I couldn't care less about any of that. You know why?"

"Why?" I ask, even though I'm not sure I'm ready to hear his answer.

"Because you made me a husband and a father. In one day." He smiles. "Not just today, but our night in Vegas. I assume that's when it happened, and that will now forever be the best night of my life."

"We don't even remember it."

"We might not be able to remember that night and our actions, but it will forever be the night you took my last name, and we started our family."

"Family?" I croak.

"A baseball team." He smiles.

I close my eyes, willing myself to stay strong. He says all of this now, and I'm sure my father did too. I know how that turned out. "I refuse to make you feel trapped."

"Trap me, Kenna. Fuck, baby, tie me to the bed, lock me in the house. I don't give a fuck as long as you and our baby are with me. I love you, McKenna."

I nod. "I know. I love you too."

"Then why are you pushing me away?"

"My parents," I croak, and his face goes white.

"No. No, McKenna. That's not us, baby. No way. I love you, and I love our baby. I would never do anything to hurt either of you in any way."

"He probably thought that too. My dad, I mean."

"Fuck him. I am not him. He was a piece of shit. They both were, in my opinion." He takes a deep breath. "Look. I'm sorry. I shouldn't talk about your parents like that, but fuck, Kenna. You can't compare me to them. They put you in situations a little girl should never be in. One I can guarantee that my children will never be in."

My mind races, and thoughts of the fights, the screaming, the fists, the tears— "I need to go."

"Please don't go."

"I need to. I just… I need some time."

"What does that mean?"

"I don't know."

"Where are you going?"

"Home."

"This is your home."

"I don't live here."

"You're my wife."

"On a piece of paper."

"In my heart. Right fucking here." He bangs on his chest over his heart. "You're the mother of my child," he tries again.

"I won't keep you from the baby."

"No. You won't. You won't have to because we're married, and we're a family. You and me, and this little one." His hand drops to my belly again. "I love you both, McKenna."

"I can't do this right now. I need to go." I can't think right now. My mind is racing, and my heart is breaking. There's a tightness in my chest that I fear will never go away.

"Let me drive you. I don't want you driving upset," he says sadly.

"It's a half a mile down the road."

"I don't care. You and this baby are everything to me. I want you safe."

"I'll be fine."

"Please? I'll have Lara follow me and bring me back here. I'll give you some time to process this, but I'm not going to stop until you understand that I'm not trapped, Kenna. I'm in love with a woman who has held my heart longer than I realized. That same woman is making me a father. There is no greater gift than you, love, and our family."

He keeps his hand on my belly as he digs his cell phone out of his pocket. "Hey, I'm going to drive Kenna to her grandparents'. Can you follow me over and pick me up?" Silence. "She needs some time to process this." More silence. "I don't need to process anything. I found out the woman I love is already my wife and making me a father." More silence. "Thanks, Lara." He ends the call. "Let me drive you home."

I nod because what else can I do? My eyes won't stop leaking tears, and I really do need to go see my grandparents. Maybe they can help me work this mess out. Maybe I can have them talk to Rip and explain. Climbing out of the car, I pass him at the rear, and he pulls me into a fierce hug.

"I love you so fucking much, McKenna," he says, his voice cracking.

I hug him back. "I love you too." I do. I love him, and I love this baby, our unexpected surprise. Never a mistake. Always loved. I'll make damn sure of it.

He drives me to my grandparents' place, and without a word, I climb out of the car, not looking back as I head inside. I hear the car door slam, and then another, telling me he's driving away with Lara. Good. I need time. Opening the front door, my grandparents are sitting in the living room. When one looks at me, they both become alert.

"What happened?" Gramps asks.

"Come here, Mac," my grams pats the couch next to her. "Tell us what's going on."

So I do.

I take the seat next to her and let her hold me close and let the words spill. I tell her about Vegas and how we got married, finding out only today, and I tell them about the baby. I tell them that I'm scared out of my mind to lose Rip and to do this on my own. I also tell them I don't want to make him feel trapped like my father. "I don't want us to turn into them," I confess.

"McKenna," Gramps sighs. "Sweetheart, your parents didn't just start down a path of drugs when you were born. It started when they were young. That's how they met. You didn't cause them to turn down that path."

"I remember," I tell him. "Dad would tell me I ruined his life. That I was a mistake." As soon as the words leave my mouth, I realize I've never really told anyone but Rip, Laramie, and Colby the truth. One night in high school, we had a bonfire, and I was drinking, and it all just kind of came out.

Gramps' fists tighten. "Listen to me, and listen good. You are not a mistake. Never ever a mistake. They let drugs and alcohol take over their lives. They were both addicted long before you were born. They cleaned up their acts because of you. We didn't know things were as bad as they were until we got the call that your mother had been taken to the hospital."

"We didn't know about how he talked to you, or we would have explained this to you sooner," Grams says softly.

"I thought it was me," I say, losing control of my tears again. "I thought it was my fault, and I didn't want to do that to Rip. I love him too much." I sob, placing a hand over my belly. "I love this baby too much."

Gramps stands from his chair and sits on the other side of me on the couch, and together, the three of us embrace as my tears fall unchecked. "That boy loves you, Mac. Anyone who sees him with you can see it."

I nod. "I love him too. But I never wanted to trap him. I love him enough to let him go."

Before he can reply, there's a pounding on the door. "McKenna!" Rip shouts, and my tears fall faster.

Chapter Twenty-Nine

RIP

I LASTED ABOUT THIRTY MINUTES AT MY PLACE, LONG ENOUGH TO CONVINCE MY SISTER I was fine and to send her home to tell her husband about their baby. I hugged her tight, told her I loved her, and sent her with a promise to call about tonight's plans. It was maybe three minutes after she pulled out of my driveway that I grabbed my keys and headed to McKenna.

I can't sit back and wait for her to believe that she and this baby are what I want. I have to show her. I have to fight for them. There's no other option. I won't ever stop fighting for my family.

I don't think when I pull into her grandparents' driveway, I just climb out of the truck, race up the porch steps, and bang on the door. "McKenna!" I pound again until the door opens. My arm is midair, getting ready to bang again, but I stop when I see Harold standing there.

"Rip." He nods.

"I love her," I blurt. "I love her so much I can't breathe when she's not with me. I want her to be my wife more than anything, and our baby." I swallow hard. "She's carrying a part of me, Harold. I don't know what to do with that but smile and feel like I'm ten feet fucking tall. She's having my baby, and I love them both." I tap my chest over my heart. "Please, can I see her? I need to tell her. I need for her to understand that I'm not me without her. I want our family," I say, breathing hard.

He watches me as I run my fingers through my hair. I'm ready to yell for her again. I need to see her, but when he pulls the door open further, I see her standing with tears rolling down her cheeks. I rush inside, past her grandfather, and pull her into a fierce hug. I breathe her in, willing my heart rate to slow. When I finally pull away, I cradle her face in the palm of my hands, wiping at her cheeks with my thumbs. "Kenna, I—" I start, but she stops me with her words.

"I heard you."

"I meant every word. I'll tell you every damn day for the rest of our lives."

"I'm sorry. I thought—" She stops and swallows hard. "I thought that I was the reason," she cries. "He told me I was a mistake and that I ruined his life. I didn't want that to be you. He told me he was trapped because of me, and I didn't want to trap you. I love you too much to do that."

"Listen to me." I wait for a few heartbeats, until I know that I have her full attention. "There's nothing in this life that I want more than you and our baby. I don't know what I need to do, but I'll prove that to you. I will. I swear to you, McKenna."

I hold my breath, waiting for her to tell me to kick rocks and disappear, but a slow smile tilts her lips. Her eyes are still wet with tears, and her cheeks are stained, but she's never looked more beautiful. "I believe you. I freaked a little, and I still need to process what my grandparents told me today about my parents when I always thought that it was me, that I was the reason, but I believe you. I love you."

I suck in a breath and press my forehead against her. "Oh, Kenna." I laugh. "I more than love you. You are the air I breathe. You and our baby." More tears stream down her face. "Come home. Please? Even just for a few hours. I just need to be close to you."

"Okay."

"Okay." I nod. I don't know what I expected when I headed here other than that I was ready for a fight. I was ready to plead my case, and I guess I did. I didn't expect her to be willing to come home with me, but I'm so damn grateful.

"Take care of them," Harold says, speaking for the first time since I arrived.

Lifting my head, I keep my arm around McKenna, holding her close. When I look over at Harold, he's holding Agnes the same way. And I know in my heart that McKenna and I will be them, living out our forever, guiding our children and grandchildren in life.

"Always." I nod.

McKenna pulls out of my arms to give them both a hug, and because they raised such an amazing woman, and they let me in their home to plead my case, and just because they're remarkable people, and I'm feeling all kinds of my feelings, I hug them both as well.

With my hand on the small of her back, I lead her to the driver's side door of my truck. Opening the door, I help her inside, following after her. With my hand resting on her thigh, I drive us to my place. Neither one of us speak a word as we enter the house. I make a point to lock the door once we're inside and lead us up to my room.

"Are you hungry or thirsty?"

"No." She shakes her head. "I'm exhausted, though. I guess all the emotions."

"Sit." I point to the bed. She sits, and I remove her shoes from her feet and pull back the covers. Kicking my shoes off as well, I crawl in beside her and gather her into my arms.

"I'm sorry."

"Nothing to be sorry for. We had a lot thrown at us today," I say, sliding my hand under her shirt, resting it against her flat belly.

"Yeah," she agrees.

"I want a little girl," I confess. "I want her to look just like her mamma."

"Really?" She's choked up, but there's also surprise in her voice as well.

"I'm really fucking happy, McKenna. I know this isn't what you would have wanted, and if you want to get married again in front of our family and friends, we can do that too, but I don't want a divorce. I want you, and I want our baby. This is our time, beautiful."

She rolls over and rests her hand against my cheek. "I used to fantasize about you being my husband. Laramie and I both thought it would be amazing to be sisters for real."

"Sisters who are having babies at the same time."

She smiles. This one reaches her eyes. "I guess we are."

"So, we're doing this? We're married and having a baby."

"Are you sure—" I cut her off with a kiss.

"I've never been more certain about anything in my entire life. This is us, baby. This is our family, and we have a lot of bedrooms to fill."

She giggles, and the sound wraps around my heart.

"You're my husband," she says over a yawn.

"Fuck yes, I am." I kiss her again. When I pull away, she snuggles close, and I hold her until I know she's asleep before letting myself drift off as well.

I WAKE SOMETIME LATER TO MCKENNA LYING ON HER BACK AND MY HEAD RESTING ON HER shoulder, my hand lying over where our baby grows inside of her.

Our baby.

My wife.

Careful not to wake her, I move down the bed and place my head on her belly. "Hey, peanut." I keep my voice low. "It's daddy."

Daddy.

I wait for the panic to hit me, but it doesn't happen—nothing but pure elation that the love of my life is making me a father.

"I love you so much. Your mommy and I both do. You are the best surprise we've ever had. Well, that and the fact that Mommy and I are married. I love her, peanut. She's beautiful, smart as hell— Oops, don't tell Mommy I cussed. Anyway, she's an incredible woman, and she's going to be the best mommy. She has so much love to give. I just found out about you a few hours ago, and already my heart is bursting with love for you and your mom. I promise to be the best daddy that I can be, but I'm sure I'm going to mess up. That's okay because we both have her."

I feel a hand brush over my hair, causing me to turn and look at her. "Hey, beautiful." I smile when I see her eyes are indeed open and focused on me. They're also shiny with tears. "Good tears?" I ask.

"The best."

"How much of that did you hear?"

"All of it."

I nod. "I meant every word."

"I know you did." She smiles as her phone rings. "Hey," she answers, keeping her eyes locked on mine. "Yeah, I imagine girls' night is going to be a little different." She chuckles. "I'm good. I'm home. Well, with Rip."

"You're home," I chime in.

"We're good." She listens and smiles. "Hold on," she tells my sister. "Laramie wants to know if we still want to come over. There's a change of plans. Girls' night is now family night."

I hold my hand out for the phone, and she playfully rolls her eyes but hands it to me. "Hey, sis."

"Everything good? She sounds good."

"We're perfect."

"Good. That's good."

"So, what do my wife and I need to bring to his family night?" I ask her. She squeals so loud I have to pull the phone from my ear.

"Just you and your wife," she replies, getting choked up.

"We'll be there," I tell her.

"Rip?"

"Yeah?"

"Congratulations, Daddy."

"Congratulations to you. And I'm pumped. Daddy and uncle in the same day."

"I'm going to be a mommy and an aunt," she says, not able to hide her emotions.

"Go snuggle with your husband so I can snuggle with my wife."

"I love the sound of that. I love it for both of us."

"Me too, little sister, me too." Ending the call, I drop the phone to the bed. "Looks like it's now family night." I grin.

"I can't believe we're having babies at the same time. It's crazy that a silly plan we had as kids is now real life."

"Well, Mrs. Callahan, you better believe it."

"I love you, Mr. Callahan."

"I love you. Both of you." I place my hand on her belly and kiss the hell out of my wife.

Epilogue

MCKENNA

TWO YEARS LATER

"NO, NO," I TELL MY DAUGHTER. SHE'S SIXTEEN MONTHS OLD AND INTO EVERYTHING. SHE grins at me and takes off, running down the hallway to where her daddy is swapping out the laundry. Not only is she into everything, she has her daddy wrapped around her little finger.

"Got ya," Rip says as he comes out of the laundry room and scoops her up into his arms.

Gemma's laughter fills the house and my heart. I had an easy pregnancy, even with Rip preaching that I needed to take it easy. One week after finding out we were not only pregnant but married, I got my results, and I passed the bar. I immediately started working with Gramps. At first, I was putting in some long hours, much to my husband's dismay.

It's not that the workload in our small Texas town is out of control. It was more me just wanting to get my feet wet. I'd busted my ass all through high school to graduate with an associate's degree and then again in law school. I was eager to start my career.

"Are you ready to go see Grammy and Pops?" Rip asks our daughter. She claps with delight at hearing their names. "Are you ready?" Rip asks me.

"Almost. I need to run upstairs and grab my earrings," I tell him.

"Sounds good, Mommy." He bounces Gemma on his hip. "I'm going to load this little princess up in the truck. Anything you need me to carry out?"

"No. Just the diaper bag."

"Got it." He leans in and kisses me before grabbing the diaper bag off the counter and heading outside.

And me? Well, I do need to run upstairs, but not for my earrings. You see, this may be a retirement party for Gramps, but I have a little surprise for my husband and the rest of our family. Grabbing what I need, I rush back downstairs, sure to lock the house up behind me.

"What's in the bag? I thought we got them a cruise?" Rip asks.

"Oh, this is just something small," I say, blowing him off. He shrugs like I hoped he would, and we're off.

Gemma babbles in the back seat all the way to the restaurant. Inside, we find my grandparents, Rip's parents, as well as Colby and Laramie, and their daughter, Dallas. We have a small party section of the restaurant reserved for us, and I'm thankful we can all sit together to share this moment with my grandfather.

"If I could have your attention," my grandfather says after our plates have long since been cleared. "Thank you all for being here." He stands and walks around the table, stopping behind me. "I can't tell you how proud I am to know my granddaughter is going to be taking over the law practice. My Agnes and I have paid our dues, and it's time for some traveling with my wife." He chuckles. "But not too much. I have my grandbabies to spoil," he says as he reaches for Dallas, who is crying for him. She's not his granddaughter, but he thinks of her as if she were all the same.

"McKenna, I have something for you." He nods to my husband, who pulls a small white box out of the diaper bag. He sets the box in front of me and takes our now sleeping daughter out of my arms.

"What is this?" I turn to look at Gramps over my shoulder.

"Open it," he urges.

Doing as I'm told, I open the small box that appears to be business cards. Pulling one out, I feel tears well in my eyes.

"You'll always be a Dawson, but you're a Callahan now too. I thought it was fitting that the office that is now yours takes your name."

Looking down at the business card I just retrieved from that box, I see Callahan Law in bold lettering at the top. "Gramps," I say, swallowing back my tears.

"There will be a crew there on Monday to change the signage on the building. It's all yours now, McKenna. You've earned it, sweetheart."

"I love you." I stand and hug him, and then Gram.

"Speech!" Colby calls out, and I smile. He couldn't have made this any easier on me, and he doesn't even know it.

RIP

MY WIFE SMILES THROUGH HER TEARS. SHE'S BEAUTIFUL, AND I LOVE HER MORE EACH AND every day. I glance down at my little girl sleeping in my arms, and I can't help but think that I got my wish. She looks just like her mommy, and that thrills me.

"Thank you all for being here. Gramps, this is supposed to be your party." She laughs.

"Humor me," he tells her.

She nods. "When I was seven years old, you and Gram took me in. I was broken and scared, but then you introduced me to the little girl next door." She smiles at Laramie. "We became fast friends, and she brought me out of my shell.

"Then, there was her brother." She looks at me with so much love and adoration that I'm glad I'm sitting down because I'm certain that look would bring me to my knees. "He was always looking out for me, and one day he found me in the treehouse, playing on my own, and he offered to marry me." She smiles.

"The best decision I ever made," I tell her.

"Anyway, fast-forward, and I felt so much love and protection, and I attributed that to Gramps being an attorney and fighting to keep me. Even at a young age, I knew I wanted to be that person for some other little boy or girl. I wanted to be the one to fight for those who couldn't fight for themselves." She wipes at her eyes.

"Somewhere along the way, with all the studying and planning for my future, I had a dream of a man who would sweep me off my feet, and we'd live happily ever after." She pauses to collect herself. "When I came home from college, and these two and Corbin convinced us to reenact that moment all those years ago, I thought they were crazy. Little did I know that was the path to our future.

"Two years ago, our lives took a turn." Her eyes flash to Gemma, where she sleeps in my arms. "It was unexpected and wonderful. Life has been good to me. I have the two of you," she says to her grandparents. "My best friend, who is now my sister." She smiles at Laramie. "A niece I adore, a brother-in-law and in-laws that I couldn't love more if they were my own," she says, glancing at my parents.

Everyone murmurs how much they love her and that they're the lucky ones, and then her eyes land on me. "And my husband and our beautiful baby girl. Rip, you fought for our family. You didn't let me push you away, and I can't tell you how thankful I am for you. For your love, for Gemma." She smiles, blinking hard to keep her tears at bay. "I actually have something for you." She hands me the small gift bag.

"Let me," Dad says, taking a sleeping Gemma from my arms.

"What is this?" I ask my wife.

"Just open it."

Knowing she's not going to tell me, I reach into the bag and pull out a picture frame. It's a picture of Gemma standing in what appears to be the hallway of our house just off the kitchen. Beside her is a chalkboard. I read the writing and then read it again to make sure I'm reading it correctly.

My role as an only child is coming to an end. Mommy is due with my new best friend.

"Kenna?" I look at my wife, and she nods.

I stand and pull her into my arms, kissing her tenderly. "We're having a baby?"

She nods. "We are."

"When?"

"In about seven months."

"I love you."

"I love you too."

I hold her close, unable to contain my smile. "I knew it would happen," I tell her.

"How? We weren't even trying."

"Oh, yeah, that too, we have a house to fill." I wink. "But that's not what I meant."

"What did you mean?"

"Us. I knew we'd live our 'forever after all.'"

Tears spill over her cheeks. "You remember that?"

"Yeah, baby. I remember. That was our first wedding." I wink at her.

"At least we remember that one," she says, and the room erupts in laughter.

ACKNOWLEDGEMENTS

To my readers:

Thank you for taking the time out of your busy lives to read my words. Thank you for shouting from the rooftops, and referring your friends. I love your messages and emails, and stories about how you connect to the characters. Thank you for your support and loyalty.

To my family:

I love you. You hold me up and support me every day. I can't imagine my life without you as my support system. Thank you for believing in me, and being there to celebrate my success.

Wander Aguiar & Andrey Bahia:

I love this image! Thank you for being amazing at what you do and for another cover worthy image.

Jersey Girl Designs:

Thank you for making the Forever After All paperback beautiful. I can't thank you enough for working me into your schedule.

Hang Le:

I gave you very little to go on, and you still managed to give me the cover I wanted. Thank you so much for being patient with me. I love this cover so much.

My beta team:

Jamie, Stacy, Lauren, Erica, and Franci I would be lost without you. You read my words as much as I do, and I can't tell you what your input and all the time you give means to me. Countless messages and bouncing idea, you ladies keep me sane with the characters are being anything but. Thank you from the bottom of my heart for taking this wild ride with me.

Give Me Books:

With every release, your team works diligently to get my book in the hands of bloggers. I cannot tell you how thankful I am for your services.

Tempting Illustrations:

Thank you for your graphic skills.

Julie Deaton:

Thank you for giving this book a set of fresh final eyes.

Becky Johnson:

I could not do this without you. Thank you for pushing me, and making me work for it.

Marisa Corvisiero:

Thank you for all that you do. I know I'm not the easiest client. I'm blessed to have you on this journey with me.

Kimberly Ann:

Thank you for organizing and tracking the ARC team. I couldn't do it without you.

Stacy Garcia:

Thank you for your graphic talents. I would be lost without you!

Lacey Black:

You are my person. Thank you so much for being a constant confidant in this crazy book world. This might not be a co-written book, but you were still there every step of the way. I can't tell you how much I value our friendship.

Author Friends:

There are so many of you who are always there in my corner. Evan, Kelly, Catherine, Niki, Molly, S, and so many more. Thank you for being my tribe.

Bloggers:

Thank you, doesn't seem like enough. You don't get paid to do what you do. It's from the kindness of your heart and your love of reading that fuels you. Without you, without your pages, your voice, your reviews, spreading the word it would be so much harder if not impossible to get my words in reader's hands. I can't tell you how much your never-ending support means to me. Thank you for being you, thank you for all that you do.

To my Facebook reader group (Kaylee's Crew):

I'm honored to have you on this journey with me. Thank you for reading, sharing, commenting, suggesting, the teasers, the messages all of it. Thank you from the bottom of my heart for all that you do. Your support is everything!

With Love,
Kaylee Ryan

Made in United States
North Haven, CT
19 June 2024

53846698R00174